The Glass Girl

Sandy Hogarth

For Katrina

and

For Jane

PART I

Prologue

5th April, 1975

They called me VL, Virgin Lips, because I'd never kissed a boy.

Sex wasn't mentioned at home. We were supposed to be good, whatever that was.

Once a year our church put on a social in its small hall. It was really just us girls huddled together, stuffing ourselves with cakes and sandwiches while the boys, in what my mother called their 'Sunday best', ambled about, looking embarrassed. No dancing or alcohol.

'Look after your sister,' my mother said to Alexis as we left, 'and back by ten, no later.' The village would be asleep by then.

We stopped under a lamp a couple of streets from the house while Alexis hitched her skirt up by five or six inches, took off her cardigan which she had worn buttoned up to the neck. Underneath she wore a blouse with a low neck. I waited, impatiently, hopping about, while she put on her make-up. She bent forward to pick up her bag and most of her breasts showed. I laughed then stood still while she put make-up on me.

She showed me a small bottle in her handbag and put a finger to her lips.

Arm in arm we walked down the hill. I wanted to run but Alexis couldn't in her heels. I felt great. Alexis was eighteen and doing her bossy big sister thing but I didn't care. I call her my big sister but she was only an inch taller than me. She was back from

3

London with her 'London ways'. That's what my father called them. She could be a pain but it was great that she'd come back, if only for a couple of days. I was sixteen, had just left school and was wearing make-up for the first time.

I rushed ahead when we got to Mrs Jackson's house. In the hall I hurried to the toilet to see what I looked like: weird. I'd have to get rid of the make-up before I got home.

A while later I was with my friends, standing around, picking at the food, waiting for something to happen, when Damien sauntered in. He was wearing black jeans, tee shirt and boots. Alexis went to his twenty-first birthday party last year. My father said Damien was a bad lot, mixed with the wrong crowd but he was the son of mum's best friend Auntie Dot so my father had to let Alexis go.

Damien looked around then winked at Alexis. She flashed him the smile she practises in the mirror and picked up her handbag. Alexis was too beautiful. She made the rest of us feel ugly.

We all watched as they disappeared outside. Gorgeous Damien.

Much later Alexis came back alone, that smile again, but wider so that even her gums showed. She pulled me to the door saying there was someone waiting for me outside. I stepped lightly into the night.

*   *   *

A car backfired as he shoved me against the house. My shoes dug deep into Mrs Jackson's flower bed. Lights shone through thin curtains and a television groaned and flickered. In the shadows he plucked me off my feet. He tore my new skirt, my pants. I opened my mouth to scream but heard only my fear as I struggled to pull away sure that he would break me apart the way my doll had snapped in half in my sister's hands. He breathed hard, grunted. Pain.

4

He stepped away.

I sank down into the dirt. There was something sticky between my legs. I was sure I was bleeding.

His laughter was deep as he strolled off into the blackness. He stopped, turned back, a shadow grown five, ten times. 'Say thank you to your sister for me.'

Chapter 1

Australia 1978

It's my eighteenth birthday, September 6th and one of those days when even my shadow annoys me. It's only a wisp of a thing, easily appropriated by some needy person.

The solitary road through the desert runs from east to west or west to east. I came from the east.

It took more than six months to get here, hitching lifts, working in pubs along the way. The drought was bad. They said that when it did rain the sand would turn the colour of raw flesh and the desert would bloom. Or something like that. I didn't believe them. Some children had never seen rain.

The hotel, hundreds of miles from the nearest town, litters the red desert like an abandoned toy.

Fifteen months ago I pushed open a door and stepped inside a dimly-lit, cool room. A man, a bit older than me, stood there: stocky, medium height, wearing baggy shorts, a not too clean tee shirt and flip-flops. I walked into his eyes and their smile.

'G'day. So what've we got here?' he said, and put out his hand. 'Steve.'

I stopped running and embraced the desert with the false hope of the irredeemably lost. It's all horizon escaping into the distance. Lizards bury themselves under the sand to wait out the heat. If exposed to the sun for too long they change colour and die. The rocks crack and crumble during the freezing darkness and the dry winds chisel them into fantastical shapes.

Steve offered me a job and his bed. We tried the bed part but it didn't work. My fault…

'No worries,' he said.

I took over one of the cabins some way from the main building: a small tin room that burns by day and freezes by night. It has a mean double bed, a couple of hooks behind the door, a battered chest of drawers and in one corner a washbasin and small mirror. The toilet and shower block, which I share with six other cabins and the campers, is twenty yards away. There's always mosquitoes breeding in the water that collects in the bottom of the showers but I don't care. I love my cabin; fancy myself as some sort of hermit.

There are four guest bedrooms in the main hotel: large dingy pockmarked rooms, each furnished with a large metal double bed, a table and a wardrobe. There is one bathroom down the passage. I suggest to Steve that we might paint the bedrooms.

He shakes his head. 'I won't stay here forever,' he says. 'Another few years.'

'Why?' I ask. 'I thought you were wedded to the place.'

'I'll leave before it collapses round me.'

I look around.

'Look closer.'

I do and see the tiny holes.

'Termites,' he says.

The bar is a thirty foot U-shape with plenty of elbow room to lean and chat or space to drink alone. Scattered around are wooden tables and chairs and a couple of lumpy sofas against the walls. Many of the drinkers are also a little shabby.

A noisy generator thumps night and day. Nearby the birds chatter around the only water for miles.

My days: sleep in late unless there's a desert crossing. The travellers become friends in the few short days they are here.

They leave shortly after dawn. We wave them off; wave, until the pennants attached to high poles on their vehicles disappear behind the sand dunes. Then I'm in the bar at lunchtime but there's never many in so I get them served as quickly as possible. It only gets really busy at dusk. The days switch off with a conflagration of vermillion and orange skies followed by swift dark night. Perhaps that's what I miss most about home: the long summer evenings.

The travellers, when they first arrive, come in blinking, fleeing the relentless light and the temperatures in the forties. Some remind me of my father, just sitting, saying nothing. It's mostly men. They like having a girl behind the bar, even an English girl. They call me the Little Pom, not a compliment. They pick up the accent and ask me why I'm here, in the middle of the desert.

'I love it,' I say. The impermanence, the solitariness is something I need right now. And there are no little girls in the desert.

They leave generous tips, luck money. Steve says I'm an asset even if a bit of a chatterbox. But I know when to shut up. Mostly.

Each day, after night falls, swiftly, uncompromisingly, the desert way, I adopt different personas: running from a violent husband (older men like that one, feel protective); hints of an unhappy love affair; the only daughter of rich English parents just pleasing myself, playing my way round the world. I mention Japan although 11th century Japan is all I know: Lady Murasaki and her *Tale of Genji*. Eleventh century Japan seems right for the desert.

'It's just a game,' I say to Steve later.

'Not a good choice,' he says. 'Some of the older men fought against Japan and have not forgiven. Or forgotten.'

I blush and remove Japan from my list of mythical countries.

I assess the listener and give him what he wants to hear. Only men. They only half believe me. They too have their stories in this ephemeral land. They smile and say that the desert is the place for whoppers.

I can't fool the women. I tell them all that I love Australia and

8

we become friends but in a day or two they move on.

Some of the travellers are old hands, like Harry. Three or four times a year he brings a party for a desert crossing. He selects them carefully.

'Too many fools,' he says. 'The desert attracts too many fools who need the stuff of cities and don't really see this.' He waves his hand towards the red sand and the spinifex grass. He promises to take me across one day. Steve says many don't make it across but Harry never fails.

Harry is big, bluff, and very old. Sometimes we sit together on the veranda with its red tin roof. On one side are four large chairs with tubular steel frames and sagging stained hessian seats and on another, piles of junk: machinery, sheets of rusting corrugated iron, old beer barrels, a broken bike, bits of a car wrecks, broken bar stools, a baby's high chair and a knackered fridge. The hard baked earth pushes up to the building, clamouring for admission.

'Marvellous mechanics,' Harry says, without preamble.

'Who?' I ask.

'Black fellas,' he says, and pushes a thumb towards half a dozen Aboriginals squatting on the floor of the veranda, facing east into the afternoon sun. Malnourished dogs lie, scattered around on the floor.

I turn towards them and smile. Earlier that afternoon I'd sold one of the men a case of beer. They come to the back door.

They drink until the pub closes and then carry one another into the darkness. I ask Steve where they go.

'They have their places,' he says. 'White fellas get pissed too.' He grins. One night Steve put me to bed, out of it. The next morning he brought me coffee, propped me and my hangover up and said that the desert was full of runaways and drunks. I was already the first and fast becoming both. I'm a sucker for New Year resolutions so I made one early: cut out the booze. It worked. I'm an all-or-nothing person.

Then there are the bad days, the days when I can't get out of bed or I tell Steve I am sick – I am, but not in a way he understands – and I walk. It's not safe in the hot sun to go so far from the hotel but I don't care. The heavy air tricks me: I hurry towards small girls, baby girls, holding out their arms to me.

We only get the post when Steve goes to Alice or the tanker drivers bring it. Letters: sometimes four or five at once, sometimes none for weeks. My mother writes every Saturday.

I sit on a tussock of spinifex the other side of a small rise of red desert sand, a few hundred yards from the hotel. It's still early morning so there's a slight chill but the sun will soon chase that off. I can hear voices, conversation from the campsite although it's some way off. Sound carries in the desert.

A bundle of letters in my hand.

My mother writes that there is a new butcher in the high street. In my head I hurry down the narrow cobbled street with its stone-built shops on either side, holding her hand, dragging her to the sweet shop. It's our secret. My father says the sweets are just sugar, bad for us.

The shop is dark inside and filled with rows of large glass jars: sweets of every colour and size. My favourites are the big hard pink ones. I can stuff one in each cheek and make them last ages. The man behind the counter fills a bag. Alexis likes the small caramel ones so I ask for those. We will keep them hidden. My mother gets out her purse. I am still at the village school. Alexis is at the grammar.

But it's the stories and books I think of when I am missing her most.

A letter from Lucy. We've been best friends for years. She's getting married. 'You have to come back and be my bridesmaid,' she writes.

Thinking of Lucy always makes me smile.

I don't get to her wedding.

Chapter 2

England 1969

St Jude's was to be the start of my real life, an adventure. Every day I travelled thirteen miles on the bus with Alexis. My big school in the nearby town with its endless playing fields, gym, library, tennis courts, everything. I was not yet eleven.

What a disappointment I was; the bright star from the village school that had sailed through her eleven-plus turning out to be a dunce barely able to put two words together, tongue-tied, stupid and bottom of the class at the end of the first term.

It was almost Christmas, twelve weeks since my mother left. I counted the weeks. She missed my eleventh birthday.

My father put me on his knee – I couldn't remember the last time he'd done that – and said, 'Your mother is sick.'

'Will she die?' I asked, although I was sure that she was already dead.

'No. I saw her last week. She's getting better.'

'Can I see her?'

'She'll be home,' he said. 'Soon.'

He lied. She didn't come back for a long time. It was my fault.

Lucy came into my life, unstoppable, like a big wave rolling up the beach. She walked into the classroom towards the end of my second term at St Jude's, March 1970. She was a bit fat and not very tall. She must have heard the sniggers but they didn't seem to bother her. She just stood there ignoring us all while Miss Carpenter introduced her, telling us to make her welcome. I wasn't paying much attention as usual until I saw her smile at me. That was it.

Later I asked her why she smiled at me. She said that I smiled at her first. No matter.

I ran up the hill from the bus shouting through the front door, 'I've got a best friend, Mum. She lives in the village.'

'That's great,' she said and hugged me. She had only been home a few weeks.

'Her name's Lucy,' I said, dropping my school bag.

The village is called Lower Newhouses. There's no Upper Newhouses. Lucy's house was on an estate about a mile away. She liked going to an all-girls' school, said it got her away from her four brothers. Her mother was always rushing around after them. 'Boys,' she said to me once, 'never have boys.'

I wasn't going to have children.

I took up the clarinet and Lucy the saxophone. We played a duet at the school concert, both of us dressed like the jazz players Lucy had seen on TV. We borrowed her brother Mike's clothes and played Frank Sinatra's '*Fly me to the Moon*'. The kids loved it. Even Alexis clapped. I know because I looked to see. The head wasn't much chuffed, nor was Dad. Mum clapped the loudest.

Lucy always had an endless supply of bubble gum (banned at home). I could blow larger bubbles than she could: the size of a small apple.

Our real coup was to put a bra on the statue of St Jude. Lucy had the biggest tits in the school – the boys on the bus were always saying stupid things about them – and her bra would have been a giveaway so she pinched one of her mother's: size 34B. The head lectured the whole school about respect, vandalism, and reputation. It took her a week to get through that lot in daily chunks. We were never found out.

In my fifth year I persuaded Lucy to go to the nearby cinema to see *Lacombe Lucien*. Lucy liked to call herself Jeanne, even asked our French mistress how to pronounce it. I told her that Louis Malle was a famous French director. That clinched it. We thought the film was sophisticated. We liked sophisticated.

After that Lucy and I skipped every sports afternoon and went to the cinema. We saw *Great Gatsby* and I fell in love with Robert Redford and cried buckets at the end. Lucy was already in love with Sean Connery. My pocket money wasn't enough so I raided Mum's purse. The school eventually caught up with us and *Jaws* was the last film we saw together. The head wrote to our parents and gave us endless detentions. I've never seen my father so angry: cinema was not for decent people, (he meant the elect like us with a direct line to God), gave girls wrong ideas; he was disappointed in me. He went on and on. Sin and the devil came into it and I was forbidden to see Lucy but she caught the same school bus. My mother didn't say much.

Lucy was going to be an actress and I was going to be a poet. Lucy liked my poems. For a while I carried a notebook and pencil with me but I gave up after I couldn't think of anything much to put in it.

Chapter 3

Early July 1975

Lucy and I were sitting side by side on the river's edge.

'What will you tell your mother?' She dug her feet into the steep riverbank to stop herself sliding into the water.

'Sorry about before,' she said, meaning the laughter when I told her. 'It's just...' She shakes her head. 'I still can't quite believe it. You don't even have a boyfriend. Pregnant.' She turned to look at me. 'You've been keeping secrets.'

Lucy and I told each other everything.

I stared into the brown sluggish river and took a deep breath to hold back the tears.

I couldn't tell my mother, couldn't say the words. 'It would hurt her too much,' I said.

'But...'

'The wedding dress,' I said, almost to myself.

'What do you mean the wedding dress?'

'Nothing,' I said, quickly. 'A long time ago.'

She didn't push it.

'Your father then, he's a doctor.'

'I don't know why, I just can't. You don't know what it's like, our church, all the stuff about sin and everything that we get thrown at us. They don't say sex but that's what they mean.' I added, 'Fallen women and all that. Remember Charlotte. She lived near me and disappeared last year. And her family. One Sunday they

14

were all sitting in the front pew, heads down, while the priest went on about purity and the Virgin Mary, even more than usual. Charlotte was all belly. We never saw them after that Sunday.'

I heard Dad say that the family had moved. 'Our daughters will never shame us like that,' he said. Mum didn't say anything.

'What about the…?'

'It shouldn't have happened,' I said, interrupting and turning away from her.

She looked hard at me.

'I have to go somewhere no-one knows me.' I didn't know that was what I was going to do until the words slipped out. Thoughts are like that, they tumble out unannounced. I heard my words and was surprised. And afraid. It might be real after all.

Lucy was usually pretty quick with answers. Not this time.

Neither of us spoke. I heard the soft plop of a fish and saw the water ripple. 'You can do this,' I told myself. 'You must.'

'She hasn't noticed anything?' Lucy asked, so softly, that I almost missed it.

'Well she wouldn't. There's nothing to see yet,' I almost shouted.

Lucy sat up quickly and nearly toppled into the water. 'I know,' she said. 'You can go to my aunt in Australia, Aunt Davida. She's great; a bit old but fun. I'll write today.' Lucy wriggled excitedly and slipped further down the bank. 'She has a boyfriend, Malcolm. He's odd, but OK.'

Australia. I grabbed Aunt Davida. It sounded so easy: a year away then back here to university. But even in that brief second I was afraid. I wanted to run to the one person I couldn't: my mother.

How stupid.

'Aunt Davida will know what to do. She's good in emergencies. That's what Mum says, although I don't think she meant…' Lucy coloured then leant over, awkwardly balancing on a root (her white trousers already covered in mud) and looked hard at me. 'She's good at secrets. I know; I've told her a few. What if you want to keep the baby? You'll love it,' she says. 'I know you will. I bet it's a girl.'

'What would be the point of going away?' I said, irritated.

She stood up, brushed down her trousers as if she was going to fly off to Australia that minute. 'I'll come too,' she said. 'We'll go together. Aunt Davida has always wanted me to come out. I'll find a way.'

I didn't get up, I didn't believe her. I put my head in my hands. I had to find Alexis.

Chapter 4

Mid July 1975

A stranger in the church

'Lucy's aunt will look after us. And Lucy is nearly eighteen,' I said. That didn't help. For my father Lucy might as well have had 'Catholic' tattooed across her forehead.

We were sitting at the dining room table, empty rice pudding plates in front of us. Rice pudding was Saturday night's ritual. My father's outrage was in the air, and my mother's sadness. Alexis was in London. Somewhere.

'I'm going away to university anyway and Miss Abbot says (that was my big gun, my English teacher at St Jude's) it would be a good idea to take a year off. Ask her.' It was true but I knew he wouldn't ask. 'Just a year,' I said. 'I'll be seventeen in a few months.' If I'd wanted to go to Africa, to the church's mission station – we were always collecting money and clothes and toys for it – he might have agreed.

My father's face and lips were tight, his blue eyes determined: his 'I'm not going to argue' face. Alexis and I called it his 'go fall off a cliff' face.

'No,' he said. 'That's the end of it. You are too young.'

'Mum?' I said, turning to her.

She just shook her head. It wasn't even a 'not now; we'll talk about it later' shake.

I almost cried out, 'But I have to go.'

At church the next day my father climbed the steps of the pulpit. He often gave the sermon. Our church is on the edge of the village, squat and plain. It was built about eighty years ago, for the workers building the dams up the Dale.

It's not like the big parish church with its tower. Or the Catholic's on the other side of the village.

Through the clear glass windows I gazed out at the hills; my hills. I didn't know anywhere else except for a couple of weeks a year to Whitby. And I didn't know what I was going to do. I sat with my head down and my fists clenched tight on my lap.

My father often spoke, in his sermons, of how we were the select, predestined to be with God, a God that is love. But it was sin he talked about most: pictures of hellfire, unimaginable pain and suffering forever. I can't remember a time when I was not trying to avoid one sin or other.

'Luke 7:37,' he said, looking down at us from the pulpit. 'There was a woman in the city, a woman we would call loose, a sinner.'

When I heard that I stared up at him but he didn't notice me.

'She approached Christ, and knelt at his feet. She was ashamed and afraid but she washed his feet with her tears and dried them with her hair, anointing them with sweet smelling oil.'

He paused, waiting for the weight of his words to fall. He always did that.

Heads nodded.

He spoke more then came to the story of the two debtors. He asked the congregation 'which of the two debtors did Christ love the most?'

There were murmurs. We all knew the answer.

'The one who owed the most,' he said softly, looking around.

I heard a strange noise, a gasp.

He was leaning on the front of the pulpit. Shock was in his

18

face, his lips had almost disappeared. I followed his eyes. They were fixed on a stranger, a woman with loose flowing hair on her shoulders, a beautiful woman. My mother also followed his gaze from the front row of the choir.

The congregation waited, shuffled.

Finally he said, in a voice that was not like his, a voice that shook a little, 'The greater the sin, the greater the pardon. We are all sinners, let us go in peace.'

He closed the Bible and walked down the steps.

I dawdled in front of the church until the woman came out. She was different to everyone else. Her face was soft and she wore a flowing ankle-length dress of bright yellow and around her shoulders a deep green shawl. But it was her hands that I really noticed. She had a ring on three fingers of each hand.

She smiled at me.

That afternoon I heard my mother and father arguing in the sitting room. I couldn't make out much except my mother saying, in a voice, loud for her, 'She must go.'

Fear and hope fought in me. I wasn't sure that I could really go. I wished Lucy's aunt had never existed. I ran to my room.

Much later I came back to the door and pushed it open. My father was kneeling in front of her, holding out two white pills. 'Take these,' he said. There was a small brown bottle on the carpet beside him. My mother was in the armchair, collapsed into a sort of ball. I started to run towards her. He put out his arm. I knew what her eyes would look like: dead.

I turned to the record player and recognised Violetta's lament from *La Traviata*. My mother wasn't singing but her lips were moving with the words: Violetta's lament from *La Traviata*. 'Love me, Alfredo, you cannot imagine the love in my heart for you.' I knew the words almost by heart. Betrayal, my mother had told me years earlier as we sat together listening to her music. I had heard it played too often.

'Take these,' he said again, his voice gentle. 'They'll help.'

She shook her head.

'Turn that thing off,' my father almost shouted, drowning Violetta.

My mother was wearing that dress again: the wedding dress.

Not long afterwards, still wearing the dress, my father took her away in his car. I stayed in my room. I didn't want to see her go.

He returned alone, late in the evening. He looked tired. 'You'll need a passport,' he said. 'I'll see to that. Go into town and get a photo taken.' He had something in his hand: an airline ticket.

'Three weeks,' he said, 'your flight is in three weeks' time.'

I lay on my bed, shaking. I put my hands on my stomach. I didn't want to go anywhere. I wanted to wait until my mother came home. I buried my head under the pillow and sobbed. I could not do it.

Chapter 5

August 1975

Alexis left for London over two years ago. She couldn't wait to leave school, said it was stupid, a waste of time, except for the art classes. She was fantastic at drawing and painting and made up her mind to go to art school in London. I didn't expect Dad to agree but he did.

She hadn't been back for four months and she never answered her phone. I tried and tried. I was beginning to think she lived somewhere else. I thought of going to London to find her but that was madness. I wrote telling her to ring me. She never replied. I hated her.

My mother didn't come home and my father stayed out of the house even more than usual during those three weeks before I left home. Auntie Dot, Mum's best friend, brought us casseroles every few days. She said she was missing her too. 'She'll be back soon,' she said but I didn't believe her. She was curious about Australia. I told her all the lies I was telling everyone else.

The house was silence and lies.

Over the next days I heated Aunt Dot's casseroles for my father and me but he mostly said he wasn't hungry so I ate them.

I left my packing to the last moment, dumping almost everything I owned on my bed and the overflow on to Alexis'.

Then I shoved most of the clothes back into my wardrobe and put things, almost at random, into a small suitcase.

My trousers were a bit tight so I put on a dark blue dress and court shoes. I longed to be in my tracksuit running the hills. When I came back everything would be the same.

My luggage, one small bag, was at the front door. I was sitting at the kitchen table. Something banged. I swung round hard and looked out. My father stepped back from the boot of the car.

Neither of us had been to the airport before. In the car he gave me a road atlas, opened it to the right page and showed me the route. I wouldn't be much use. We quickly left the village and too soon were on the road leading to the airport. I stared out the window, hoping we would never get there.

'Mum,' I said to the windscreen, unsure whether I'd spoken aloud.

'She sends her love. She's sad she couldn't get home in time. She'll write.' His tone said that was the end of that conversation.

Then he said, 'Lucy will be with you soon. When is it?'

My father had telephoned Aunt Davida although I didn't know what they said.

'Two weeks,' I lied. 'Aunt Davida will be at the airport to meet me.' Lucy had promised. I had to believe her.

Lucy hadn't bought her ticket yet. There was trouble with one of her brothers and her mother said she had to stay and get a job.

My father and I didn't really speak again until he was parking the car.

'Your mother will miss you,' he said.

I looked at him and wondered whether he would miss me and what had made him change his mind. He's never been good with words.

We were far too early. My father strode ahead, (he always did), carrying my case. Neither of us knew where to go and there were so many people, queues everywhere.

'Sit here,' he said pointing to a chair. He put my bag down beside it. I wasn't used to seeing him look so lost.

I checked my shoulder bag for my passport and my ticket: a return ticket, valid for a year. My father had paid for everything and given me some traveller's cheques with instructions to open a bank account in Melbourne. I expected his usual 'money doesn't grow on trees' but it didn't come.

We joined the queue for my flight. It was long. Everyone else had loads more luggage than me. I began to regret some of the stuff I left behind. We stood together, moving slowly.

At the desk the girl in uniform wasn't much older than I was.

I gave her my luggage and handed over my ticket and passport. She smiled and said, 'Change at Singapore.'

'Put them somewhere safe,' my father said as we left the desk, pointing to my passport and boarding pass. His lips parted, I waited, but he didn't say more.

I tried to look as if a great adventure was beginning.

My last morning. I couldn't stop thinking of it like that, an execution, the prisoner's last wishes. (Dickens, too many books, an overhyped imagination.) What were mine? Not to go through those dark doors in front of me, to stay with my mother, go to Durham and read English, spend hours at Lucy's, listening to her tapes, watching their telly.

The other thing I pushed away, making my decision the way I usually do: blindly, impulsively. 'You fool,' I told myself.

My father offered to get me a Coke. I stared at him. I didn't think that word was in his vocabulary. I grabbed it as love.

The final call for my flight.

He held me by the shoulders and hugged me, a big hug for him. 'Be good,' he said, then asked if I had my Bible. 'Yes,' I said. A lie. I was done with that stuff.

'Write to us,' he said. A quick wave.

I waited but he didn't look back.

It's not too late: a small whisper in my head. You can stay here.

23

A different whisperer attacked: she's gone away. Don't be a coward. Go, then you can come back and nothing will be changed.

I walked through the 'Passengers Only' door. There was no-one to help me now. What had I done? I asked myself over and over. Why had it happened, and I cried out in anger against my sister.

A couple of nights ago, in a dream, I saw my mother standing in my bedroom doorway. She was singing but I couldn't recognise the song or understand the words. I put out my arms to her and as I did so she grew smaller and smaller, then disappeared.

Chapter 6

Melbourne Airport

I stood a little way from the double doors, my bag at my feet. People rushed past, excited voices clouted my ears. Aunt Davida must be somewhere.

'So here you are, Lucy's best friend.'

I swung around and a woman flung her arms around me. Lines at the corners of her mouth ran upwards, her face was all smile and her brown hair flowed loosely around her shoulders.

'Lucy's description was perfect,' she said.

I wanted to throw myself into her arms and cry. The long hours in the plane and blank fear had snatched away my words. My tongue lolled, my jaw snapped closed. I had barely spoken for nearly thirty hours.

'Sorry, Malcolm says I talk too much, but then he hardly speaks at all. Sorry, my dear, I hope Lucy warned you about me. You'll meet Malcolm at home. He agrees that my intentions are good. You must be deadly tired. Please call me Davida.'

She reached up and placed both her hands on my shoulders, hands that were strong but gentle. 'We must get you doing some yoga, get those shoulders back. Welcome. Welcome.' She stared into my eyes, catching me like a startled rabbit, then she picked up my case and walked briskly towards glass doors marked 'Exit', continuing to talk, flinging words back over her shoulder. 'It will do me good to have someone in the house. I'm too used to my own way. That's what Malcolm says. He has a house around the corner; he lives half there and half with me. It suits us both. He's into architecture and the rights of the individual, a funny mix.'

I didn't know what to say so I trailed after her, her clothes floating, ghostly following. We wove around people and shops.

'I don't know anything about babies, but I have students who do.' She stopped briefly and turned to me. 'Enough of me, we must get you home.'

It was winter in Australia but the fields were brown, (I learned to call them paddocks) strung with desultory wire fences and dotted with occasional sheep. I was trying to get my head round calling a woman nearly as old as my mother by her first name.

'It's so different; it's not what I expected.' The words limped out.

'We've had a drought but that's normal. It's not like this everywhere, just between the airport and the city. These paddocks don't know if they are countryside or city in the making. You'll love the bush.' Davida turned and smiled.

I didn't think so. People got lost in the bush and were never seen again.

Davida drove slowly in the middle lane as cars flashed past on either side. Some drivers hooted, their mouths opening and closing like the goldfish in my dentist's surgery.

'You must miss the green.' Davida pointed again and the car swerved, following her finger. Car horns blasted.

I grabbed the dashboard.

'Oops, sorry, Sophie has a mind of her own. We've been together ten years; we understand each other. I don't work her too hard; she's too old for that.'

'There's lots that's beautiful,' Davida continued, hunched over the steering wheel.

I started to say thank you. She waved the words away.

'It's years since I've been to Yorkshire. How's my lovely niece?'

'Lucy's great,' I said. 'She's going to be a teacher. The kids will love her. But she's got a job right now. She's working in the chemist in town.'

Davida nodded. 'She'll come out here. I promise.'

To show I was not a total moron I told her about my family. My silly voice went on and on, and still I dribbled out more: that my father worked too hard at his practice and the church. She smiled when I mentioned the church and I remembered that she might be a Catholic like Lucy. She didn't look like one.

I couldn't talk about my mother and there wasn't much more I could say about my father so that left Alexis. I put on my best bright voice and said, 'Alexis lives in London but doesn't come home often.'

'What about you?' Davida asked. 'What are you going to do?'

'I'll go to university next year.'

'I meant what will you do until the baby comes?' Davida said softly.

The baby, I said to myself. If I could say the word 'baby' it might be real.

I watched the countryside flit by.

'You could help me with my yoga, she said. 'I have a small studio built on to the back of the house. It takes up most of the back yard. I teach six students at a time. Malcolm says I'm hopeless with money and keeping records. I expect I am. Mind you, he's not much better. You could help with the admin.' Her voice was warm and low. Her students must love her.

'Or there's a coffee bar around the corner that might give you a job,' she said. 'I live near the university so there's plenty your age around. Have you done any yoga?'

I shook my head.

The paddocks gave way to a sprawl of houses until the freeway ran out and we turned left following the signs to the university. Trees and grass divided the wide road into three: single lanes down the two far sides and a very wide central carriageway for trams and cars in both directions. The trams were noisy green beasts. I grew to love them. The streets were busy with students just as Davida had promised. I spotted an Italian ice cream bar, restaurants and several cake shops. Davida pointed to a wine bar: 'Jimmy's,' she said, 'very popular.' It was lunchtime and tables and chairs were set up on the pavement, all occupied.

Davida manoeuvred Sophie into a side street. 'This suburb was originally mostly Italian,' she said. 'It's still great for food shops and restaurants.'

We turned into an even smaller side street narrowly missing a car parked close to the corner. The houses were all different from each other: large and small, brick, stone, wood, huddled together like tents at a fair. It wasn't anything like home where everything was built of stone. Davida angle parked in front of number 32, a narrow two storey semi-detached house. It and its neighbour had wrought iron fences enclosing small gardens and balconies on the first floor decorated with pretty iron lacework. The garden in front of us was wild and overgrown.

'We're home.' She reached over and hugged me.

The front door opened and a man stood there smiling.

Later, in the room that was to be mine, I stood naked in front of the mirror and looked at my belly.

The next day, I wrote to my mother. She would get the letter somewhere. I asked her to telephone me as soon as she was home. I made up all sorts of stuff about a church and its minister and congregation. God hadn't helped me so the lies didn't bother me.

Two weeks later she telephoned. She got the time wrong so it was 6 a.m. Davida didn't mind. She was always up early for her yoga practice.

'Hello Pet,' my mother said. Her voice was that of one who had forgotten how to speak.

'Mum.' I couldn't keep the sobs from my voice. She always called me her brave little warrior. That was gone.

Davida heard and came running. She chatted to my mother, while I got myself together. I heard her say what a lovely girl I was, what fun we were having. She even mentioned the coffee bar. I don't think my mother said much.

'When did you get home?' I asked my mother. She sounded tired.

'Today.'

I wanted to ask about the place where she'd been. Instead I told her about Davida and Melbourne; made life sound great.

'You sound happy,' she said. 'I'm glad.'

'I'll write, Mum,' I promised. 'Often.'

Davida is like no-one I've ever known. 'You manage your own destiny,' she told me, over and over.

I loved Malcolm from the beginning. On the weekends he and I took the tram to the beach. If it was hot he wore the same clothes: tee shirt, old shorts and sandals. Despite the sun he had white skinny legs that never got brown. He didn't seem to notice when my belly grew big. He swam, I paddled in the shallows.

Or we walked to the park and sat together on a bench. He taught me the names of the trees.

'Over 600 different species of eucalyptus trees,' he said. We could only find a dozen or so.

And birds. Chocolate brown birds with black heads and yellow bills the size of thrushes were everywhere. They bounced along the nature strips. 'Mynah birds,' Malcolm said.

My favourite were black and white slender birds, smaller than our magpies: 'Magpie larks,' he said.

I laughed, 'Two birds in one.'

He'd never been to England so I told him about our steep green fields with walls wandering over them, of sheep and of Lower Newhouses with its cobbled street and brown flowing river. He was impressed

29

I made friends at Davida's classes, especially Jo. She was a few years older than me, was already married and had a six-month-old baby, Mario. We went to the Italian coffee bar round the corner after her class on Monday mornings. It was only small, almost like the front room of a house. I always had the same: cappuccino and a piece of cake. Jo only had black coffee. 'Trying to get rid of this,' she said, patting her tummy.

I kept putting off asking but finally, when I was nearly eight months I said, 'What was it like?'

'The birth?' she said and looked hard at me. 'No fun, but he was worth it.' She pointed to Mario in the pram beside us.

I didn't ask any more. I'm good at that, hiding away stuff I don't want to think about, putting it in a box and closing the lid.

Davida sent me to her doctor, a kind old man. She must have told him about me because he didn't ask any awkward questions, like about the father, or why I was here, so far from home. He said I was strong and healthy and should have no problems. Then he asked, 'Are you keeping the baby?' His eyes were soft.

I didn't reply.

'There are plenty of good people who would look after your baby and love it,' he said. Davida must have told him what I was going to do.

I told him I wanted a girl. He just smiled and gave me details of what he called antenatal classes but I didn't go.

I made up my mind long ago but I still longed to ask my mother what to do.

Chapter 7

January 1976

Malcolm was there when the pains started. He drove me to hospital. Davida said she was too excited (she meant worried) to drive, so she was in the back seat.

I should have listened to what Jo was not saying. My stoicism fled, or perhaps didn't exist and when the pain drove me to cry out I hated the thing that was tearing me open and turned away from the white bundle that the nurse held out to me.

Lucy sat beside my bed with Clare in her arms. Clare made noises for her (she kept her real speaking for me, that's what I told myself) grunted and waved her chubby feet free from her blanket.

No longer school kids, either of us.

'They call you 'Mrs',' Lucy said. She looked tired. She'd arrived too late for the birth but with the largest bunch of flowers I'd ever seen.

She looked along the ward. I watched her count: twenty mothers and twenty-one babies in two clinical soldierly rows.

Lucy still wanted me to keep Clare.

'What sort of mother would I make?'

'A good one,' Lucy said, looking cross.

'I left, remember, so Mum wouldn't find out,' I said a little tartly.

The bottle, that's when it happened.

The nurse lowered her voice when she said, 'It's not a good idea; the bonding will make it too difficult…' She tailed off, and didn't say what 'it' was. I watched other mothers fix their babies on their breasts, tiny hands pressing into soft flesh. I cried to see such love. Nothing had prepared me for it.

She tried to curl her hands around the bottle, her perfect fingers in miniature, with the nails not much bigger than a matchstick head, the tip of the second finger bent slightly back, replicating my own and my mother's. She was not a changeling, she was mine: my daughter. I said the words over and over.

But I would do as I planned whatever it took. Too young in my head or too silly to think beyond the next day; too frightened to look into my mother's eyes and say, 'I'm pregnant.' (She would not have stopped loving me. I know that now. I should have known it then.)

A woman in a formal grey suit and carrying a briefcase, a strong purposeful woman, came to the hospital and stood at the end of my bed. She said I could keep Clare for six weeks. She offered me that blink in time as a gift. I wondered why six weeks, why not seven or five or… Then she saw Clare and softened, put down her briefcase and bent over to touch her. 'She's beautiful,' she said.

I lent her to strangers to admire and cuddle, but she was utterly mine.

Clare talked to me but I couldn't understand her.

Before we left hospital I counted the feeds for the allotted time: 228 plastic bottle feeds.

I took her back to Davida's. She had her own miniature yoga mat. She laid there, the sun streaming through the window, while we did sun salutes, triangles and headstands; stretched and chanted. She gurgled and did her own stretches.

Lucy was sleeping on a couch downstairs. It was quieter there than sharing with Clare and me and the broken nights.

My mother sent me a newly knitted cardigan, turquoise. It fitted perfectly. And three books: a curious collection of *Madame Bovary,* a John Updike and Paul Theroux's *Great Railway Bazaar.* Perhaps she thought of me as the great traveller.

'You can't be my niece and not do yoga,' Davida said to Lucy.

She was hopeless at first, knew it and didn't care. We all laughed with her and after three weeks of daily classes she did a passable headstand, so passable it was better than mine.

Lucy and I went to the coffee bar every day. It had a large metal container of not very good coffee but delicious buns and cakes. I ordered my usual and gave Clare her bottle. Everyone there made a fuss of Clare.

Lucy picked her up and held her on her knee. She looked down at Clare and said, 'I'm going to have lots of kids.'

'All girls.'

'Of course.'

She's given up on teaching.

'London,' she said. 'Climb the career ladder.' Her full cheeks dimpled. 'Quickly.'

She had to leave after three weeks, go back to work.

I walked Clare everywhere. I pushed the pram down the streets to the gardens, found a seat, lifted Clare out, wrapped her in her light blanket and held her on my knee. Or to the beach where we sat on the sand and watched the children and the waves. I built elaborate sandcastles for her while she slept and knew that one day she would make her own.

Malcolm was away and Davida saw that it was time for Clare and me, just the two of us. I wanted inside her head, to answer the questions in her eyes, to interpret her small grunts. I watched the curling of her fingers and the waving of her exquisite chubby feet. I told her about Lower Newhouses and the green hills.

33

I told her about her grandmother.

Someone else would name the birds and the eucalyptus trees for her.

I wheeled her through the streets, waiting for the women to stop and admire her. They saw in Clare their own miracle, their own umbilical cord attached forever.

I told her I loved her, that I was letting her go to a mother and father that would always love her.

'It's not too late to change your mind,' Davida said. I just shook my head.

I didn't say that I had not foreseen this love. I had imagined nothing. That is what flight is.

Chapter 8

A timid moon glimmered. There was nothing to mark that day out as exceptional. It was Wednesday 25th February. A hot Melbourne summer had passed and it was yet to wane.

I lay on my bed at Davida's; Clare propped on my stomach. She would be six weeks old tomorrow.

I talked to her through the night, tried to tell her everything she would need for a lifetime. She gazed at me, wanting more stories: of the family, the village, the dales, our wild bleak countryside and the white Christmases she would marvel at. I prayed she wouldn't burn her fair skin in the unrelenting sun. I told her stories about pretty little girls, happy little girls. She listened, screwing up her perfect nose and responding with small grunts. There was no time to speak of boys.

Then she slept. I talked softly on. She must not to be afraid of anything. If there were shadows let them flicker and be brief; smile always, have fun, have music in her life.

She trusted me to watch her through all her nights and listen to her dreams.

Dawn of the 26th and still the clocks counted time while my world tiptoed by. At noon I gave her the last bottle. (Two more in total than I had calculated.) She sucked greedily, waving her perfect legs and curling her toes. Her small hands gripped the bottle tightly. I gazed and gazed more.

A new dress that day, the prettiest I could find. No hand-me-downs from the charity shop. I laid her on the bed, changed her nappy and buried my face in her tummy, kissed it, gazed into her eyes, willing the love in my heart to follow. I put on her dress, buttoning it up carefully. Then her leggings and bootees.

I carefully manoeuvred her chubby small arms into the cardigan and wrapped her loosely in her shawl. The shawl had pink edging which matched her bonnet, her going-away outfit. In a bag I packed a spare bottle and a clean nappy although the one she was wearing was pristine.

'The most beautiful baby in the world,' I whispered to her.

Clare stared at me, trust in her eyes. She didn't know of the betrayal to come. Perhaps she was hoping for another trip to the beach.

'Don't let anyone tell you I didn't care,' I whispered. 'It will be like you have died when you go. Don't try to persuade me with your eyes. I want you to be happy.' I touched her errant finger and kissed her shapely nose, her unwrinkled forehead, her flushed cheeks and her tiny full lips that still tasted of milk.

My daughter, I whispered to her: 'I have spread my dreams under your feet. Tread softly because you tread on my dreams.' I kissed her softly on her full mouth. She would find Yeats for herself later.

The doorbell rang: the tall woman with big hands and functional shoes. She repeated what she had already told me.

'Have you done this before?' I asked. I knew her name but refused to say it, even in my head.

The woman looked puzzled, her mouth pursed, her long straight thin lips gyrated. My eyes begged her. She said, pain in her voice, (so she was a good woman and I almost liked her) 'She's going to a good home; they will take great care of her.' She added, 'She will be special.'

'She's that already,' I said. The woman looked away.

What was her new mother like? They would give her a name

36

of their choosing.

We sat: the woman, Davida and me and a baby. The baby, my baby, let her eyes wander, trusting eyes. From my lap she uttered small, contented noises. We made noises: the weather, the traffic and other banalities until we faded into silence.

I held Clare for a last time then passed her carefully to Davida, holding on to her tiny right foot for a second before tucking it into the shawl. Davida kissed her gently on the forehead and didn't hide her tears.

I would not let the woman see mine.

Leaden feet carried me back up the stairs to my bedroom and the empty cot. I asked myself over and over: had I made a terrible mistake? I would never know.

The front door slammed shut.

I gave her away just as I told myself I would. The woman with the functional shoes said it would get less, the pain that brought on moments of madness and disbelief that life was worth living.

My daughter – I wanted to watch over her all my life – has gone to another mother who cannot fail to love her.

My daughter – I love to say those words. Time stopped when Clare went.

I went to the supermarket and bought a bottle of gin. I didn't bother with the tonic or ice and lemon. Half and half – water and gin. I was horribly sick. The next day I found cuts on my hands and face and couldn't remember how they got there. I threw out what was left of the bottle.

The pain of her, of her beauty, the way her full lips pursed, the smile.

Davida and I walked and walked: through and round the nearby gardens day after day. She waited for me to speak. I couldn't. My fingers ached to touch Clare's silk-soft skin. Sometimes Malcolm came but nothing changed.

Finally Davida said, 'Clare is beautiful. You have a beautiful daughter.'

'No longer mine,' I dragged out.

'She will always be yours and you will always be hers.'

'She has another mother,' I said. One who will feed her, dry her tears, prepare her for the world.

'And a father,' Davida said. 'You couldn't give her that.'

I had, purblind, followed a path that I might regret forever.

I lurked round women with small babies, peered into prams. They turned away from me, afraid. I wanted to tell them that I had a baby, once, that I had made a mistake.

My exhaustion sucked the light from everyone I met. At my coffee bar they hesitated to approach. Strangers gazed at me oddly then faded away. My trousers and tee shirt were not clean but not outright dirty. I still washed. Sometimes. I tried not to go outside until dark, hurrying into the shadows and avoiding casual encounters, fearing the shutting of tram doors, the quiescent bay water lapping the sand.

It was winter inside my head, an English winter, not the mild Melbourne slide into autumn. Snow, lots and lots of it, piled up, suffocating; flaky stuff that got into everything. I welcomed the nothingness.

I run and run to the point of exhaustion, to the point of hope: that I may find her in Davida's arms waiting for me to run back to her.

Outside the mild winter passed. October. It would soon be summer. I gathered all the evidence together and carried down the big things first: the cot, the pram and next the toys, then the clothes. All back to the charity shop. I pushed my face into her small vests and pants: nothing. A sealed loop of memories ran through my head, second by second, again and again.

The photographs. For two whole days I sorted them, a kaleidoscope of love: baby in mother's arms, Clare and Davida, Clare in the pram, Lucy and Clare, Clare lying on the grass in the park, Clare under the trees, baby sleeping, smiling, crying: Clare, Clare.

When I could hold a conversation I telephoned my mother and father. 'I'm going to stay here a while,' I said. 'Travel.'

There was silence. Then, 'I half expected that,' she said, a catch in her voice. 'You haven't mentioned university for a time.'

I hadn't.

'I'll get a job here. I can still go to university when I get back.'

Would I ever go back? Leave Clare?

PART II

Chapter 9

1979 The Desert

I write back to my mother but not often enough. I write about the drought. It will be hard for them, in their wet countryside, to understand. I tell her I am happy and make up things to stop myself writing 'my daughter'.

She sends me news of my sister. I don't want to know but I read the words. Alexis married, not long after I left Melbourne, more than two years ago. She has a son. He's a year and a few months younger than Clare. My mother and father didn't go to the wedding. I'm curious but don't ask why.

Another letter and it's the church fete. 'I cooked for days,' she writes. 'I missed my helper.'

It's a long time since I've been that.

The kitchen was my mother's, her dominion. I can see her now, sitting at the table, the sun shining in the window and playing with her brown hair, teasing the tight waves that she has permed every couple of months. She often brought her knitting or sewing and sat with us while we did our homework.

Saturday was her baking day and mine when I was still at the school in the village. I had my own apron in a drawer in the dresser. 'Your apron, Pet,' she would say as she put hers on and got out her recipe books.

Together we decided what to make, usually sponge or butterfly cakes. Or biscuits.

I loved getting my hands into the mix but mostly she made me use the wooden spoon. Sometimes we sang hymns. My favourite was '*All things bright and beautiful...*' The cooker brooded hot and dangerous. I called it my green dragon. We weren't allowed to touch it. Later we sat at the long kitchen table while I stuffed myself. The kitchen was warm and fusty with the fug of freshly baked cakes.

Often Aunt Dot joined us. She's thin and wiry and runs everywhere. She was in and out of our house almost every day except the weekends, drinking tea, gossiping and laughing with my mother. I eavesdropped sometimes but it was pretty boring.

Alexis was always out somewhere.

'The best fete yet,' my mother writes.

In another letter Alexis has a new job. The way my mother describes it she might be cooking for the Queen. 'Cordon bleu,' my mother says. I don't know what that is and I don't think that my mother does either but it sounds good.

Behind her bright chatty words my mother's missing me, says she will have to come and see me if I don't come home soon. We both know she won't. It isn't the money. She's not strong. Those are the words my father uses. And she won't leave my father.

He writes sometimes, mostly about God and forgiveness. I write back, not often, about the birds I've seen: corellas, budgerigars, cockatoos and one hobby. I identify them using the book he gave me just before I left home: *Birds of Australia*.

I long for books. Some of the travellers leave theirs behind. I used to be fussy but now I read anything.

I've started a diary, a notebook really, and call it *Clare's Story*. I'm terrified she'll escape from my head. I have the photos. Not enough. I put things down on paper, make them real: the way she stretched and frowned, a tiny furrow creasing her forehead and the way she gazed at me with love and trust. Yes, I know babies don't focus that young but she was different. Don't all mothers know their babies are different? And I was a mother. For six weeks.

I struggle to recall her smell and the way her soft flesh surrendered to my touch. I wrap my empty arms around my body.

I write poems for her. They are rubbish.

On bad days that can segue into weeks I hide behind my hair and carry her in my head on random walks in the dawn while the sun loiters like a prima donna. The light, delicate and coy, teases: a little further, come, come, a few more steps. I never reach anywhere except more parched earth that stretches over hundreds of miles to Alice and beyond. I suck in the light, directing it inward to my shadows.

I cadge a lift from one of the travellers and arrive in Melbourne a couple of months after her third birthday.

I check in to a cheap hotel near Flinders Street Station and go to Myers to buy new clothes. I must look good for her. Schools have been back a little more than a month and summer is waning. I don't let Davida know I'm here.

In my new clothes I catch a bus to Melbourne's most expensive suburb, Toorak. I have the address of two nursery schools where the houses and gardens are large and the streets are populated with sleek new cars that probably cost the same as a small house in the country. Her parents are well off. That's about all I know.

I'm there early enough to see babies and toddlers carried on their fathers' or mothers' backs and in prams; small hands reaching up to hold big hands and short legs, chubby and bursting to grow, running to keep up. Surreptitiously I examine toddlers in pushchairs. I'm certain I will recognise her.

Morning and afternoon I lurk a short distance away and watch the mothers and children laugh and chatter together, an exclusive club: the hugs, the kisses, the love. I see the mothers get out their handkerchiefs and wipe the small faces, listen to their tales, tie their shoelaces and tell them to hurry up.

Yet I will return no more. I am a ghost, they are ghosts. I can only see a baby. No first steps, no real words although she spoke to me and I didn't understand.

Chapter 10

1981

The talk in the bar is of Lindy Chamberlain and the dingo she claims took her nine-week-old daughter, Azaria.

Dusk is well past and the pub is unusually crowded with at least twenty men and a scattering of women, mostly at the bar. Only a few are sitting on the sofas in the dark recesses.

One young man, younger than most of the travellers, says, 'Not the bloody dingo mate,' to no-one in particular.

Heads nod in agreement.

'Oh she's guilty, alright,' says another. 'Those Seven-Day Adventists.'

Her husband is a Seventh-Day Adventist Minister. I haven't a clue what that means but I'm sure she's innocent. She was camping at Uluru when she was heard to cry out: 'A dingo's got my baby.' No body, just bloodstained clothes.

How could she bear it?

My father is dead. Six years after I left home, almost five of them here at the hotel.

My mother sent a radio message: 'Dad died peacefully yesterday. He loved you. I don't expect you can make the funeral. You will be with us anyway. Love, Mum.'

I was away from the hotel, one of Harry's long-promised trips, and only got the message four days later. He was buried by then.

I travel to Alice with the oil truck to phone her.

'I'm so sorry Pet,' she says. 'A lovely service. It was packed.' She sounds proud. 'You were missed,' she adds. I can hear her trying not to let the part about being missed sound like an accusation. 'Love you,' she says. She doesn't cry but doesn't say much either.

'I'll write,' she says. 'We gave him a good send-off.' She makes it sound like a holiday. 'Your father was a good man.'

Perhaps he was. I don't really know.

I tell Steve a little about him, say he was strict.

'My father was the opposite,' says Steve. 'Didn't care where we were or what we did.'

Chapter 11

1982

The travellers bring the latest news and sometimes the newspapers. Britain is fighting for those remote islands that the Americans and Argentineans call the Malvinas and the British call The Falklands. One of the men says, 'We should've been there, we'd have shown them.' The *Belgrano* is sunk while steaming away. Over three hundred dead.

'And a woman too,' a man not much older than me says, meaning Maggie Thatcher. I hear admiration in his voice.

Just when I'm thinking about leaving (there's more to life, I tell myself) and I'm getting bored, an old man arrives at the hotel. He drives a battered blue car and erects a compact tent on the campsite.

He's a small, tidy man with greying hair, neatly cut beard and a face tanned by the harsh sun. He wears dark coloured shorts and vest. High up on his right arm is a small tattoo of a desert flower. It's his eyes I can't miss: intense violet eyes the colour of stained-glass windows, eyes to trust. He is old.

He says that names don't matter, that Bill will do.

The next day I see him sitting by the water and I join him. The few trees are crammed with noisy flocks, mostly corellas and galahs. An enormous spoonbill perches twenty feet up on the metal frame of the water pump. It's there for days. The old man says it must be lost or sick. One morning it's gone. All the living

49

is here for the water.

I take time off from the bar and we drive into the desert. The blue car floats over the corrugations. We head over the spinifex-speckled sand, crossing the polished pebbles of dry riverbeds their banks spotted with mulga bushes. Birds screech at us, offended by the encroachment on their territory. The rivers don't flow for long, but keep their secrets, hunching their silvered shoulders and slipping underground to the cool darkness where they flow on. The old man knows how to find water in the dry beds.

The roads are sparsely dotted with cars turned on to their roofs. 'Aborigines,' he says. 'Easy to get their wheels off that way.'

Later we stop, seek the shade of a meagre tree. We lean against its thin trunk, our shoulders touching. The car crouches low in the searing heat, its doors flung wide.

He points to a carcass: skin and bones. 'A camel,' he says. It is lying on the earth a short way off. 'Been there years,' he said. 'The soft bits, the guts, get taken and the dryness preserves the rest.'

We are both silent. It's a harsh land but I love it.

'I have a son,' the old man says softly, 'a boy. Well, he's grown now.'

'How old?' I ask and shift a little to move into the speckled shade.

'Old enough,' he says. 'He left home after a fight. There was just the two of us. We were glass-blowers. It was good working with him; he was full of ideas.' The old man falls into reverie then tells of the transformation of lumpish dullness to crystalline wonder, the ordinary into the remarkable, the inert coming alive in the white heat of the furnace.

'Timing is everything in glass making,' he says. 'You need two pairs of hands to make glass. We worked as one although we were searching for different things.' His face softens. I read in it love for his son. And the glass.

'His wanted to create glass the colour no-one has known. I wanted that for him too.'

'And you?' I say.

He is silent a moment, as if reluctant to say. Then he says, 'Mine was to create the figure I have carried in my head all my life.' He moves his hands to form a shape but it is too vague. His forehead is creased with concentration.

'I made hundreds but they were never quite right.' He talks on, a lot of words for him. 'My son grew restless, impatient and the heat of the furnace got to him. He left saying not to look for him, that he had his own way to find. He knows how to survive. I taught him that,' he sighs, 'and the glass.'

After a time I say, 'Six weeks, six wonderful weeks.'

I dig in my pocket and take out a photograph. I carry it with me, always. It is sweaty and mangled. 'Clare,' I say. 'She's six now but I haven't seen her for a very long time.'

I look at it before I pass it over. It was taken two days before she went.

He takes it carefully.

I'm wearing a bright yellow dress and Clare, lying across my knees, has on her white dress and cardigan and is squinting a little.

'The sun was strong,' I say. 'Melbourne, late February.' But I know the exact date: 14th February. 'Hot,' and I add, 'not as hot as here.' She's wearing a floppy hat but I'm shading her from the sun so the brim is pushed back.

'The bay,' I say, 'Port Phillip bay. We went there a lot. A couple of tram rides away.'

'We?' he says. He thinks I am speaking of her father.

'Malcolm. Not her father.' I look at him. 'He's about your age. Malcolm and Davida. They took me in. Davida's a yoga teacher. I owe her.'

'Ah,' he says. 'Yoga. I did yoga until I got too old, too stiff.'

We look together at the photograph. My giant hand cradles her shoulder and her diminutive one, with its nails still soft, is raised beside her face, fingers lightly curled, except the one. Her bare feet are tucked under her dress but I know what they look like: neat, regular toes, chubby toes, bursting with growth. We are smiling for each other.

'The water was warm.' I turn to look at him.

His eyes are wet: for his son? For my Clare? For us?

'We paddled.'

She gazed down at the swish and roll of the waves. The envious sun catapulted up its brilliance from the water. She closed her eyes.

The sea will always mean Clare for me. Perhaps that's why I chose to run to the desert: as far away from the sea as I could get.

'She changed me,' I tell the old man.

The temperature rises to fifty degrees, but that doesn't bother him. I burn easily so cover up and always wear a wide-brimmed hat. I have two pairs of lightweight trousers and two tee shirts with longish sleeves which I alternate. My plimsolls are battered. No-one out here cares much about clothes.

In the far distance – I still find distance difficult in the dry thin air – ten or fifteen red kangaroos with hare-like ears and excessively long padded feet and thick tails keep us company. The creatures leap giant strides on overlong hind legs, their small front legs held close to their chests like half arms, their bodies leaning forward slightly. The heat dances in waves, blurring everything. When we stop the creatures stop. The old man says that in a season of abundance (a strictly relative term) a female can have one young hopping beside her, another in her pouch, breastfed there and a third in its womb waiting for the good times.

All the desert waits. Death in this harsh burning land is easy.

Chapter 12

1982

It was my birthday yesterday, 6th September. I was twenty-three. Steve threw a party in the bar. Only ten of us. We had a cake with twenty-three candles and, a great rarity here, chocolates.

Steve's cabin door slams. In the still dawn sound carries. I turn over to snatch more sleep. It's that empty part of night before first light scurries in through carelessly closed curtains.

Not much later, when I am hovering between dozy wakefulness and sleep, Steve taps on the door, pushes it open and stands beside my bed. He's in shorts and tee shirt despite the bitter early morning cold. On his feet, as always, flip-flops.

'A radio message for you, Ruth,' Steve says. In his outstretched hand a piece of paper.

I stare at him, at his hand. He looks at me a moment or two then leans forward and kisses the top of my head before walking quietly out the door.

I hold the paper between thumb and forefinger but don't read it. I turn to look at the clock: 6.30 a.m. It would be 9.30 or 7.30 p.m. in England. I forget which. I put the piece of paper on the bed, shove on some flip-flops and walk to the toilet block. Steve's face has told me all.

Back in my cabin, shivering a little, I sit on the edge of the bed and put out my hand.

'Mum died yesterday. Telephone me. Alexis.'

I read the words again. And again.

I had a letter only yesterday. She sounded cheerful. Mothers are supposed to go on forever. And there's so much I have to tell her. Too late. She has taken my untruths with her.

Just a couple of months ago Steve was driving to Alice so I tagged along and telephoned her from the post office.

'You and your sister must stick together, look after each other,' my mother said, her voice trembling a little. 'Come home soon.'

I don't bother with a shower, don't bother with much. I put on my plimsolls, a pair of trousers and a top. I slam the door as I leave, running. It's not too hot yet but still I sweat with the effort of forcing my feet through the soft red dirt, up and over the dunes, the steepest I can find. Punishment. My feet dig in deeper and I breathe now in short desperate bursts. If I could keep running I could undo this lie also. It would not be too late; I could go home and find her standing at the front door, love in her eyes and arms to wrap around me.

I would tell her about Clare, every little detail. She would love her too. My raucous breath and the blood pumping in my ears compete. I stop and sink to the ground, put my head in my arms and bawl, howl like a toddler.

It gets hotter. I am quiet now. I have come out without water, without my hat. I'm not sure of the way back. And I don't care.

I don't know how much later it is when I feel the sand shift beside me. It's Steve.

'Followed your footprints,' he said. 'It's getting a bit hot.' He holds out a bottle of water and takes off his cap and puts it on my head. I manage a smile.

'You can send a radio message. I've booked a flight for you

tomorrow from Alice. I assume you are going.'

I nod.

I tell the old man that my mother is dead. His eyes offer comfort and I murmur that I haven't seen her for nearly seven years. Words are like water in the desert.

We are sitting, a long way from the hotel, in the mean shade of a stunted tree. It's late afternoon and the sun will soon fall off the horizon with its usual reckless flush.

'My mother,' I say.

'My mother,' I try again. 'You'd have liked her.' It seems a betrayal to put her in the past tense so soon. I am trying it out. 'Just my father, my sister and me,' I say, 'and Coriander, our cat.'

Corrie was the best purrer in the world.

My mother walked about the house with Corrie hanging over her arm, had her sitting on the piano stool beside her while she played or on her lap while she read.

'I told the kids at school that she was mine but really she was Mum's,' I say.

'A herb,' he says, almost inaudibly.

I nod and smile a little to myself. 'The neighbours must have laughed when they heard her calling 'Corrie' over and over, in the garden.'

I let the silence between us gather. He doesn't move.

'She never went far,' I say. 'Brought up on a farm, a teacher, then to our village where no-one locks their doors, day or night.' But she travelled far with her books; in her head, too far.

'She was often sad,' I say, 'and sometimes had to go away.' He looks at me and waits. I am silent, back in that first time when I watched my father put her, in her white dress, in the car, shut her door, walk round to the other side and climb in. I thought that would be the worst day of my life. It wasn't.

'This might frighten her,' I say, waving at the desert around me and the sun still powering up in the early morning.

55

'She trusted everyone,' I tell the old man. 'Books, music and God. Well, the God bit was more my father.' I'm half talking to myself.

'Your sister,' he says.

'Alexis. She betrayed me.' I pick at it like at a sore.

'You ran away,' he says.

'Yes.' I think about that. 'Yes, I ran away,' I say. 'My mother…' I don't finish.

It's hard, in the desert, to forget. I think of the dead camel, still there.

The old man tells me an Aboriginal story. He begins softly, and speaks of the Dreamtime when animals and people could talk with one another.

'All the animals were happy until one day a cockatoo fell from a tree and broke his neck. The animals couldn't understand why he wouldn't wake up.'

The old man looks up at the few birds in the tree above him. They've fallen silent; some of them have their heads cocked, gazing down at us.

'They met at the spring gathering to discuss it,' the old man continues. 'They couldn't explain it. The eagle hawk, Mullian, said the cockatoo had entered a new existence. Some of the animals wanted to test this so Mullian agreed but insisted that for a time they mustn't know sight, smell, taste, touch or hearing and return in another form. The opossum, wombat and snake all tried but returned after winter no different. Finally the caterpillars asked to try.'

His voice has become softer but I don't have to strain to hear. 'The next spring message sticks were sent everywhere, to the birds, animals and reptiles telling them of the forthcoming great event. At daybreak the dragonflies arrived at the gathering, leading butterflies and moths of all colours. The birds in their excitement sang, creating new songs and all agreed that the butterflies and moths had solved the mystery of death; they had come back in a different form.'

He pauses a moment then says, 'This happens every spring.'

He gives me a gift, a glass figurine: an exquisite glass girl, a dancer, with straight back and proud posture. Her body is draped in a mid-calf-length pink dress, the folds caress her long legs and her feet are encased in delicate oyster pink ballet shoes, the ribbons winding round her slender ankles. Her dark hair is shoulder length, her face tranquil and her hazel eyes as fathomless as the ocean. A brittle beauty. He says that it carries the desert within itself.

We embrace.

The next day Steve and I leave at dawn for Alice and the airport. I am going home.

I've slung what little I have into my small suitcase then look around my cabin. There's no evidence that I've ever been here.

Steve drives at exactly the right speed to minimise the impact of the corrugations. We pass groups of Aboriginals sitting by broken-down vehicles. They have babies and small children.

I want Steve to stop.

'Their own will look after them,' he says.

I worry.

Steve breaks the silence from time to time, to speak of India and his dreams. When we are an hour out of Alice he asks, 'What was she like, your mother?'

'Kind,' I say, 'gentle and very clever.'

'You loved her,' he says, a statement not a question.

My tears start to fall: silent, personal. Steve passes me his handkerchief.

'I'll miss you,' he says. I hear his smile. 'I'll have to train someone else. Don't suppose they'll be as quick as you and not so good with the whoppers.'

I manage a smile back.

'I'll write,' I say and turn away.

At the airport I call Alexis. We haven't spoken for almost seven years. I long for the voice to be my mother's. Already so many regrets.

Alexis gets it over quickly. 'She died on Monday.' Then, 'You need to come home.'

I nod, although she can't see me. 'How did she die?'

'A massive heart attack.' Alexis doesn't offer more.

I tell her I'm on my way and that she must not have the funeral without me. She promises. There was a time, when we were very young, when Alexis and I could tell each other anything, arms wrapped round each other, her murmuring to me that everything would be alright.

I was going home.

PART III

Chapter 13

1982

The luggage trolley slams against the scratched, opaque swing doors.

Thirty hours since I left Melbourne; the wrong time of day and a head overflowing with my mother. Excited babble clouts my ears and I ram my trolley into the naked heels of the woman in front of me. She turns and glares. I mumble an apology. The luggage mountains shuffle past the barrier overhung with people, some holding up signs with names on. I read some: James Roberts, Adventure Tours, Best Taxi Service. I spot the mothers by the tearful excitement on their faces.

One small suitcase. I push and wonder why I bothered with a trolley.

Alexis must be somewhere. The last thing she said on the phone was, 'See you at the airport.'

I pass the barriers and stand.

A few minutes later someone pulls my arm urgently and an excited high voice floats up. 'I found you. Mummy said it was you,' he says. 'She's over there.' He points through a thick throng of people to a table and a lone woman sitting there. I quickly turn away.

'I'm Ben.'

'Hello Ben.' He must be. I reckon up using Clare as the baseline: five and a half.

'I'll push,' he says, taking hold of the trolley. I'm only half listening and he's got the trolley before I can protest. Pushing is an effort for him but he manages. He looks serious, impish, in his brown rimmed glasses and an odd knitted woolly hat in blues and reds pulled down over his ears and framing his face. He wears smart khaki shorts and a yellow tee shirt.

'I know all about you. You're Mummy's sister,' he says. 'You've been to Australia; that's as far as you can go Daddy says. I'll go to Australia when I'm a bit older. Mummy says I can.' The words tumble over themselves.

Skinny legs stick out of new-looking red and yellow sneakers as he leans hard on the trolley, pushing it on an erratic path. Angry people move then smile when they spot the small figure. Looking back over his shoulder he grins with perfect teeth: Alexis' genes. He has her blue eyes too, only a shade or two more brilliant.

My mother wrote often about him. She loved him. I didn't want to know.

'Gran knitted this for me. Mummy hates it.' He points to his beanie. 'Gran said it kept her hands from seizing up. They were all twisted.' He adds, 'She's dead.' Then, 'Mummy says you have been living with black men in the desert. I'd like to do that.'

I laugh, too loudly. Passers-by stare. Ben grins, pleased.

Fifteen yards, ten.

He shouts, 'Mummy, Mummy, I've found Auntie Ruth.'

I'm an aunt.

My sister is perched on a stool at a high round table. She's reading a magazine, one hand turning a page, the other holding the handle of a small coffee cup.

I stop; look at her, a long time.

She has changed. Her once-cropped brown hair is now dirty blonde, shoulder length and hangs down past her carefully plucked eyebrows and her long, straight nose smattered with a light cluster of freckles to her shoulders. She's wearing a silky sundress, a strappy thing of abstract pink flowers with bright yellow centres; no bra. Her legs are crossed then wrapped round each other at the ankle and a sandal with a bow that matches the dress hangs loosely over the ball of one foot. The legs unravel in slow motion and the dress falls limply over her thighs to mid calf.

Ben hurtles towards her. I follow slowly and stand a foot or two away from the table.

'Hello sis,' she says. 'Forgotten what I look like?'

Ben pushes the trolley right to her side.

'You've met Ben, he's wonderful isn't he?' Her northern accent is muted.

I look away: questions, questions, one big one, but not right now. There's my mother to bury first.

She runs her eyes over me: a long slow, meant-to-be-noticed scrutiny.

Alexis pushes back her stool, walks over and flings her arms around me, a touch replete with history. 'Hiya kid,' she says.

My body doesn't yield but she doesn't notice. She jams the magazine into her handbag and leads the way through the crowds. We walk side by side while Ben, still pushing the trolley, keeps in front of us, his hat bobbing away and back. He turns every now and then to shout, 'Come on.'

I want to talk about my mother and I need a bath.

'You look good,' Alexis says. 'You were a gawky kid but you've grown up.'

'It's been a long time,' I say.

'It's not just that,' she says slowly, 'something else. Oh well.' She points to a sleek silver Mercedes. 'Here we are.'

I don't know much about cars but this one is beautiful. 'Expensive,' I say.

'A good divorce settlement helps.' Alexis' laughter is unadulterated guilt. She pauses, the car door in her hand and turns to me, 'I know what it is. You don't look scared anymore. Or lost.'

63

The sky is cloudless, a blank blue page. A clean chill pours in through the open car window. It has the feel of a spring day even though the summer is nearly spent. My mother loved these days. I shiver a little and try to push away the jet lag and hours of stale recycled air, heavy with fear and alcohol. Tiredness is making me stupid. I'd slept as many of the thirty hours as I could, longing for oblivion.

From the back seat Ben chatters, jiggling his legs. 'I have a pet parrot and a dog at home. My dog is called Great Bear, Bear for short. It's the name of a star Dad says. Dad taught me about the stars. They both came from the rescue home.' He giggles. 'I don't mean Dad.'

He carries on, 'I wanted to bring my parrot to show you, but Mum wouldn't let me. I thought you might recognise it because it came from Australia. He's red and blue and green and is called 'Lost' because he doesn't belong here.' His high-pitched voice rattles on. 'I'm allowed to take him to school sometimes.' Annoyance at our failure to reply pitches his voice even higher. 'Mum doesn't like Lost.'

'Or Bear very much,' Alexis says in a voice that I already recognise as special to Ben. 'He's a black and white mongrel and a nuisance, a sloppy thing.'

'What about Coriander?' I ask.

Ben interjects. 'Corrie was great. She used to sleep with me and she limped too, just like Gran.' He leans forward and taps Alexis' shoulder. 'Can I have a cat, Mum?' Alexis shakes her head. This is evidently well rehearsed.

'She died,' Alexis says. 'Mum took her to the vet; she could hardly walk. About six months ago.'

The hills crowd round us, now giants become Lilliputians. Once I knew the name of every one. The sky too has shrunk.

The countryside looks oddly small, broken by ambling stone walls, mostly bare of trees and punctuated with sheep, unkempt shaggy bundles on stick legs. In the valley bottoms the walls run down every few hundred yards to the river's edge, each field with a small stone barn. The sun dances with new windows in renovated old barns and their drives scar the hillsides. The disused train line, running through cuttings and for the most part beside the river, is more overgrown.

Everything has changed.

'We're nearly there. You must be tired,' Alexis says.

I just nod.

'You'll find the village changed,' she says.

As we cross the bridge I peer down at the water, a sludgy brown. It idles to the sea over a hundred miles east and starts thirty miles higher up the dale. A large park runs beside the river. There are swings and a climbing frame. I dreamt away hours on those swings. Perhaps I'll take Ben there.

Alexis points out a new flower shop in the high street, says there are now four cafes (I only remember one), the butcher mum wrote about so that there's now one at either end of the high street. And a new car park. The cake shop is still there. The grocer's looks different but the Post Office and the pubs seem unchanged. Everything huddles at the foot of the hills.

Children and old unsteady legs crowd the narrow pavements. We turn left at the top, past a couple of streets and swing into a cul-de-sac of half a dozen houses. Ours stands a little apart, two storeys, old, and built of stone. Alexis pulls into the drive to park in front of the garage.

Further down the hill is the church hall.

The lawn falls away to the footpath and the house peers down on the rows of neat cottages flanking my old primary school. Fifty-three pupils when I left to go to the grammar school in the nearby town. I count back: fourteen years ago. It looks unchanged.

Alexis steps out of the car and walks briskly towards the house, plucking a key from her handbag. Ben is dragging my case up the front path.

I don't move. I want to believe she's still here, have her put her arms round me one more time. Sixty-one. My father was seventy when he died.

Minutes later the click of the car door opening startles me and Ben puts his small hand into mine, saying, 'Mum sent me.' I climb out of the car on unsteady legs and follow him. I seem to have lost myself as well as my mother. He leads me into the kitchen.

I'm home.

'Take that thing off,' Alexis throws at Ben as she puts on the kettle.

Ben tugs off his hat and chucks it on to a kitchen chair. 'There,' he says and stomps out.

I sit at the kitchen table. There are new scratches in the table and some of the cups are grubby and one has a hairline crack. The chair feels hard, uncomfortable and an electric cooker and hob has replaced the Aga, my green dragon.

We can hear Ben messing about outside.

'Tea?' Alexis asks.

'Coffee please.' I stand, pick up my case and walk to the door.

'Ben's in the spare room,' she calls after me.

I stop and turn around. Our mother called it the guest room but no guests ever came.

'It's cold but he doesn't notice,' Alexis says. 'He loves it, calls it his room.' She gets out some mugs and puts them on the table. 'It'll be like old times.'

I stare at her. She must be mad. Has she forgotten?

Upstairs I dump my case in the bedroom Alexis and I always shared: two beds, a small wardrobe, a chest of drawers and a bookcase on my side of the room, within reach of my bed, still mostly stuffed full. The gaps are where my mother took books to send to me.

I've kept all my books even the ones I had as a kid. I count my Enid Blyton: fifteen, mostly *The Naughtiest Girl* and the *Famous Five* series. For months I wanted to be Elizabeth, bemoaning the fact that I didn't have blue eyes and fair hair (Alexis did but I didn't point that out) and couldn't go to boarding school. Then I tried to make every one call me George.

'Don't be stupid,' Alexis had said, 'it's a boy's name.'

Mum agreed to call me George when it was just the two of us but forgot after a few weeks.

One of my earliest memories is of my mother reading to Alexis and me. Another is hearing her play the piano. She gave us books and more books: for birthdays and Christmas; some from her own childhood (battered and old) and sometimes she took us to the library, a bus trip away, or to the bookshop, said to us from an early age, 'Love is sharing a book you love.'

We read the usual kids' stuff: *Wind in the Willows, Pooh Bear* and Beatrix Potter and then *Little House on the Prairie, Anne of Green Gables* and *Le Petit Prince.* The last three were my favourites. At nine I fell in love with Jo in *Little Women.* I too would be as brave as a lion, always. How I cried when Beth died. I even tried to be nice to Alexis for a while.

As soon I started at the grammar my mother moved to what she called the classics: Jane Austen, the Brontës, George Eliot, Edith Wharton. And Dickens. I didn't get on with Dickens except for *Tale of Two Cities.* I love France although I've never been there.

And poetry, loads of poetry. When I grew up I would be a poet like Emily Dickinson. I'd never marry, just my poetry.

She taught me to read before I was old enough for school and then persuaded them to take me early, so I was always the youngest by far.

I walk to the wall where I run my fingers over the pencil marks on the height chart: Alexis 5ft 7in, Ruth 5ft 6in. I had my growth spurt when I was eleven but never quite caught Alexis up.

The clothes I left behind still hang in the wardrobe. On Alexis' side are a couple of dresses and a pair of trousers that didn't come from any shops around here. I kneel down, fumble in the back and put my hand on a small furry leg, Teddy. Before I exiled him to the darkness he went everywhere with me: I read to him at night, sat him on the stairs with my schoolbooks and gave him the lessons I'd had that day. He was a quick learner. I shove him back into the dark. I was great at giving everything names, but teddy was just Teddy.

My bed is furthest from the door. The bogeyman would get Alexis first, and she'd fight like the devil. We know a lot about the devil.

I sit on the edge of my bed, head bowed. I don't know how I'll get through the next days.

The smell of coffee draws me back to the kitchen. It's large with a long pine table and is the only really warm room in the house.

Alexis and I sit opposite each other at the table. We have slipped into our usual places. Ben is outside playing some complicated game with a pile of sticks.

'Real coffee,' I say, feeling bright since what seems like forever.

'Real coffee,' she says. 'I've slung the instant I expect it's been sitting in the cupboard since Dad died. I brought coffee from London, and,' she points, 'the cafetière. They're the latest thing, make fabulous coffee. You need to give it a minute or two.'

I look at the coffee thing. It's so long since I had a decent cup of coffee anything will taste good.

She blows a puff of smoke. Her smoking is new.

'Wait till you taste it,' she says. 'And the coffee; it's the best in London: French.'

I top up my coffee and search Alexis' face for clues. She's behaving as if nothing has happened. That night then seven years of silence between us. I open my mouth, tell myself to wait and close it. I'm just too tired.

'There's not much more I can tell you,' Alexis says before I can ask. 'A weak heart apparently. Nothing could be done, no warning. The hospital telephoned in the morning and left a message to call

68

them. I didn't get the message until about six. I had a function, a major client. I called the hospital at eight. She died at 4.20 that afternoon.'

I watch Alexis slowly push down the plunger through the water to settle on the coffee grains, wait until its resistance falters then pour coffee into two mugs.

'I sent the telegram the day after she died.' Alexis adds, 'They said she wasn't in pain and it was a good death.'

I hear her indifference, boredom even. 'You don't care that Mum is dead do you?' I get up and take a bottle of milk from the fridge and slop some into my mug. I wave away her offer of sugar. She drinks hers black. I sit back down and stir my coffee and stir it again.

'Don't get cross.' Alexis reaches across to pat my arm. She leans back in her chair. 'She never loved me the way she loved you, not from the start. She couldn't look after me when I was born; Dad got a nurse in. I don't remember but that's what he told me.'

'That's news to me,' I say, putting my spoon down. 'When did he tell you that?'

'Years ago.'

'She treated us the same.' My voice rises.

'Not in ways that matter.' Alexis speaks so quietly I have to lean forward. 'You and Mum were always in a huddle over books.'

'She read to both of us.' I protest but as I speak I see myself snuggled up to my mother, her arm around me. Alexis stands in the doorway and I stick out my tongue. The door bangs as she leaves.

'She told me you were in her tummy. I pretended I could feel you kick.' Alexis reaches for her gold pack and the saucer she uses for an ashtray, lights up, and blows a perfect smoke ring.

I sit quietly and listen.

'Then when she brought you home I sat on the floor and held out my arms, wanted to hold you. She refused. She never wanted to share you.' She looks hard at me. 'You were her little star. After you came along she didn't even notice I existed,' she says. 'So why should I care?'

'That's not how I remember it,' I say but I'm beginning to doubt.

'And you were exquisite as a toddler. I adored you, dragged you everywhere; you were my doll.' She leans over to the ashtray. 'Remember your first day at school? You refused to get dressed in the morning, just stood in your knickers at the front door.'

It was Alexis who took me by the hand, led me upstairs, dressed me, and walked me to the little school just down the hill. At that school she watched over me. I told her everything: the betrayals, the excitement of new best friends, what the teachers said to me – word for word, if I could remember – and all my little victories and defeats. We lay on one of our beds, usually hers, wrapped around each other and talked. Every day I longed to have something exciting to tell my big sister.

I drag my mind back and hear her saying, 'Dad was difficult but I loved him. He bought a small TV to stop her missing you so much. It was black and white,' Alexis says. 'A small portable sin.'

'He hoped God wouldn't notice,' I smile. 'Did he watch it?'

'Only westerns.'

'Ah, strong moral tales there and clear sinners, usually the Indians.' We both laugh.

'She got a cleaner when he died, an old lady who never did much as far as I could see, just a lot of talking.' Alexis moves her elegant shoulders impatiently. 'She was a waste of money.'

'I expect Mum wanted company.'

'She had all those nutters at the church.'

'It was Dad who was into God,' I say. 'What else is there to do here?'

'Ooh, the world traveller,' Alexis says but with a smile. She looks thoughtful, 'I shall set up my own business with Mum's money. Dad left a lot to the church and the rest to Mum. I have a team of eight; most of them would come with me. There's money to be made catering for corporate special occasions and I'm sick of working for someone else.'

'Do we have to talk about that now?'

'Not if you don't want to,' Alexis says, looking unruffled.

The squirrel is tiptoeing along the stone wall at the back of the garden. I get up and walk to the window for a closer look. He's become brave since I left; no-one to chase him away. My mother said they were God's creatures and my father insisted they were vermin. He was probably right but the squirrel cheers me.

Alexis breaks in, 'Everyone loved Dad.' There are tears in her eyes. She takes a deep breath, and shakes her head like a dog caught in a rain shower. 'You weren't here and you should've been.'

'Easy for you,' I say. 'I was away in the middle of nowhere. Lake Eyre was filling up. It only happens a few times every hundred years. Millions of birds were flying in.' Alexis doesn't have a clue what I'm talking about. I carry on. 'The telegram was four days old when I got it.' I don't say that I wouldn't have come back anyway. I add, 'Mum understood.'

'The church was packed.' Her voice is redolent with pride. She empties the cafetière and says softly, 'He wasn't good at emotions. He told me he was dying. He came to London to see me.'

'He came to London! On his own. London, and without Mum.'

'Yep. Sin everywhere, flesh, bad language, bad manners.' She adds, 'A medical conference or something.'

'Sodom and Gomorrah or worse,' I say.

Alexis shifts in her chair and recrosses her legs. A few minutes later she says, 'She was away.' She pauses, 'A visit to the loony bin.'

'You don't have to call it that.'

'She never knew he came to see me. I think there was something else he wanted to tell me.' She lights a cigarette.

'Aren't you curious? I would've been. How can you be so calm?'

'A bit, but there's nothing I can do about it,' she says, and blows one of her perfect smoke rings.

I wonder what else he didn't tell her, what other secrets he kept to himself.

Alexis gets up, briskly rinses out the cafetière and puts three scoops of fresh coffee grains in it followed by hot water. She carries it back to the table and pushes the plunger down. Too soon. Water and coffee grains spill out. She gets up again, finds a cloth, wipes up the mess and sits back down.

I slump with tiredness. 'I expect Mum took Dad's death hard.'

'I thought she might...' Alexis doesn't finish.

Ben calls to us, demanding that we come outside.

'Not now darling,' Alexis calls back. He turns his back.

'I bet Mum spoilt him,' I say.

Alexis smiles as if to say who wouldn't? I watch the thrust of his chin, his tongue stuck out the side of his mouth as he concentrates on balancing on the wall, his thin arms outstretched. I hold my breath. He's already wriggled a small way into my heart. Clare would like him. Cousins.

Alexis leans forward to plant her elbows on the table. 'She adored him,' Alexis says. 'We came up for a few days a couple of times a year. Dad loved him too,' she laughs, 'but you know Dad, not one to let his feelings show. Ben was only two when he died so doesn't really remember him.'

Ben shouts again, sounding fed up. 'I want to show you something, Mum.' Alexis hurries outside.

The funeral is tomorrow and Alexis has organised it all.

Chapter 14

My mother's room is cold with only two small windows, both facing east. Immediately inside the door is a wardrobe: brown, large, old-fashioned. There are two single beds with matching blue covers separated by a bedside table and lamp. I bury my head in the pillow of the bed nearest the door; bury my head in the smell of her. It's faint but it's there.

I walk across the room and open the wardrobe. My father's clothes are gone but my mother's are still crammed together, in their usual place, on the left-hand side.

I lift a navy dress off a coat hanger, one of her Sunday best. I imagine her standing in the front row of the choir, singing. I replace the dress in exactly the same place it came from and finger her other clothes, not many. I count the dresses: seven. I can't remember seeing her in trousers. I spread them out into my father's space. She was a careful dresser but how little I knew her.

I expect to feel Coriander rubbing her soft fur against my ankles, looking up hopefully, her purr disproportionately loud for her delicate body.

Tucked in the corner of the room is my mother's dressing table, with its modest mirror and pretty blue floral material hanging down its sides. She loved pretty things but indulged herself little. I sit on the stool and pick up her hairbrush. It's in the same position as always. I pull out some grey hairs. I've never seen her grey.

While I was at the village school it was my job to brush her hair. I did it gently, trying not to disturb the perm although the brush was too big for my hands. She missed her long hair, she said, had it cut when Alexis was born. I asked her why. 'Easier that way,' she said, but with an odd look on her face.

I place the brush back in its place.

My other job was her pills. Each day I counted them out: two pale blue, round, shiny ones and a large dirty white oval tablet with a line across the middle (my mother called it her horse tablet and had trouble swallowing it) and several others I can no longer remember.

She wasn't beautiful, not like the women in magazines but people noticed her, remembered her. Perhaps her cleverness shone through, or was it her slightly puzzled air? I asked her once about that look. 'Life, it's odd,' she said, 'the things it brings and takes away.' I didn't know what she was talking about.

And her soft anxious eyes. Most eyes have a story to tell if you look closely enough.

Twenty-nine when she married my father; 1950, post-war Britain, still with rationing. I asked her, when I was too young to understand what it meant, 'Did you fall madly in love with Dad?'

My mother paused a moment and then said, 'We courted for nearly a year but I knew he was the man I wanted to be with.' She hugged me. 'I came to visit your Aunt Dot. That's how I met him,' she said.

We were sitting side by side on the piano stool.

She missed her teaching, her boys and her girls, she said. 'Then Alexis and you came along,' she said and put her arm around me.

I decided then, to be a teacher, an English teacher like her.

Her silver necklace is lying, neatly curled, near the brush. I pick it up and put it in my pocket.

In the spare room a bright orange cover is on the small single bed. The floor is strewn with toys including an oversize train. Ben's clothes are draped over the chair, another pile on the bed.

Downstairs I turn on the light in the dining room. Her lace doilies, carefully worked, still sit on the dark polished table: two large oval ones in the centre and one at each place setting. My father's and mother's ghosts at either end.

We had tea in the kitchen when my father was out, which was often. When he was home we ate in the dining room. It was freezing in there. Alexis or I had to say grace: 'For what we are about to receive may the Lord make us truly thankful'. We weren't allowed to rattle it off or mumble. He called us little savages but said it with a bit of a smile. He wanted to know about school so Alexis and I made stuff up. Sometimes we agreed beforehand but we often forgot so made it up as we went along. When it worked we would afterwards throw ourselves on our beds and laugh our heads off. Sometimes we got in a mess, my fault mostly and got sent to bed without our pudding. That didn't stop us. Looking back, I don't think they believed a word of it.

The gas fire is dead. I shiver.

I hesitate, even now, to enter my father's study.

His dark leather armchair in the middle of the room and with the ceiling lamp hanging just above, it resonates with him. After knocking and cautiously pushing open the door I would find him most often, in that chair. He had a way of sitting with his head down, one hand on his book, the other on his face with his nose between his first and second fingers. The newspaper, his medical journals and books were piled on the small table beside him.

Against one wall is his desk, Regency, with delicate tooled green leather top and gilded trim. That was where he read his Bible or wrote letters there.

He didn't have friends, not that we knew anyway. The minister came to the house to see him sometimes.

I sit at the desk and put down my orange juice. The chair has little padding and a rounded uncomfortable wooden back. In the shallow middle drawer I find his fountain pen. My mother gave him a new Parker when I was about ten but he still used his old one, said it was moulded to his hand. I place it between my forefinger and thumb. It is too big but my hand can learn. I search for a bottle of ink and find it in the top drawer with sheets of paper. I write my name: Ruth Bishop. We were a family of no-nonsense names, no excesses.

An address book. I flip through it and recognise church names. In a bottom side drawer I find his old box Brownie. It only came out on holidays.

There's a slightly grainy photo on the raised back shelf of the desktop: Mum, Alexis and me. On the back is written in my mother's neat handwriting: 1965. I was six, Alexis eight. We are sitting in bathers on the sand, one arm around each other and the other round our knees. Our mother is behind us in a deckchair looking happy and proud, not a hair is out of place. Whitby Abbey is in the background.

I pick up the juice. It has left a ring on the leather. I smile and leave it there.

Downstairs the upright piano stands solid and proud against one wall of the sitting room and on it a few family photographs.

The room has walls so thick that the sun has to be canny to find its way in, mostly only in sickly shafts. The one exception to the parsimony of the furnishings is a large Persian carpet still resplendent in its dark reds and blues, a magnificent indolent creature covering the wooden floor between the sofa and the armchairs. My father bought it when Alexis was born. My mother boasted that it would last forever and showed us the weaver's signature woven into one end. It's in Arabic and Alexis and I joked about what it really said about Christian infidels.

On Saturday evenings, in winter, my father lit a fire. Alexis and I would eat our tea fast, escape as soon as we could and run to the sitting room. Set back a little from the fire was the sofa. Alexis had that. I liked to sprawl with a book on the carpet. My father read the newspaper and my mother always had a stack of books beside her. Or her sewing basket.

I almost miss it in the corner to the left of the fireplace. Lots of things were the devil's work and television was in the top three. There one sits, leering at me. I switch it on then off again.

Her books are still in the small bookcase. Old friends. I run my fingers over them, mostly the classics. I falter on an orange penguin: *The Vagabond*. Sidonie-Gabrielle Colette. Even the name excites me. Parisian music halls. How far from my mother's life. A caged bird. Perhaps. Her name is written on the front page: Harriett Bishop. She was proud of her handwriting, copperplate she said.

I put the book back, walk to the opposite corner of the room and take a record out of a cupboard below a small gramophone. She told us that she brought the piano and gramophone to the house on her marriage. And her books.

I count the records: twenty-four, the same as she had when I left.

I sit in her armchair and tuck my legs underneath me. She always laughed when I did that, said that was how she sat when she was my age.

Best of all she loved Mario Lanza and Maria Callas, La Divina. They were the greatest singers of all time, she said. And Brahms, anything by Brahms and Mozart: concertos, operas, chamber music.

I learned to dread her sad records, the ones about despair and lost love. Sometimes this music poured through the house, like water from a pent up dam. It told us… I don't want to go there. Not today.

And the stink of overcooked sprouts, a smell like pee, and the incinerated mush she served us and seemed not to notice.

'Look after your mother,' my father would say to me and I

would run to her, put my small arms around her.

She disappeared into deepening silence and poetry, mostly Emily Dickinson. She knew the poems by heart (and I do now, some of them) and as she paced the sitting room and I sat, silent in a chair, almost hidden in the unlit room, snatches of poetry, floated over me: 'And could not breathe without a key/And 'twas like Midnight, some/When everything that ticked – has stopped –/And space stares all around… /Despair.'

I didn't understand her dark world then. I still don't.

I sit on the piano stool, open the lid of the piano and rest my fingers lightly on the keys. There's an open hymn book on the music rest. I close the book and put it on top of the piano, get up and pull out the scores from the stool. On top are my two favourites: 'Amazing Grace' and 'Swing Low Sweet Chariot'. I hum each of them quietly.

She taught me to play the piano and then, at St Jude's, I had lessons. I loved Mr Roberts, a smiling man who said 'music must be fun, must be love'.

All my early music is still there: piano duets for fun, easy duets, classics for four hands. I was eight when I started. My hands were too small. At night I stretched my fingers under the bedclothes, willing them to grow.

The silken sheen of the polished black wood caresses my fingertips. I manage a Christmas duet. No matter that my mother's hands are not playing, I hear both parts.

Ben slides on to the stool beside me. 'This is where you are,' he says and leans against me: a slight body, bare grubby knees and feet that dangle. He pulls his hat out of his pocket and puts it on. 'You can teach me,' he says.

My hands shake a little as I put my left arm around his thin shoulders, look into his earnest small face and give him a hug. He looks up at me and grins. I could love him if he would let me.

He wriggles and puts his hands on the keys, a cacophony. I

play one-handed and use my left hand to place his fingers on the notes. We manage 'Once in Royal David's City'. His hands are too small.

Chapter 15

Later That Day

Lucy flings her arms around me. 'I'm so happy to see you. You've stayed away too long.' She puts her hand to her mouth. 'That's me. Sorry. How are you? Silly question. Tired I expect.' Her words rush out and half of her hug is taken up with navigating the ample coasts of her own breasts. 'I'm so sorry about your mother.'

We part and stand, looking at each other, still holding hands.

Lucy's overlong earrings dangle down to the line of her chin and her glasses are large, giving her a pert look. Her blonde hair is moussed wildly upwards. In our second year, against school rules, she dyed her brown hair blonde. The teachers protested. Lucy ignored them and has been blonde ever since.

Neither of us wrote much when I was away but that doesn't matter. We hug again.

'Come on, let's grab the last of the sun; we can sit in the garden,' I say. I take her hand and pull her through the kitchen – Alexis looks up from her magazine and throws her a small wave – and out into the garden.

We drag two deckchairs out of the garage – old and dusty – and find a patch of sun. I give them a perfunctory wipe with an old towel.

Ben is playing in the street with his bike, a present from my mother last Christmas. He's unsteady but fearless. My old bike must be lurking somewhere. It can lurk. The desert was flat and

I'm not up to these relentless hills. Not yet.

We place the deckchairs close together, our faces into the weak late summer sun. 'It's great to have you back,' she says and waves her hands, 'despite...' then, 'How's Oz?'

'Hot, but wonderful, the desert I mean. I haven't seen Davida for years.' I swing my deckchair around to face her. We laugh as I nearly tip the thing over.

'Melbourne,' Lucy sighs. 'I'd love to be back there. Tell me about the desert. It sounded a bit weird.' She grins. For nearly a year weird was our favourite word. Everything and everyone was 'weird'.

'When I got back from Oz your mother kept asking me about that job we invented for you in the coffee bar. You should've heard me.'

We smile at each other, remembering the story we concocted together.

'The desert,' I say, 'I loved it.' I find it hard to explain that somehow I found myself there. 'I'll miss Steve and the others,' I say. 'He's quiet but interesting.'

She raises an eyebrow, knows that will make me laugh. I tried to copy her years ago, stood in front of our bathroom mirror but nothing would persuade my two recalcitrant eyebrows to behave independently.

'No, just mates, not that he didn't try.' After a moment or two I say, 'All the people coming to the hotel hundreds of miles from anywhere, staying a night or two and setting off to cross the desert.' I sit up, feeling excited, 'I'm definitely going back one day,' I wave my hand, 'I'll take you there but you'll have to sleep in a swag under the stars.'

'Spiders?' she says quickly.

'Loads,' I say.

She shudders. 'No deal.'

I brush my hair back with my hand.

'I like the hair,' Lucy says. 'It suits you long.'

I lean over. 'Tell me about Mum. I should have been here.' That easy promise: 'just a year Mum'.

'It was the desert she didn't understand,' Lucy says. 'I came to see her whenever I came back from uni. We got on. I loved her.' Lucy's eyes are wet.

Me too, I say, inside my head, me too.

For a few minutes we watch Ben: his head down, his legs moving quickly, the bike steady. He's got the hang of it. The tip of his tongue is still sticking out of the corner of his mouth.

'I've seen him once or twice in the village, with his father,' Lucy says as she turns her chair a little to follow the sun. 'She spoke of visiting you but it was too remote, too expensive and your father wasn't well although he kept working,' Lucy says. 'The whole village turned out for his funeral.'

After a thin silence I say, 'The desert wasn't real, I didn't feel real.' I give up trying to explain. I had to be in her country.

'Clare was lovely,' Lucy says. 'And so small.'

'Just as well, it was painful enough,' I say and try to keep the catch out of my voice.

Alexis sticks her head around the corner of the house and calls to Ben to come in. He dumps his bike and stomps in, annoyance in every step.

I take a deep breath, one of Davida's yoga breaths.

'And you?' I ask Lucy. 'Not the boyfriends, they can come later when I feel stronger.' We grin at each other. 'Shame you didn't go ahead with teaching. You'd have been a great teacher.' The children would love Lucy and the head would probably hate her. 'And marketing, what's this all about?'

She digs into her oversize handbag and pours a clutch of small cosmetic samples on to the grass. 'For you.'

I scoop them up, put them in my lap and pick each one up and examine it. 'Great, just what I need.' I grimace. 'The sun in Oz.'

We smile at each other.

'So what happened to London?'

'Don't know. Too many people. Turns out I was a country girl after all,' she says. 'I'll marry and have kids, lots of girls,' she says.

'You couldn't settle for just one man,' I tease.

Ben runs out of the house and picks up his bike. I turn to Lucy, shading my eyes, 'I'll have to think about my life now, not just drift. Davida was a great one for preaching that.'

'You need time,' Lucy murmurs.

I put the samples down and get up, 'There's something I want to show you.'

Back in the bedroom I dig into my bag and unpack the glass girl and carry her carefully back outside.

Ben sees me holding something, dumps his bike and comes running over.

'What is it?' he says excitedly.

'Something precious I brought from Australia.'

'Can I see?'

I tell him to sit in my chair and then hand him the glass girl. She's a little longer than his small grubby hands.

He stares at it. 'It's pretty,' he says, but he's disappointed.

'It's glass,' I say, 'a dancer, made from the sand in the desert.' The desert bit impresses him, although a boomerang would impress more.

I take it from him and pass it to Lucy. She examines it carefully and finally says, 'It's wonderful.'

She leans over to hold me while Ben runs back to his bike shouting, 'Watch me.'

Ben shouts again and we turn to look in time to see him crash on to the grass. He picks himself up and gets back on.

An ugly, rasping noise surprises me. I'm bawling, blubbing like a two-year-old. Lucy puts her arms around me. I let myself go rag-doll loose.

Chapter 16

The funeral

The next morning I'm up early: jet lag and a mind that won't close down. There's a slip of a moon in the west and a male blackbird sings in the garden, thrusting out its chest. I hurry down the ginnel steps, slippy and niggardly, two by two, and past the primary school. A tractor glugs below along tracks worn by the cows, clarty with mud and excrement. In spring the ground is swathed with bluebells with their drooping iridescent heads. The woods face east and already there's a smell of dank rotting vegetation from too much rain and too little sun; lichen plasters the trees and fungi form strange appendages on the north-facing side of the trunks. No bluebells in late summer.

The heron is there, standing on one yellow grey leg, etiolated elegance. At other times it can be as squat and frumpy as an old tramp. It has a matching yellow beak and a long black nape. At dusk I sometimes heard its croaking call. The heron and I stare at each other.

I find a dry rock on the river's edge, sit quietly and dream of my mother. I hold her hand. I want to skip but I walk beside her, helping her over the uneven stony ground. We both pretend. Reaching the edge of the woods I let go, only for a minute or two and run ahead. Ten or twenty yards later I leap out from behind a bush. She screams and stops. 'It's you,' she says, and bends to cuddle me. We settle under our tree. It's generous, broad and shady with roots spreading above ground to make a seat for us. We sit close, the two of us, and talk.

My body clock says it is evening, village time is 10.45 a.m. My red and yellow summer dress looks too bright for faded English skies but my mother would want me in colourful happy clothes. I force my feet into shoes that pinch.

Alexis wears four-inch heels and a black and grey dress that reaches to just below her knees. It has large shoulder pads and over it she wears a black jacket with a magnificent sinuous emerald crocodile brooch on the right lapel.

Alexis, Ben and I walk down the hill to the church with its square tower. Ben occasionally holds both our hands, but mostly runs around us.

The clear blue sky stretches itself out in a giant yawn over the bare green hill. The air is still and smoke from the chimneys below struggles upwards. Jackdaws on the treetops are silent and high above the church a kestrel circles lazily on a thermal. Black clad figures stream along the streets leading to the church. They see us and pick up their pace and their sticks.

We pass Mrs Jackson's house. I quicken my pace. Alexis drops behind a little. I look back. Her face is passive with a hint of resignation.

Outside the church people stand silently. I recognise many and we smile, hug, briefly touch. Mr Murray, the minister, is among them. He's a big man with fair hair and a smile that gallops over his face. When he arrived a few years back my mother wrote that she liked him, said he had new ideas, was just what the church needed but my father thought he was too young, a bit soft on sin.

Mr Murray takes my hand. 'I've heard so much about you,' he says. 'Your mother was a wonderful woman. We were good friends. I'll miss our chats about books and the world.' The world bit surprises me.

Inside the church Alexis and I walk side by side down the

aisle, with Ben a little ahead, twisting his face back towards us. I don't look to either side but sense the curiosity, the silent nudges and the grief. The church is brimful. I want to hold someone's hand.

We take our seats in the front pew, Ben between us. He is wide-eyed and fidgeting, peering over at the coffin. His body wriggles independently of his smart navy jacket and grey trousers, so that from time to time he faces one way and his neat jacket buttons another. His tousled hair is undefeated by some sort of gel.

I fix my eyes on the plain dark brown coffin. It is dead centre, raised on a rectangular slim-legged support between the choir and the pulpit and on its lid a profusion of red roses, slim, exquisitely formed buds.

Behind it, on the back wall hangs a wooden cross.

On the other side of the coffin the choir is replete with serious-looking women and a few men. They will miss my mother's contralto voice.

Lucy is sitting a few rows from the front on the other side. She must have got here really early. It's not often she's on time for anything. Her smile warms me.

Aunt Dot is in the pew in front of Lucy. She has lost weight and looks ill. She moves a paper-thin wrinkled arm and smiles love at me. There was a note from her waiting for me when I got home to say that she was not well but wanted very much to see me and talk about my mother.

'The Lord is my shepherd, I shall not want/I will dwell in the house of the Lord for ever.' The words wash around me, high female voices and solid male voices. I know the psalm by heart. Alexis doesn't sing. None of the regulars need the hymn books. I glimpse others looking embarrassed. I want it to be over.

An oversize fly crawls across my book. I am back in the kitchen with my mother armed with a massive yellow fly swat. She hated flies and chased them round the kitchen. I asked her once if I would be swatted by some enormous hand and killed. She smiled and said, 'Of course not'. I didn't believe her.

The choir sings one of my mother's favourite hymns: 'All in an April Evening'. There's soft sobs from somewhere in the church. If there is a God I want him to lend me blankness for this day. If I can get through this hymn I will hold myself together. I try to remember the words of love, the light-hearted chatter she wrote to me; not her eyes full of pain.

Ben nudges me. Everyone is kneeling except Alexis and me. I kneel and smile at him.

I hold Ben's hand when he offers it, which is not often enough, and tell myself there will be time later to cry, not now. But I fail. Alexis leans across Ben and takes my hand.

Mr Murray walks the few steps up to the pulpit. He is above us, but not by much. He speaks to us, to Alexis and me.

'We are here to celebrate the life of Harriet Bishop.' There is something triumphal about the word 'celebrate' that I can't take. I drop my head.

'She was part of the fabric of the church. She will be missed.'

I look up, glimpse heads nod, hear small murmurs of assent.

He insists that she is in heaven with her husband Robert, also a loved member of the congregation, sadly deceased.

He fixes his gaze on the three of us. 'Everyone loved her,' he says. 'Her God and mine was a God of love, of forgiveness, a generous understanding God.'

Ben whispers to Alexis, 'Is Gran really in heaven?' She doesn't reply so he repeats the question to me. I nod. He is young.

Mr Murray offers prayers for Harriet's family and friends. He mentions us by name and Ben nudges Alexis and looks pleased. The church reverberates with prayer, good intention, pain, and hymns sung with fervour.

My mother is carried out by the church elders. The men look too old and frail for the job. I would like to carry her on my shoulders.

The earth is torn open and a giant cloud blots out the sun. My father's headstone marks the grave: Robert James Bishop, 1911 – 1981, loving husband of Harriet, father of Alexis and Ruth and grandfather of Benedict. There's space below for my mother's name and dates: 1921 – 1982. She will be buried beside him.

Ugly heaped-up earth on one side and the dead weight of people on the other. Leaning forward I pluck a single red rose. Ben nudges me so I take another and hand it to him.

I reach into my handbag and fold my fingers over the glass girl. The curves of the girl's body fit perfectly into the contours of my hand and I imagine the changing colours of the red-gold desert, the shimmering silver lakes and in the distance the small girl with the outstretched arms. She would have loved her grandmother.

We stand inside the door of the church hall to welcome everyone. Ben slips away. I try to emulate Alexis' graciousness. Mourners shuffle past. Soon we both are tacky with the press of soft earnest flesh, with hands held overlong, moist sweaty hands, chubby damp hands, skinny bony dry hands and kisses; and plain unmade-up faces.

The last black clad figure filters past us.

The interior is bright. Sunlight pours through the large pristine windows, overpowering the harsh glare from the neon strips running the length of the ceiling. One errant sunbeam lights up the text at the far end above the stage: "Come and let us return unto the lord: for he hath torn and he will heal us: he hath smitten and he will bind us": Hosea 6, 1.

'The hall looks a lot smaller than it used to,' I say to Alexis as we move into the overcrowded hall.

'That's because you've got bigger,' Alexis says. 'You've forgotten.'

I banish the last time I was here.

Today the same giant tea urn stands on a table with piles of white cups and saucers stacked beside it. Women move from table to table with plates of sandwiches and cakes. Ben goes straight for a plate of cakes. Some of the older ones reach out to touch him.

He slips nimbly between them.

The men and women, mostly women, remnants from our childhood, speak of our wonderful mother and even more wonderful father and of God's promise that they are with him now, in glory. I listen and nod.

'Have we enough food?' I whisper to Alexis. 'There are hundreds here.'

'Tons. The Ladies' Guild made it,' Alexis adds quietly.

'We know quite a few,' I say. 'Don't you remember…?' I start to point.

'No, I don't,' she says.

'You had as little to do with the village as you could,' I say.

'Let's just get through this,' she says with a small toss of her head and walks away.

Many of the mourners are grown old and thick, others too thin. Women, hold their claw-like hands in front of themselves, protective of their lack of flesh, balding men with chins disappearing into their necks and one short stout man with hair pulled across the top of his head. I wonder what he does when it's windy.

I make myself over, become what they expect; I listen to their words of comfort and speak or smile my thanks.

Alexis stands a little apart. Some of the men covertly watch her.

I am becoming hysterical. Tears would be safer than the uncontrollable laughter that is welling up inside me. I don't know what to do except flee. Someone touches my arm and I swing hard around.

Lucy.

She's in her trademark white baggy trousers, a long burgundy top and a bright pink scarf that almost but not quite clashes. Her right wrist is fashioned in three or four inches of thin, bright Indian bracelets. She flings her arms round me. We hold each other long.

We disentangle. 'I like the earrings. New?'

'Newish.' Lucy's laughter tinkles softly, an oddly light laugh from such a solid body. 'Do you know all these people? There are so many.'

'Quite a few,' I say. 'Mum will have told them I was the desert adventurer.' I nod my head towards the stage. 'There's my Guide leader, Miss Brown.' A tall athletic-looking woman of about forty catches my eyes and smiles. She was fun. 'You refused to join the Guides because you didn't like the uniform,' I say to Lucy.

'Probably,' she says and squeezes my arm.

Lucy waves a chubby ring-weighted hand, 'I recognise a few that you really liked. There's one of them, your Aunt Dot.'

Aunt Dot beckons. Someone has found her a chair and placed another beside her. I can still hear her at our back door calling, 'Harriet, yoo-hoo.'

'I'll be back,' I say to Lucy and walk quickly over to the empty chair, saying hello to people as I pass. Aunt Dot and I hug. She feels frail so I'm careful.

We sit together and she takes my hand. 'She won't have suffered.' She adds, 'I didn't have a chance to say goodbye.'

She's pushing hard at my 'no tears' resolution. I squeeze her hand.

'God will look after her.'

I don't reply.

'She missed you,' Auntie Dot continues, still holding my hand tightly, 'but she wanted you to have your own life. She talked about you all the time.'

We sit quietly for a few minutes.

'We were such good friends,' she says sadly. 'I'm sorry, Ruth, I'm tired. It's time I went home but promise you'll come and see me.'

'Soon,' I say and hug her again before taking her over to the man who is driving her home.

Auntie Jean, another faux aunt and one of my favourites, is there, dressed in pink including pink hat and shoes. 'Your mother liked this dear,' she purrs looking up at me and waving her hand at her clothes. 'I wore it for her. I don't like black.'

I bend down and kiss her wrinkled forehead. 'Mum would love it. I wore this dress because it was her favourite.'

I find Miss Brown. She tells me to call her June. We reminisce about Guides but I'm only half listening. I loved Guides, especially the weekend camps. Not far, just to the woods further up the dale. My mother loaded me up with easy-to-hide cakes that I could eat in my tent.

She smiles, then says, 'I knew about those cakes, you know.'

We both laugh.

The mourners are enjoying themselves now, meeting friends they haven't seen for years. Noise levels rise, hammering my head: snatches of village gossip, children's illnesses and achievements, pros and cons of a new head for the primary school all compete for attention.

I talk to faces I half know, half remember, see mouths opening and closing. I am received with love. Many remember Alexis and me as children, my father as their doctor. Some ask me about Australia. It would be easier if I could claim good works in Africa. Some ask about the Aboriginals. That gets them closer to Africa. I don't mention the booze or the dispossessed in Alice Springs. I give them Ayers Rock (rather than Uluru). I don't mention working behind a bar and wonder how my father finessed that one. I suspect some of them see me as the servant in the parable of talents who buried their talent instead of multiplying it. Most are kind and invite me to their homes. I plead uncertainty of plans.

I remember little of what is said.

Alexis disappears. A cigarette probably. Ben hovers near the food and is much patted on the head.

I ache for it to be over.

The plates of cakes and sandwiches are almost empty, stained teacups pile up.

Lucy promises to come over tomorrow.

Ben's hand finds mine and with the other he holds out a book. 'Can you read to me?' he says. 'I asked Mum and she said you would, that you are an ace reader.'

I squat down to meet his eyes. 'We'll take some food around first. There's not much left.'

He nods, rearranging his wild curls and looks seriously at me, 'I've had four cakes; they are great.'

'When we get home,' I say, 'I'll show you a blackbird's nest.' He nods. 'But we must be careful not to disturb her.'

The hall is almost empty, the urn and dirty dishes cleaned and taken away. Empty cake plates are claimed and the few remnants of food forced on the stragglers. Mr Murray stays to the end. He gives me his kindly smile and I ask him if he would like to have some of my mother's books. He would.

Ben and I walk back. Alexis left a short time earlier to make some phone calls. Ben gambols and I trudge.

I'm relieved to throw off the red shoes and change into trousers and blouse, light sweater and plimsolls that I find in the wardrobe. Ben is waiting for me where the stone borders planted with small bushes rise steeply up. The birds nest here, living off my mother's birdseed and the copious autumn berries.

'Do you know how many nests the male wren makes to win the female?' We're peering into a bush where a blackbird usually nests at this time of year. Disappointingly the nest is empty.

'Two.' He sounds confident.

'A good guess but five or six or up to ten, then the female selects the nest she likes best.' I grin at him, 'Very sensible of her.'

He looks nonplussed.

I ask him what bird he might be. Before he can answer I tell him the Aboriginal Dreamtime story of how the birds got their colours, how, long ago a giant rainbow broke into a million pieces and fell to earth as birds. The crow was frightened and cried a black, ugly 'aaaah' and the kookaburra laughed with joy, and still laughs.

He thinks a moment then says, 'I'm a kookaburra. Can we go to the river? Please, yes please.' His feet jiggle with excitement but his voice is solemn.

I can't refuse his eager thin face.

'Of course.' I tousle his hair.

'Gran told me this was one of your favourite places.' His hair is completely hidden under his hat and he's wearing the shorts and tee shirt of yesterday. 'Mum said to tell you that she'll do some food later. I told her I was stuffed.' His cheeky grin envelops me.

'So you should be,' I say. 'All those cakes.'

He grins.

We sit side by side on the riverbank, his body flopping over my knee. I badly want to hug him. Instead I say, 'Your grandfather taught me about birds.'

He sits up. 'Will you teach me?'

'Of course,' I say. 'We'll start tomorrow.'

He crouches down, looking for trout. 'Perhaps I'll go to Australia and live in the desert when I grow up.'

Chapter 17

Alexis nods when I tell her that I'm going for a walk. We've not spoken much since the funeral.

Outside the night spreads like wrinkled old skin and the air, smelling of woodsmoke from a chimney lower down, comforts.

I walk down to the graveyard carrying a cushion under one arm and wearing a thick sweater. After the desert I'm feeling the chill of the summer evening.

The village has shut down and the silence is almost total except for a little owl bark and the answering reply.

I perch on the cushion and rest my chin on my knees. My loneliness deepens.

I let the memories flood in: the beach and my mother's white legs, her just-crawled-out-from-a-century-under-a-rock white legs and my father in his old-fashioned baggy bathers; the cakes, our game in the woods, her hand, holding mine.

'I have something to tell you, Mum,' I murmur to the flower-covered earth mound. 'She had clear, trusting eyes and just before she went they were turning our colour. That's what I hoped.'

There, I have told her. 'Clare, your granddaughter. The name will surprise you. It just happened, like everything else.'

'You will want to know how much she weighed: 8lbs 4oz.' I carry on the monologue in my head, sometimes my lips soundlessly moving. A good weight the nurses said. The white band on her arm was overlarge and slipped a little as if the flesh was waiting to grow into it. Her face was scrunched and cross and she held her knees tight up against her belly, against the world. (I don't say that at first I turned away from her.)

'She had the same bent finger as you and me.'

Through the night I watched her, guarding her, waiting for her to wake; delighting in her flawless nose, a shapely nose that like marshmallow left no trace when touched and took back its shape, still perfection. I watched her stretch, snort, fart and smile. She had a little frown. I couldn't imagine her growing up otherwise I might have remonstrated, told her that frowning leads to wrinkles. That's what Alexis told me.

She was a serious person, my Clare. There was fierce concentration in everything she did: sleeping, eating yawning, crying and dirtying her nappy.

She will be six years, eight months and eleven days. That's the way children count their age, is it not? She will be at school, her first year over. I wonder if she can already read.

I shiver and regret not wearing more clothes. I'm still partly in Australia. Steve and the crew will just about be getting up to another cloudless day. I wonder how many are setting off to cross the desert. Steve is a mate but I doubt he'll come here, too many people for him. I'll have to get back there one day. When I find myself.

Chapter 18

The next day we are tired, even Ben. Alexis has phone calls to make and Ben and I run/walk to the village for milk and a few other things.

We pass the butcher and a teashop. Ben sees the cakes and wants to go in. I tell him 'no', that there's something better. His face lights up and he takes my hand. My head is full of my mother's hand holding mine as I skipped down the high street all those years ago.

The bank. I will have to set up an account, get some cash. Time for that later. The library and estate agent, a pub, the local store and just before the newsagent on the corner, the sweetshop.

Ben runs into the Aladdin's cave of dozens of large glass jars bursting with bright colours. The jars still line the walls but there's now a separate glass case of chocolates that say handmade and a counter full of chocolate bars. Ben goes straight for the glass jars but takes his time to choose. I go over the top and let him select an enormous bag. Ben does the same as I did: picked the brightest and the biggest.

We walk the length of the high street, cross the bridge and into the park. Ben pronounces the slide boring, for babies and demands that I push him on the swing. Then the two of us race to the top of the climbing frame. Children stare.

There's no escaping my mother: 'nice service', 'lovely woman', 'we'll miss her'. Some cross the street to touch us and offer sympathy; others keep their distance but smile. God is in most of the greetings.

Back at the house I dig out an old tracksuit and running shoes. They just about fit. I put them on and run out the front door. Ben sees me and shouts that he wants to come. I wave and shout back, 'next time.' I've forgotten running, forgotten the joy (once the first pain barrier is passed) of filling my lungs and emptying my head. And the opposite, filling my head with dreams.

I run out of the village and up the hill.

After lunch I shower, dress and lay myself out on my mother's bed, limb by limb and stare at the ceiling. There's a small crack in the plaster. The bed is a little hard. I'm tempted to try my father's bed but don't.

Alexis' perfume announces her. Cigarette in one hand and an old plate in the other, she slides on to the bed beside me and I move over to make room. She puts the plate on the bedside table. When her body touches mine I shuffle away.

'Ben's watching telly. You two are getting on well.' She offers me one of Ben's sweets. 'He told me to give you one,' she says. 'You OK Ruthy?'

'Ruthy.' I chew it, nurture it. There should be comfort in the childhood naming but it won't change things. 'Everything alright in London?' I ask.

She laughs and ignores the question. 'It went well yesterday,' she says and leans over to tap the cigarette ash on to the plate. 'I'm surprised she didn't die sooner; she seemed lost without him.' Alexis' voice is flat.

I want this over with. I get off the bed and stand a few feet away. 'It must have struck you as odd, my sudden departure.' My voice sounds hard. I intend it.

'Why? You always did what you wanted, had Mum around your little finger.'

'I went to the other side of the world. And you didn't bother coming home. I telephoned, wrote to you. You never answered.'

She looks away.

'You weren't there, were you?'

She looks defiant. 'I'd moved. I didn't want them to know.'

I laugh. 'Don't bother telling me his name.'

'I won't,' she snaps back.

'You're my sister. I wouldn't have told them.'

'I'm sorry,' she says and puts her hand out to touch my arm. 'I'll tell you one day.'

'I had to go. You know why.'

'How the hell should I know? I was in London,' she spits out. Her anger is back. She's always been mercurial like that.

The words slip out. 'I was pregnant. Remember the Easter social when…'

'The Easter social,' she says slowly, then sits bolt upright, eyes wide. 'I don't believe you.' Her voice is loud, her stare hard.

'It's true.' I look into her eyes and say his name.

Silence shuffles between us.

She flushes. 'I don't believe you.' She's shouting. 'He wouldn't.'

I shout back, 'He raped me, Alexis.'

Alexis swings her legs over the side of the bed, stubs out her cigarette and strides along the hall. 'I don't believe you,' she says again over her shoulder.

'You disappeared, never came home.' I shout at her back. 'You should have helped me. It was all your fault.'

She turns round.

'That's rubbish Ruth. I'd just met Peter and I had other problems.'

'What problems?' I say, although I don't care.

'None of your business.' She strides back and stands in the doorway, her lips tightly shut just the way our father's were when he was angry.

Slowly, like some old woman recovering from a stroke, learning to speak again, I get out the words, 'He said, "Say thank you to your sister for me".'

98

There's fury in her eyes. 'You've made that up. You and your imagination, it was always out of control.'

'How do you explain his words?' I say, very, very quietly.

'I don't believe you,' she's staring at me, her hands on her hips.

We're now standing an arm's distance apart.

'You're lying.'

'You gave me to him,' I say. 'I was a stupid kid. I didn't know what to do. I ran.'

She walks down the passage.

I sit down on the bed and try to shut out that night. I fail.

It seems hours later but can only have been a few minutes when I hear her footsteps. She sits down. 'I'm telling the truth. I never guessed. Any of it.'

'Why should I believe you?' I say although I am beginning to doubt. Alexis has always been good with the lies. We often shared them, laughed about them but I can usually spot her lies. Not this time.

'Because it's true,' she says, her face tightening, her eyes hard. 'You were such an innocent, more like a silly fourteen-year-old.'

'I was, until that night,' I say quietly. I'm back in the dark in our bedroom, curled, foetal position, pillow over my head to stifle my sobs. Waiting. She didn't come home, just left a note on the kitchen table saying she'd gone back to London early. Dad was hopping mad.

'Pregnant,' she says slowly. 'Why didn't you tell me?'

'Oh, I tried. I've just told you.'

She starts to speak.

I don't let her interrupt. 'You weren't around. You just disappeared.'

'Things were happening,' she says, 'and how was I supposed to know? Telepathy? You were such a homebody, tied to Mum's apron strings.'

'You're a shit Alexis. I went to the other side of the world, for God's sake.'

'I've told you,' she says, anger in her voice. Then more softly, 'There was Peter and it was getting serious.' She tails off. 'I was away for a while. When I got back you'd gone.'

'I'll never forgive you. He raped me.'

She stands. 'It was nothing to do with me.' She's silent a moment then says, 'You must have...'

'What!' I shout. 'Don't you dare. What a fool I was to ever have trusted you. Rape Alexis. Don't you understand the word?'

She begins to move away. 'Don't go,' I spit out. 'We haven't finished.'

'I never thought...' she says. There's still anger in her voice but it's not at me. 'Anyway, you could've...' She pauses. 'Got rid.'

'How could I do that? I wouldn't have anyway.' I've never worked out why. Except perhaps that I didn't have a clue how to go about it or didn't really believe it was happening.

'You didn't tell Mum?'

'I couldn't hurt her. The shame. It would have...'

Alexis' voice cuts in. 'The nut house. I rang after you left. Dad said that's where she was. Well, he said she was away but I knew,' she says tight-lipped.

'Mind you, they would probably have sent you away to one of those homes, you know the ones girls go to for four or five months looking a bit fat then reappear thin six months later.' She sniggers. 'Remember that girl, what's her name, who disappeared.'

'Charlotte,' I say.

'They wouldn't have let you keep it,' Alexis says.

She's making Clare sound like a toy.

'Who wouldn't?'

'Mum and Dad.'

'I never put it to the test, did I.' I snap back at her.

'I really believed the Lucy's aunt story and you were too young for university.' She stubs out her half smoked cigarette. 'And what did you do out there, for God's sake. You didn't have to go so far.'

I breathe deeply, try to calm myself. 'Lucy's aunt is in

Melbourne,' I say. My voice rises. 'What do you think it was like away from everyone?'

'You had your fat friend Lucy.' Her derision stabs the walls. 'And you could have come to London.'

'And what would you have done?' I ask.

Alexis walks back to the bed, sits down and looks at me. 'Dad? He's a doctor after all,' she says, the anger gone from her voice.

I shake my head.

'Tell me,' she says.

I leave the room and come back with the photo on the beach. 'A baby girl,' I say. 'Clare.' I hold it out to her.

'She looks lovely,' Alexis says. 'You look good, a real mother.'

I'm still thinking about that when I hear her say, 'You had her adopted so it's turned out alright.'

'What do you mean turned out all right?' I say, whipping round to face her. My hand itches.

'You didn't have to give her away.'

'Are you stupid,' I say. 'What would be the point of going away if I kept her? Turn up here with my bastard?' (Oh Clare, I cry out to her. How can I call you that?)

Alexis gets up with her 'I'm not going to fight' face on. She brushes her hand through her hair and yawns, 'It must have been hard. We'll talk more in the morning.'

'Hard is a good start,' I shout after her. 'What about the rest? You're a shit Alexis, a self-centred shit.'

She turns back. 'I really am sorry I wasn't around.'

Alexis grew up way before leaving home, my childhood following more slowly after, even allowing for the two years age difference. In her last years at school she stopped having much to do with me and with Mum and Dad, if she could get away with it. She didn't really care about any of her school friends either. They eventually worked that out for themselves and drifted away.

I'm awake much of the night. Bewildered and confused; utterly alone.

Chapter 19

The next morning we sit at the kitchen table warming our hands on mugs of coffee. I don't know what to believe, what to think.

The sun struggles towards the kitchen windows. The air is chill.

I'm wearing my mother's dressing gown. It's an old woman's garment but I snuggle into the smell and the memory. Alexis wears smart blue trousers and a white blouse with a high collar. She already has the scent of London about her.

'Ben's still asleep,' Alexis says. 'He'll sleep for some time yet and then we have to leave for London.' She looks defenceless without her make-up. 'Let's start again,' she says quietly. 'I'm really sorry Ruth. You must believe me. How could you even think I would hurt you like that?'

Easy for you, I think, but notice how exhausted she looks, dark circles under her eyes. The two years between us has shrunk, almost to nothing. There's something inexpressibly sad about Alexis this morning. Her mouth is tight, her eyes hard; she looks lost.

'You must know I would have helped you if you'd let me.'

Too much has happened. I don't know what to believe, haven't the strength to start the argument again. I want to be on my own.

'And I would have loved to have seen Clare. I'm sure she's wonderful. Perhaps you'll see her again one day.' She gets up, walks around the table and rests her chin on the top of my head, her arms on my shoulders. I quiver under the touch and wrap the dressing gown tightly around me.

'You must come and stay with us. And Ben would love that,' she says. 'Ben adores you already; we can be your family.' Alexis walks back and sits down. The touch of her arms on my shoulders is still there.

I nod but am not yet ready. I get up and put two slices of bread in the toaster.

We hear Ben moving about upstairs. She shouts to him to have a shower. There's no answer but a few minutes later we hear the rush of the water.

Alexis pauses to put down her cigarette and take up her coffee. 'I came home a few months ago. She talked about you.'

'What about?' I hold my breath.

'Your childhood. She was obsessed by the belief that you were unhappy, that there was something she had not been able to make right for you.'

'What? Didn't you ask?' I lean forward to look closely into her face.

'No.' She stubs out her half smoked cigarette and I wonder if she really enjoys them.

I slide off the chair and walk around the room to the window and watch the shadows on the hillside but can't recapture my old game. The stories have fled leaving only cloud reflections.

As I turn back Alexis says, 'The school thinks that Ben's clever but too much in his own head. He's going to Peter's old school when he's twelve, as a boarder.'

'How can you bear to let him go?'

'It's a good school. He'll do well there.'

I collect the toast on the way back to the table, put it on two plates and take the butter and marmalade out of the fridge. I butter my toast. I don't really want marmalade so I get up and rummage in the cupboard and find some old honey.

'Tell me about Peter,' I say.

Alexis rinses the cafetière, makes coffee and places it on the table between us. 'There's not a lot to say about Peter. He was over the moon with Ben.' She butters her toast and adds a thick layer of marmalade. 'He's a lot older than me, a lawyer, pots of money.'

'Mum and Dad didn't go to the wedding.'

'No, she never got her wedding,' Alexis says. 'Dad's fault. Peter's a Catholic, well Catholic enough to want a nuptial mass and that meant Dad wouldn't come. Peter's brother gave me away.'

Part of me wishes I'd been there.

'It wasn't a big wedding, just a few of his legal friends and their wives. Then we went on honeymoon to Barbados.'

'You look good in the photo, the one on the piano.'

'The whole village has seen it,' she laughs and chews half a slice of toast, slowly, delicately, making it last twice as long as mine. 'I brought Peter up here a few times. He and Dad got on and he was good with Mum.'

She has a special face when talking about Mum, smug and dismissive. She's wearing it now.

'After Dad died Peter and I drifted apart. We bored each other. He worked all the time, still does. It was a civilised divorce.' She adds, 'Peter met someone else but he still sees a lot of Ben. I might not have divorced if Dad had been alive, not so soon anyway. Mum worried for Ben I expect, but he's fine, you can see that. Dad adored him,' she says. 'He was softer than I've ever seen him when they were together.' She picks up the other half slice. 'I see Peter sometimes, when he comes for Ben. He takes him on holidays, usually to France and Switzerland, just the two of them, male bonding and all that stuff. Ben has quite a few words of French. I'm surprised he hasn't tried them out on you.'

We can hear him thumping about upstairs.

I butter more toast, spreading honey on it. 'He's very confident.'

'He went to nursery from his second birthday and loved it. He's not shy.' She gets up, clears her plate and puts her hand out for mine. 'Finished?'

I haven't, but pass her my plate with one hand and hold my toast between thumb and forefinger with the other. The honey drips and I lick it off.

Alexis puts both plates in the sink and shouts up the stairs, telling Ben to get a move on. Minutes later she turns towards the door her face lighting up, 'Hello darling.'

Ben runs in, his hair wet, dark, plastered to his head, a few curls escaping on to the nape of his neck. He's dressed in pale blue pants, a smart dark blue shirt and a dark blue pullover. He kisses Alexis then darts around the table to kiss me, soft skin to my cheek, thin arms around my neck. I want to cry. He sits and sluices down a large bowl of cereal in silence then grins as he spreads generous swathes of honey on his toast.

I point to the waterfalls of honey cascading off his fingers and I describe the bees' waggle dance, a dance that directs other bees from the hive to the pollen. He listens seriously then sucks his fingers. 'Can we go to the river, Auntie Ruth?'

'Not today, Ben, you know that,' Alexis interrupts. 'We're going soon. You can help me pack the car.'

He pulls a face then grins at me, shows me one of the sweets we bought yesterday sticking out of his pocket and goes outside to play with strict instructions from Alexis not to get dirty.

I follow Alexis into the sitting room. Alexis sits upright on the arm of Dad's easy chair. 'Mum left you her piano.' She adds, 'I don't suppose it's worth much these days. I don't want anything,' she says, looking around. 'Sorry I can't stay. I have a lunch for twenty to get ready for Friday. I've cleared the food in the kitchen cupboards. You take what you want.' She waves her hand around. 'I don't expect you'll find anything exciting.'

I watch them down the street. Ben swivels around on the back seat and waves until they are out of sight.

Chapter 20

The soft mist outside is backlit by weak sun and a rainbow drapes itself over the curve of the hill. The house is ghostlike, a shriven shell. I hear my mother's voice: soft, loving, and see her in the shadows.

I start in the kitchen. The church will get most of the things I don't chuck. And the local charity shop.

I find cardboard boxes and newspapers in the empty garage. I pack up the kitchen crockery and label it village.

While I work I rerun my conversations with Alexis, over and over. I don't know what to believe. I torment the words, seek out nuance, lies. The shock and anger on her face. These past years I've imagined the conversation so many times, a different one; was ready to have it and walk away.

It's not so simple.

The sitting room. There's not much to pack up here except for the china cabinet.

Alexis doesn't want the furniture and on looking at it, nor do I. It can wait until the house is sold then I'll get a charity to take it. Except the Persian carpet. I'll store that. It will need a big room and I don't see the prospect of that for me any time soon.

There are three photographs on the piano. There were two long before I left home. One of the old ones is missing: mum and dad's wedding photo.

In the school photograph Alexis and I are in school uniform. Alexis looks grown-up, secretive and I am gawky and wide-eyed. Our mother took us by bus to the nearby town. It was our first holiday after I started at the grammar school and we had to wear our uniforms on a Saturday. Alexis said we'd look stupid but I loved the red and navy uniform. Kids on the bus laughed.

In his photograph Ben is in short pants and shirt and wearing a wide smile, his curls falling around his face.

I pick up the last one: Alexis in an elaborate full-length white dress and carrying a bouquet of white flowers, her lace veil flung back and almost reaching the ground. Peter is in a morning suit. They are a handsome couple.

The china cabinet is about five feet tall with two glass doors. The key is in the lock.

I pack up a Wedgwood fine bone china tea set with small pink flowers and gold rims. Lucy might like it, otherwise I'll keep it, but know it will live out its life packed away. I am not a fine bone china sort of person.

There are still a dozen or more delicate pieces: small fine bone china jugs, figurines and plates. I helped my mother dust them although she only ever let me touch the more robust pieces. I put to one side a fine art deco silver teapot for Auntie Dot. That will remind her of all the cups of tea she and my mother drank together.

Tucked in a back corner I find the musical jug, 'my jug', I called it. My mother never let me wind it. I wind it now, gently, cautiously and play it over and over: 'There's a long, long trail a-winding unto the land of my dreams/Where the nightingales are singing and a white moon beams/There's a long, long night of waiting,/Until my dreams all come true,/Till the day when I'll be going down/That long, long trail with you.' It's unbearable so I shut it up.

The clothes are easy to deal with: bras, knickers and things of that ilk into black sacks and dresses, jackets, coats, hats, into two piles: rubbish and charity. Everything else I lay out on the bed, so little for one lifetime. Ten pairs of tights – hoarding against what eventuality, or simply a marker of not getting out often after my father died; six boxes of handkerchiefs, all unopened, pretty floral patterns – gifts to the elderly when imagination fails, and four packets of lavender soaps in exquisite floral boxes. Face powder, lipsticks, some jewellery of little value, and the cameo brooch.

I place the brooch on the dressing table. The rest is packed into boxes and stacked in the hall. The church women will see that everything goes to good homes.

I sit on the bed and take the elastic band off a bundle of cards and flip through them. They are all the birthday cards we ever gave my mother. A separate smaller bundle, six in all: the cards I sent from Australia.

The last thing in the wardrobe is my mother's treasure box. We were forbidden as children to touch it. The secrecy of the thing got to us. I feel uneasy even now, and excited.

In an envelope a hospital baby's name card: Ruth Bishop. I look for another. There's none.

The afternoon begins to lose its heat. I'm tempted to phone Lucy but tell myself the sooner I get this done the better.

A few family photographs including a small one of my father and mother on the beach. My father is wearing capacious maroon bathers with a white belt. My mother looks good in a black swimming costume. She is lying on a towel, resting on her elbows. They are both laughing. It must have been Alexis or me taking the photo. I like to think it was me.

I don't remember many burning hot days on those holidays but we still loved them. On holiday my father noticed us and he and Mum seemed happy. I wanted to stay there forever. We went to the same boarding house and on Friday nights we had fish and chips. The same families came every year. I had my gang. We swam every day, whatever the weather and played ball on the sand. There was a fish and chip shop in the village but we never went there. We stopped going to Whitby when Alexis left home. Dad said it was a family holiday. I sulked for days over that. Mum said he didn't mean the family bit (he did) but that we had outgrown Whitby.

A small black and white photograph of a birthday party. I count the candles on the cake: eight. I look as if I already have a chunk of cake in each cheek. Mum and Alexis are leaning close to me to get into the picture. I'm wearing a dress that reaches my knees and is made of thin pink cotton with flowers. Most of my clothes were hand-me-downs from Alexis. It didn't bother me but my mother pleaded with my father for 'new clothes for the girls'. She didn't win. 'Waste is a sin Harriet. There are years more wear in them.'

The photo flutters to the carpet. Reaching for it I see something under the bed and stretch out full length. The worn fibres of the carpet scratch the side of my face and my arms can't quite reach. My fingers scrabble millimetres away from what looks like a large brown parcel. I get on to my knees and push the bed over by a foot. The dust where it has stood is thick. Flat down again on my stomach my stretched out fingers grasp the edge of the parcel and pull.

It is about eighteen inches square. I place it on the bed. Attached to it is a large envelope. I pull it off, turn it over, hesitate. The outside of the envelope is blank, the glue failing so the envelope opens easily. Two pieces of paper fall out. I open one of them. It's in my father's terrible handwriting.

3rd March 19 June 1949
My Dear Harriet,
I do not think that this letter will come as a surprise. I am not a man of many words and I hope you do not hold that against me. I'm

afraid that I may not be able to find the right words. I see our life as man and wife within the church, and in time, our children in the church. Perhaps one day we might do God's work in Africa. I pray that you can share my vision of our life together.

Yours in Jesus, and I hope, soon to be your loving husband.
Robert

I stay seated on the edge of the bed. I'm finding this father too late; a romantic even, in a religious sort of way. I'm stunned by the love and hope and the certainty in his words in his strange letter: thirty-eight, my mother twenty-eight.

I look at the letter again. There was a condition: she had to love God as he did. Few could do that. She tried, gave up her teaching, threw herself into the life of the church. She never spoke of her parents. Perhaps she gave them up too.

They married a year later. Except for the Africa bit my father stuck to his vision and tried to make sure we did. Was it a meeting of two lonely people? No children for five years – Alexis, then me two years later.

I put the letter carefully on the bedside table, 1949.

I don't pick up the second piece of paper, I'm too excited. Instead I pull out the bulky item from the envelope. It's the missing wedding photograph.

I push it away, then place it face down on the bed. I don't have to look. It's in black and white. They are standing in front of the church porch but the photographer is too far away: July 1950. My mother is wearing that dress: a modest full-length white wedding dress. She looks younger than twenty-nine. Her hair is long, pulled loosely back from her face and tied at the back with a red ribbon, hopefulness and joy in her eyes. My father is in a grey suit, white shirt and light grey tie, and mirror-black shoes; a good-looking man. He looks happy, loving. There's a softness about him.

I leave it face down and open the second letter.

My father's handwriting again. Disappointing. I was hoping it would be my mother's reply. The letter slips easily from the envelope as if happy to be free at last.

I look first at the date. Six years later.

16 September 1957
My dear Harriet,

I have been on my knees all night praying for God's guidance. He has told me to hold nothing back, to be entirely truthful, that his love will look after us both.

Nothing can prepare you for what I have to tell you. I should be there with you but it's not possible and I cannot delay.

You are a good woman Harriet, a faithful, caring woman, my wife.

I have not been attending a medical conference this week. I lied to you, one of many, evidence of my fall into the devil's keeping, into lust and adultery.

I have been with another woman.

I promised myself to tell the full truth so I will confess that I have known her the past year. Her name is Beth. The devil tempted me and I fell.

I grasp the letter so tightly that the paper tears. Part of me wants to laugh. My father and a mistress: impossible.

'Known her,' I sneer.

I sit down. Were you too scared to come and tell your wife, look her in the eyes and say I have another woman? You wouldn't put it crudely; your God might not like that. How could you do it, any of it?

You hypocrite Dad, I breathe. Married less than five years. It didn't take you long, and what about all the man of God stuff? No Africa for you, just another woman.

Mum, I cry out. Mum. I stand, as if I might do something, anything to change what I've just read.

I find the place where I left off.

I have strayed from the path. I am a sinner Harriet, but not, I hope, damned forever. With your help and God's teaching I can live the rest of my life doing God's will and stray no more. You and I were married in the sight of God and marriage is the bedrock of our church. In sinning I have fallen from the true path and abandoned God and you.

I take a deep breath, put the letter down and shout out: 'What crap Dad. What utter crap.'

But I'm not prepared for the next blow.

Beth has given birth to a healthy girl, my daughter. I tremble at the pain this will give you.

She is unable to care for the child. She has promised she will not seek to contact us or the child.

You and I can bring her up as our own. God has not blessed us with a child of our own, and I know that is a great sorrow for you. The child belongs with me. Can you bring yourself to love the child as our own? I pray that you can.

You are my wife. Will you have me back? May God find it in your heart to forgive me and accept a daughter into our lives.

Your loving husband,
Robert

The baby is Alexis. My sister.

Stillness permeates the room. The furniture ceases its groans of old age; the tap in the bathroom stops dripping, the sun goes out and the wind dies. I throw the letter down. My heart doesn't know how to cease its terrified beating, my hands shake. I watch them, curious, detached.

I need to get out; run.

Shoving the letter into my pocket I slam the bedroom door

behind me, run from the house and up the public footpath; run until I'm out of breath, then run/walk/run until I can see nothing but sheep and hills and sky. I find the place where the ground dips slightly and provides a bed of heather. I kick off my shoes. I'm not wearing socks and my toes look naked. I rest my head on my hands and knees and gulp in the unsullied air.

I smooth out the crumpled letter as best I can and read the words again, one by one: adultery, God, forgiven, my daughter, love, mother, our lives and all the rest.

My mother loved my father. I'm sure of that. But did she forgive, forget? Forget, I think not. She kept the letters.

The other woman did he love her? I don't really care but I gnaw at it. Did my father want to stay with her? The three of them.

Divorce. He could not, would not do that. It didn't exist in our church, would be driven away.

The woman gave her child away but who am I to fault that. He took the child back to his barren wife to nurture and invoked God in the argument. No wonder she went mad.

I want to fly from this, back to the desert.

I hate you, I say out loud. You were too unforgiving, I tell him, for a man who has so easily forgiven himself.

I throw myself back on the grass. Sheep graze nearby.

My thoughts whirl about in my head, poison the grass around me. The letter has shredded my memories, rearranged my life.

My father arrived home with a baby. What did he tell the people at church? An abandoned baby rescued. He's a doctor and few would doubt the story, would be glad for my mother with her brave smile. My mother – she must have had a week perhaps a little more.

How much did he tell her about the other woman?

Then I remember Alexis' words: 'She never loved me the way she loved you, not from the start.' And the bit about a nurse caring for Alexis.

She loved Alexis, I'm sure of that. But those cuddles with my mother flash into my head; Alexis standing in the doorway.

We both gave a child away. Perhaps this Beth also lives with her ghost baby in her head, imprinted on her soul. What did she do with her days after Alexis went? She knew where her daughter lived. Surely she was tempted to come and look for a girl Alexis' age, just to catch a glimpse.

A lamb butts its mother's belly, demanding milk. The ewe stands placidly chewing, acquiescent. Her lamb suckles.

Did my mother, during those years, seventeen at least while Alexis was at home, fear a knock on the door and the woman, a stranger standing there?

She kept the letters for us to find; for Alexis to find. Now she will have a new mother, a phantom that may still be alive.

I want to shout to everyone: 'My father was a bastard, a hypocrite.' I want to spit the words out, tell the village about their beloved doctor, the church about their saintly man of God.

Back at the house I sit in the kitchen and try to plan. I consider burning the letters, pretending I know none of this. But the letters have changed our lives: Alexis' and mine. I make up my mind. I have to go to her.

I pack a small bag, telephone Alexis and leave a message. 'I'm coming to London; I've some things to show you.'

I leave with the other woman in my head. The word 'mother' has lost all sense. I do the sums in my head: he must have been forty-four. How old was she?

Where is she?

Chapter 21

At King's Cross I stand bewildered.

Typical, I chastise myself, I thought it would all be so easy. At an information desk I ask, in my best sophisticated voice, the route to Fulham. A man in uniform reaches under the counter and pulls out a small map that he spreads over the top. His thick black forefinger traces a route along a blue line from King's Cross. I watch carefully.

'Change, there,' he says, 'at Victoria. Then it's the District Line to Wimbledon. That takes you to Fulham Broadway. It's all signed.' Then he smiles, as he straightens, 'First time in London then?' I nod, take the map and thank him.

On the Underground I pick up a discarded newspaper. Grace Kelly is dead. Princess Grace of Monaco. I never saw any of her films but I mourn her and her story anyway.

Twenty-five minutes later I get off at Fulham Broadway marvelling at how it has all worked.

It's a bright summer's day and I walk past flower shops with minimalist window displays, a couple of off-licences, small grocers, mouth-watering delis, antique shop windows with exquisite pieces small and large and no prices to be seen, and tempting coffee shops. The elegant terraced houses are imposing, stretching three stories up, each with a skimpy front garden, orderly receptacles for weekly dustbins and the kerbsides sated with expensive cars.

Number 62 Austen Road. I walk slowly down the short path

peering in through the large window with its curtains pulled right back. I'm sweating and it's not wholly the muggy city weather.

'Hi Ruthy.' Alexis' hug is long and close; her hair gets caught in my sunglasses and she laughs as we disentangle ourselves. 'Your first visit to London. What's so urgent?' She looks a little irritated. 'I should really be at work.'

I look for the other woman in Alexis' face but it's just Alexis looking back at me.

Bear falls against my legs, pinning me to the spot. He's black, big and sloppy and I fall in love with his wistful eyes.

'Bear, kitchen,' she says.

Alexis waves at the bare walls, then puts her arm around my waist as we walk down the hall. 'I've barely started on the house. I only bought it a few months ago. Ben and I moved into a small place after the divorce and now here. It was a good move, I made heaps.' She touches a white wall. 'The guy I bought it from loved white as you can see. It's all like that, all the rooms except Ben's room. That's finished, but nothing else.'

I dump my bag and follow her into the front room. It is large and high-ceilinged with an elaborate central plaster rose but a room strangely desolate with bare badly marked walls and sparse furniture: a sofa, a television, one small chair and a side table replete with photographs of Ben in elegant silver frames: Ben on the beach, Ben in school uniform, Ben as a baby, Ben with Alexis and... I count them, thirteen.

'Yes, overkill I know,' she laughs. 'He's with Peter tonight. I didn't tell him you were coming; he'd have insisted on staying home. You have a fan there.'

'Ditto. I'm sorry I won't see him.'

She turns and walks briskly out the door and down the hall. 'Come on,' she flings back over her shoulder, 'you must be starving. The train down and then the Underground; your first trip to London. I can't do any real cooking here until the kitchen is done but there's a marvellous deli around the corner.' Alexis pauses, placing her arm around my waist.

We sit at the table. The kitchen does look pretty bad: a very old refrigerator, an equally ancient cooker, a few kitchen chairs, a couple of cupboards and a small rubbish bin.

She sees me looking around. 'I know, awful. Wait until you see it next time.'

I get up, retrieve my bag, pull out the bundle of papers. I pass the school reports across the table as I sit down. 'Your school reports: a mixed lot.'

'History. Sling them in the bin. It's over there.' Alexis points to the corner of the room.

I leave them on the table.

Bear gets out of his basket and settles on my feet resting the side of his head on my calf. Leaning down I run one hand over his head and up one ear and with the other hand finger the letters in my pocket. The longer I delay the harder it gets. Part of me is trying to work out how much Alexis will care.

She jumps up, picks up the reports and chucks them in the bin.

I take the letters out of my pocket and hold them out to her. I have to get it over with.

'What's this?' she says, ignoring them, 'And what's the rush? What about a coffee?'

I nod, and let my hand with the letters drop by my side. She gets a cafetière out of the cupboard and coffee from the fridge.

'It's from Robert to Mum,' I say.

'So it's Robert now,' she says, pouring the coffee, forgetting I take milk. I get myself some from a bottle in the fridge.

'Read this one first.' I separate the letters and give her the first letter.

She scans.

'I hope no-one ever proposes to me like that,' she says, 'and all that religious claptrap.'

I pass her the second letter.

117

She reads quickly, slows and stops. I get up and go to the window, put my back to her and wait. A long time.

'I think it's time for a drink,' she says finally and gets a bottle of white wine out of the fridge. Her coffee is untouched. 'Opener in there,' she points to a drawer, 'and glasses there,' waving her hand at a cupboard.

She looks pale.

I open the bottle, pour two generous glasses, sit back down and drink.

Alexis says nothing for a time, simply gazes out of the window and sips her wine.

Finally she says in a voice so low I have to lean towards her to hear. 'I always knew I was different; it explains a lot,' she says. 'I shall never forgive him for not telling me, both of them. They've lied to me all my life.'

'He promised Mum.' I don't know why I'm defending him.

'Your mother, not mine,' she snaps back.

I push the bottle towards her. She tops up her glass.

'She loved you,' I say quietly, revisiting old ground. I don't know what to say about the other woman. I'm being ripped apart here.

'No she didn't.' She half snorts. 'I was invisible. Everyone had to tiptoe round her. The house held its breath: she must not be upset.'

Her voice is low, each word precise. Her anger is loud.

Alexis and me: the good times when we knew what each of us was thinking; when we ganged up together against Dad or Mum; when we lied for each other. That's what sisters do. And the Alexis who grew steadily away from me.

She takes a large mouthful of wine. 'I saw her face light up when her little darling came in,' she says. 'Never for me.'

I say nothing. My glass is half empty.

'She shouldn't have kept me if she wasn't going to love me.' Alexis speaks calmly, softly.

'Robert didn't give her much choice,' I say.

'He should have told me.'

'Yes.'

'She's not my mother.' She adds, 'Thank God.'

'So that's it; she doesn't count.'

She sniggers, 'At least I don't have to worry about ending up in the nut house.'

I force myself to stay silent. 'Will you find her, this Beth?' I ask. 'If she's still alive.'

'Dad's bit on the side,' Alexis says.

'I wouldn't expect you to be prissy about that.'

'I'm not. It doesn't sit well with all that holier-than-thou stuff. And anyway that's not what I mean.'

'Will you?' I ask again.

'No,' she says. 'I shan't forgive her either, for giving me away.'

'I gave Clare away,' I say so quietly I can only hear my voice inside my head.

Alexis looks startled. 'That's different.'

'How? You won't know,' I say, 'unless you find her.'

'I don't want to talk about this again,' she says. 'Never.'

'OK,' I say and don't mean it. 'And us?'

'Oh us,' she says. 'We're alright,' and puts her hand out to mine. I'm surprised to find I am pleased.

Bear wriggles then settles back down on my feet. Alexis finishes her wine, gets up and walks to the door. 'You're in Ben's room. You'll find it two floors up. My bedroom's on the first floor. You can hang anything there,' she says. 'I need to go to my kitchens. I won't be long. You'll find plenty in the fridge if you're hungry.' She turns back, 'Oh and no carpet yet so watch out for splinters in bare feet.'

The front door slams.

Ben's room is beautifully decorated: toys in a cavernous yellow box, stacks of books on the shelves; red and yellow curtains with trains running across them and a red chest of drawers. In the corner in a bright yellow cage that must be two feet high and eighteen inches across Lost sways gently on a swing. He eyes me imperviously and finding me wanting closes his eyes. I will enjoy sleeping in this room. I unpack my few things.

Her room has a large mirror, wardrobe and a king-size bed. I hang up my dress. A door off one corner leads to an en suite. She was right about the previous owner and his white fetish. The heavy red curtains are new and the bed is covered with a matching bedspread. As I gaze around, wondering what her plans for it are I spot two photos in large silver frames. I move closer. One is of Ben, the other of a man in his fifties: Uncle John.

I stand rooted in another time, another place. The mind is leisurely in its attack.

Chapter 22

1969

The day before Alexis and I left for Uncle John's, Mum and I baked. I climbed on to my special stool, measured out the flour and carefully cracked the eggs the way she had shown me. The Aga blasted out heat and I shouted and pointed to a cloud the shape of a sheep in the sky. My mother tried really hard to see it.

I was ten.

'You can take these cakes to your uncle's. You'll have fun.'

I watched her hands mix the cakes. She stroked my head making my hair floury. She laughed and got flour in her own hair when she pushed back a wisp from her forehead. There were always bits that escaped. We called them the runaways.

'You'll be back in time for your new school,' she said as she poured the mixture into paper cups and then put the cakes in the oven. I had to listen for the timer – fifteen minutes.

Later, when they were cool, we would ice them and I could choose the colours and the decorations.

'Perhaps I'll come next time,' she said when she was packing the cakes into a tin. She won't. She never does.

'I'll see Blackie and Jet, and Uncle John will take me on his tractor. He doesn't take Alexis.' I giggled. 'The wind messes her hair.'

This time I would give the cats names, and the cows. They would have to be girls' names. I ran through the names of the girls I knew. Not enough.

Alexis liked going to Uncle John's and started to nag Mum about going way before the school holidays even started. She said Uncle John was handsome and taller and stronger than Dad. I wasn't sure about that.

Uncle John had the sheep and cows to look after and Aunt Judith worked in a hospital. Uncle John said she wasn't a nurse or a doctor but bossed them all. She didn't seem bossy to me but we didn't see her much because she was at work most of the time. She was always tired when she came home and complained that it was too far to drive every day. They had no children. Last year I asked Aunt Judith about that. She said that it just hadn't happened. I'm not sure but I think she had tears in her eyes.

Aunt Judith never made cakes.

We left late because Dad was reading the newspaper in the kitchen for a long time after breakfast and talking quietly to Mum. In the car he told us that something serious had happened, that Bobby someone in America had been shot. He was a good man, an important man, Dad said and wouldn't say more. Alexis said this Bobby someone was the brother of the president who had also been shot. We never heard talk about things like that at home, just village stuff. I was frightened and asked Dad if we would be all right. He smiled and said we had nothing to worry about; we were safe.

We left our dale with its woods and crossed into another that was almost bare of trees. I played a game with myself, following the wriggles and twists and turns of the grey stone walls up the steep fields, fields littered with sheep.

'Are we nearly there?' I kept asking although I knew we weren't and Dad hated that question.

He drove fast. I liked that. As usual Alexis got the front seat. She said she got carsick in the back. It wasn't true. I don't think even Dad believed that but he still let her have the front seat.

Uncle John and Aunt Judith lived a couple of hours' drive from our house, in another dale, further west. Dad called it 'the wild country'. He was quiet on the drive there. He usually pointed things out to us and asked us both about school and asked me about Brownies.

When we got there mist was curling round two of the chimneys even though it was midsummer. It was always windy there and the hills were bigger than ours at home. There were no trees except for a few around the house.

As soon as the car stopped I ran to Uncle John. He lifted me off the ground and swung me round so hard I thought I might fly away into the sky. My legs flew out wide and my skirt blew up in the wind and I screamed. He had a big grin on his face. Dad just stood and watched.

Alexis left us and walked towards the house practising her smooth gliding walk and grown-up smile that didn't show too much gum.

Dad carried our bags into the house and the bedroom Alexis and I shared. Alexis' bag was twice as big as mine and Dad cracked his usual joke and asked her if she had the kitchen sink in it. Every year he asked her that. She just looked cross.

I ran outside to look for Jet and Blackie, the sheepdogs. They weren't tied up by the tractor but I heard them barking and found them in the big barn behind the cowshed. They knew me and gave me great licks all over my face. I was glad Dad didn't see. Blackie was my favourite. I put down a bowl of water for him. He looked at it and at me and then put his paw inside the bowl and tipped it over. I always laughed and patted him when he did that. He just sat, waiting for the bowl to be refilled.

By the time I got back to the house Dad was gone.

The next day I found the cats and told them their new names: Tigger and Thomasina. They were sisters so I liked the names both starting with T. Uncle John said they were good ratters and when I tried to save food for them he told me not to. 'They have to be hungry or they won't catch the rats,' he said.

Every day I got up at 6 a.m. for the morning milking. The cows knew to come to the shed and it didn't take Jet and Blackie long to get them in when Uncle John whistled. He said they knew what each whistle meant. When the cows were in their stalls Uncle John put on the machines that collected their milk – he said I would be able to give milk one day but I didn't believe him – and I gave each one a cuddle. I loved their warmth and the way they plodded to their stalls and pulled at their feed in greedy mouthfuls.

Thomasina had kittens a couple of days after we got there. They were tiny. Then they disappeared. Alexis said Uncle John drowned them. He laughed when I asked him and said he had given them away. But he never left the farm and no-one ever came.

The sun shone for the next two days and with Aunt Judith's help I named all the cows. I even remembered them all. As they came into their stalls I told them their new names. Uncle John just laughed.

The following day it was bright and sunny and, unusually, no wind. After Aunt Judith had left for work and the milking was done Alexis prissy-walked round the table in the kitchen and sat on uncle's knee. I wanted to sit there too but there was no room. Alexis pushed her chest tight against uncle, burrowing down into his lap. She wound her arms around his neck and kissed him on the mouth.

'I'll dance for you, Uncle John?' she said, using her gooey voice and pirouetting off his knee.

'I'm going to find Blackie,' I snorted.

'Be careful, don't go near him.' Uncle John's voice was muffled.

I found Jet and Blackie in the barn. The three of us raced up and down, the dogs barking. And I had a butterfly in a jar with the holes in the lid. I liked butterflies next best after birds. I'd show it to Uncle John.

After lunch Uncle John said he would take me to Far Hill. 'Come on', he said, walking to the back door.

124

Alexis slammed out of the room. I stuck my tongue out at her back.

Usually I took Teddy on the tractor with me but Uncle John told me to leave him in the house. It was a long way and I had to hold on tight. He let me take as many biscuits as I wanted.

He lifted me high into the air then on to the tractor seat. 'There, princess,' he said. He had never called me princess before. I was sorry Alexis didn't hear him. 'Put your arms tight around my waist,' he said, 'so you don't fall off.'

I looked back at the house. Alexis was staring out of the sitting room window. It was that look that said she would kill me. I didn't care.

It was ages before we reached Far Hill, checking all the sheep we could find on the way there. 'Nothing as daft as a sheep,' Uncle John said. Blackie was excited and ran behind barking and the wind was chasing the clouds in the blue sky as they scudded around trying to escape.

My legs were bare and I was wearing sandals.

'You look good,' Uncle said, pointing to my shorts.

'Better than Alexis?' I asked.

'Much,' he said, 'but don't tell your sister I said that,' and he laughed.

He drove the tractor fast over the rough hillsides. It was very bumpy and I had to cling on tight. I screamed sometimes. Just for fun.

We stopped in a valley and he lifted me up and put me in front of him and told me to lean on the steering wheel. I didn't come much higher than his waist. 'Can I drive,' I said although I didn't really want to.

'Quiet,' he said and bent forward and slipped his hands up the legs of my shorts to the top of my thighs, to the place my mother said was private, only for me. He asked, 'Do you like that?' I didn't know what to say, so I nodded but his hands felt like rough, wooden paddles, the sort I played with on the beach. His fingers moved, seemed to go inside me but that couldn't be. It hurt. I felt something hard between my legs. It hurt so much I pulled myself up and on to the steering wheel of the tractor and started to cry.

'Stop crying.' He'd never shouted at me before.

I put my hands between my legs. I was frightened. 'I want to go home,' I sobbed.

He sat back, looking cross and said I must never tell my mother or anyone, not even Alexis.

'You hurt me,' I whispered.

He laughed and said again that it was my fault. 'You will be in trouble. No-one will believe you,' he taunted. 'They will say it was your fault.'

I wanted my mother. And Teddy.

When we got back to the farmhouse Alexis ran out and flung herself at him.

'Hello princess,' he said.

Our father came the next day to take us home. It was my turn in the front seat but I crawled in the back.

'What's up,' Dad said. 'Cat got your tongue?'

When we got home I ran to Mum. I flung myself at her.

'Had a good week, Pet.?'

I nodded and with his words in my ears ran to my bedroom.

The next day I told my mother I was sick. She said, 'I expect it's all the sun,' and let me stay in bed all day. I wanted to stay there forever. Or run away.

Chapter 23

London 1982

I'm still sitting on the bed when I hear the front door slam and Alexis slipping off her shoes.

'Ruth.'

'Here,' I call back.

She looks calm when she comes through the door. She's like that, changes from one minute to the next. She sits down on the bed and points to the mantelpiece. 'Uncle John.'

I turn away.

'We went there as kids,' she says.

'Yes,' I say, very slowly, 'then we stopped.'

'I didn't.'

I don't believe her. I hear my mother saying, 'You'll never see him again, neither of you.'

I look at Alexis. 'We stopped going,' I say and add, 'Thank God.'

'I never stopped seeing him. We met secretly. He took me places – hotels, cinema, dancing even.' She giggles, 'Dad would have had a fit.'

'John,' I say. The word takes forever to leave my lips. Such a little word.

She's not listening. She's enjoying herself.

'He's our uncle, he's too old.' I haul myself back, feeling sick.

'Thirty-two years older if you really want to know. I like older men.'

Our eyes lock.

'What about Auntie Judith?'

'What about her?'

Oh Alexis, I cry inside my head. I sit absolutely still. I want out of the room.

'All those times you stayed with school friends.' I say slowly, 'A tall skinny girl. I can't remember her name.'

Alexis says impatiently, 'Annabel.'

'Yes, Annabel.' She laughs. 'I stayed with Annabel, I'm not stupid but I wasn't with her all the time. She had her own secrets. And that's why I persuaded them to let me go to London.'

'Art school,' I interrupt her.

'Oh that, yes. That was fun for a while. John bought a flat in London so we would have somewhere to meet, although he hates cities.'

'Peter?' I ask.

She looks serious now. 'I didn't see John for a couple of years. It was hard for him.'

I look at my watch. It's five. 'I could do with a glass of wine,' I say, standing.

'OK,' she says and springs up. She runs down the stairs. I follow slowly.

Alexis gets the half-full bottle of wine from the fridge and pours some into two glasses. We sit down at the table.

'The farm was a lot of work for him, especially later after Aunt Judith died. I was in London by then.'

I can't resist, 'Getting too old I expect.'

Alexis throws her head back and laughs. 'Not in the slightest.'

'Did Ben meet him?'

'He didn't meet him until after Peter and I divorced and I got my share of the marital home. John was good with him.'

She comes to stand beside me. 'Come on Ruthy, let's not quarrel.'

It's dark outside, already late. It's been a long day.

'I couldn't stand the flat and we needed more space,' she says. 'It took me time to find something I liked and could afford.' She adds, 'I don't expect you have any idea what houses cost here.'

'I had a look in an estate agent's window on the way here. I probably couldn't even afford a garage in this street.'

'I've bought some stuff from the deli. Let's eat.'

It's getting dark outside.

Bear is on the bed waiting for me and Lost hears me come in and clicks his annoyance at being disturbed. I wash my hands and face, drying them on the towel Alexis has put out for me. Ben's mirror is too low so I have to stoop. I wrap myself tightly in the duvet, for comfort, not warmth. Alexis' house is hot. I listen to the street noises: a couple of boys boasting about their conquests, a motorbike starting up and reverberating down the street, a randy tomcat calling, and a fox screaming.

The next morning I find Alexis in the kitchen, sitting at the table reading the paper; a pale blue silk dressing gown clings. She gestures absently to the coffee pot, the toaster and a loaf of bread, some exotic fruit.

As I sit down I hear the front door open and footsteps running down the hall. Alexis pushes back her chair and holds out her arms. Ben pours into them like a river in spate, then swivels his head towards me.

'Auntie Ruth you are here, Dad said you were.' He turns indignantly to Alexis. 'Mum, why didn't you tell me?'

Bear emerges from under the table and pushes himself against Ben's legs. Ben laughs and kneels down to hug him. His jacket and shorts are navy, his hair is combed down and wet, but already the curls are escaping on his neck.

'A kiss, darling.'

He flings himself at his mother, and then stands shyly in front of me.

'A kiss for your aunt,' I say.

His arms twist around my neck, my body relaxes into a hug. I feel weepy but control it.

'You should be at school. Your father was supposed to drop you off there.'

'I know,' he says, 'but I told him I wanted to see Auntie Ruth.'

Alexis continues. 'Now I'll have to take you.' The words smile and caress, belying their rebuff. 'Talk to your aunt while I dress and get ready for work.'

Ben chatters, full of his time with Peter, demanding to know if Bear slept on my bed. He looks a little disappointed when I say 'yes'.

'Lost was annoyed that I woke him last night.'

Ben giggles, 'He's a bit of a bully.'

'I like him,' I say.

Alexis comes in, smartly dressed in a dark grey suit, scarlet silk blouse and her trademark very high heels. 'You can look after yourself, London is big,' she says and smiles. 'Ben will give you his key. I'll see you after work. Have fun.'

Ben fishes in his pocket and detaches a key from a hook on his belt.

We hug.

I go upstairs and pack, check the room and the bathroom and carry my bag downstairs. Then I sit at one corner of the kitchen table and write a note.

Dear Alexis,

There's still things to do at home so I'm going back today. We need time, each of us, to sort things out. Perhaps we can talk more later. I'd like that.

It was good to see you and Ben. He's great. I'll telephone in a couple of days.

Love Ruth. And a big hug for Ben.

Alexis was done with Lower Newhouses years ago.

I hope Ben will come but it will need to be soon. We can talk about my mother and he can wear his silly hat. I will show him my secret paths, teach him about birds.

I go into Alexis' bedroom one last time, for the photograph on the mantelpiece: Uncle John, a colour photograph, his curly auburn hair glinting in the sunlight. A foot away another photo in a matching silver frame, more curly auburn hair: Ben.

I wrap my arms around myself to keep out the chill, hear Alexis' laugh. I sit, a long time, looking at nothing. When I get up I turn one photograph to the wall.

I put Ben's key through the letterbox as I leave and walk quickly to the Underground, noticing little. The train journey just happens and the house is as I have left it.

Alexis is out when I telephone. I leave a message saying I called.

Chapter 24

Yorkshire

I walk the hills. Lucy comes over when she's not working. She thinks I need taking care of. She's right. Everything crowds into my head, jostles my pain, tells me it will never end. I consider going back to the desert.

There will be a letter from at least one university soon. Or I'll travel: Milan, to the opera and to Paris. My mother's money will stretch if I'm careful.

I don't intend to tell Lucy about the letters but I do. She's surprised, says my mother adored Robert. She's more forgiving than I.

'Just a slip,' she says.

'With terrible consequences,' I say. My laughter sounds manic in my head.

'She brought Alexis up, that's what counts,' Lucy says, 'and loved you both. I bet Alexis looks for this woman, Beth, one day.'

I'm not so sure.

'You're still sisters,' she says.

'Yes.'

Mr Murray calls. He takes my abstraction for sadness. We go through my mother's books. I tell him of the excitement she and I shared as the date got closer to the monthly parcel from the book club. She always let me help choose. I leave him while I make a

132

cup of tea, urging him to take what books he wants. I've already culled them. I intend to travel light.

When I bring the tea in he has a pile of half a dozen books sitting on the small table beside him, on top *The Canterbury Tales*. I urge him to take more. He selects Saul Bellow's *Humboldt's Gift* (not Bellow's best, I've already taken that) and William Styron's *Sophie's Choice*.

He says that he will send one of the lads from the church to help me with packing and dispersing the things in the village.

We drink our tea in the kitchen – everywhere else is too cold – and talk about my mother but it is my father and Alexis in my head so I am reluctant and he doesn't push. He says my mother was a good friend.

'She had her demons,' he says.

I sit up and listen. He must have known, perhaps the whole church knew: those unexplained absences. My father would not have told. My mother, in her loneliness, her shame, her depression, perhaps, sought Mr Murray out.

He shifts in his seat and leans his elbows on the table. His face looks troubled. 'We all have them. She tried to hide hers and mostly succeeded.'

'Was she happy?' I ask.

'She wanted a lot out of life,' he says. 'And marriage can be difficult.'

I look straight at him a minute or two and give up.

He says he would love to look after her piano until I am ready for it. I tell him I will pack up her music, that he must borrow that too.

I catch the bus to the nearby town to buy clothes and have my hair restyled. I return with a whole new wardrobe. I throw out my old clothes, every one of them, as if that's an answer. It's that or go mad. I try telephoning Alexis, once, twice, three times a day. Not even an answering machine. 'Déjà vu,' I can't help thinking.

I get out my father's mower. It's as old as the hills around us. It was his baby. I push it up and down.

The newspaper is still full of the Shatila massacre and the second worst recession in Britain's history. I read about Michael Foot and the Labour Party and know I have some catching up to do.

A couple of weeks go by before Alexis calls back. She will not be drawn so we speak of small things.

I go to Aunt Dot's and we sit together on her sofa in front of a fire although it is warm. She holds my hand and speaks of my mother, of their endless cups of tea, the sewing, the chat and the laughter. That cheers me.

'She was earmarked for promotion, you know, headmistress, she was good.' Aunt Dot lets go of my hand for a minute, sips her tea, then says, 'She had a hard time getting away from her parents. They expected her to stay on the farm and look after them.'

Now that Dot has started she doesn't want to stop.

'In some ways the church was too small for her, our little world, especially for the women,' she says.

'Her books,' I say.

'Yes. And she had her girls,' Aunt Dot says and puts her cup down to hold my hand again.

My tea sits, undrunk.

'She loved your father,' Dot says. But I hear reservation or is it my rewriting of my life, their life. I look at her, hoping for more.

Into the silence I ask her about the place my mother went to. Lucy knew about my mother's disappearances; no-one else. When Auntie Dot came to look after us she said our mother was visiting friends. We didn't believe her. Dad always looked hassled so I didn't give him a hard time.

'She had to go,' Dot says, 'when everything became so dark. It was a quiet place for the unhappy, a place with doctors and nurses. Expensive, you could tell that by looking around.' Then she says,

134

'There was a small chapel and a minister who came every day but Harriet wouldn't see him or go to the chapel. I never understood that. The place didn't welcome visitors, said the patients needed rest, no excitement, an environment away from what they were used to.'

She sighs and is silent a few minutes before going on. 'I pestered your father until he agreed I might write to her. I never told him I was going to visit and when he found out he was angry, said I put her recovery at risk. I don't believe that but I didn't go again.'

'What happened to her there?'

Aunt Dot pauses a few moments then says softly. 'They gave her electric shock treatment. She hated it, said it made her forgetful. She felt lost afterwards, in a different way.'

I remember how she was when she came home, sort of empty, drained.

'All she wanted to do was get back to her girls.'

'Why did she have to go?' I ask.

Aunt Dot looks away.

'The first time,' I prompt.

She hesitates. I squeeze her hand.

'Before you were born and not long after Alexis,' she says. 'It was hard for her, those first couple of years with Alexis.'

I wonder what she knows but before I can stop myself I say, 'How could he do it?' I don't try to hide my anger.

Dot lifts the teapot and refills her cup, notices she needs milk and adds some. 'A mistake,' she says sadly, 'we all make them.'

She concentrates on drinking her tea. I notice her hands: crooked and knobbly. They tremble a little. I get up and give her a hug then sit back down.

'I miss her; I tried to help her.' She puts her cup down. 'He loved Harriet,' she says.

Not enough, I think, not nearly enough. 'And all that God stuff.' I look at her nervously, a step too far. She just smiles.

'And Alexis?' I say.

135

'She loved her, of course,' she says.

I wonder if she is too quick.

'It was hard. At first,' she repeats.

I'm tempted to tell her about Clare but don't.

'None of us are perfect,' she says, 'and he tried to give his life to God.'

He might have given more to us, less to God, I think but I'm not going to fight.

'Yes,' Dot says. 'I always knew. She stopped coming to church, didn't want to see anyone, except me and sometimes Mr Murray. She trusted him.'

She's quiet for a minute or two, then says, 'It was the music too. She played those pieces as if her life depended on them.' She sits quietly. 'Perhaps it did.'

My mother became a waterfall in reverse, water struggling backwards against a flood of life that threatened to tear her apart. She just sat, with her music and her poetry. Towards the end I refused to help her. It did no good; she still left us. I got angry, hated her for going away. I blamed her, sulked when she returned. How that must have hurt.

'She didn't want to go away. She never wanted her girls to see her like that,' she says.

One day, when I am very, very old I may smile and say, 'My father had a mistress,' making something exotic of it for people who did not know him, know our lives, know my mother.

Chapter 25

I watch too much telly, wasting my life; get hooked on *Bergerac* and *Juliet Bravo*, my penchant for detective stories surprising me. I mop up the news programmes and can't wait for Parky's next interview. Cambridge offers me a place next year but I don't want to wait. Two others, with good reputations for sociology offer places this year if I move quickly. Not English or history. My dream of following my mother as an English teacher has gone. It belongs to my past life. The decision is too hasty but it will do.

I always planned to go to university when I returned so that's what I do. I don't waste much time but it's hardly a decision.

I tell the estate agent to make a real push on selling and agree a price, on the low side, with Alexis, by letter. She too, seems in a hurry.

I'm keeping the furniture until the last minute. A house clearance company has given me a good price and the estate agent says houses sell better if they are furnished.

I open my mother's bedroom door. There are still some things to clear. I don't know what to do with her treasure box.

The parcel is there, on the bed. I'm reluctant to go near it. It is dusty, threatening. The tape is old, peeling round the edges and clouds of dust rise from the brown paper. It opens itself up to me.

I part the tissue paper and carefully pull out a white dress, a wedding dress. I wrap it around me and lie on the bed.

Slowly a pinprick of a time reveals itself frame by frame. I try to shut it down, close off the leaks. There have been too many.

A cold wet day, the day after we returned from the farm. Sunday lunch in the dining room. Late because it was roast chicken and that took ages. Alexis or I set the table, turn about, which usually meant an argument. I hated those Sunday lunches. They went on forever, just like church. We had a reading from the Bible, and, as if we hadn't already had enough, we got the starving children of China bit if we didn't finish what was on our plates. Waste was a big sin on my father's list.

This Sunday my father was at a meeting of Church Elders that would go on most of the day so no Bible reading. Lunch: lamb chops, mashed potatoes, peas and rice pudding for dessert. As usual Alexis refused to eat the potatoes or the rice pudding. We were just sitting there arguing.

Alexis wanted to go to Annabel's house but my mother said 'No,' and added, 'If it stops raining we can go for a walk.' I could tell she really wanted to let Alexis go. Our father always insisted we give Sundays to God. 'Not much to ask,' he said.

'A walk,' Alexis said scornfully, then whingeing a little, 'He needn't know.'

I just sat there, looking down, thinking about running away.

Alexis flounced out of the room but my mother called her back to finish clearing the table. It was her turn. A few minutes, no seconds later, she was back, the same flounce in her step, her chin stuck out, her eyes flashing. She had on her 'I can't stand my sister' face. That should have warned me but I stayed sitting at the table, feeling pleased that Alexis was in trouble and sticking a fork into the lace tablecloth. My mother would have slapped my hand had she noticed.

Alexis slammed the dirty dishes back down on the table, and said, all casual-like, as if talking about the weather, 'Uncle John touched Ruth.' She pointed down towards her thighs.

Looking pleased with herself she picked up the dishes and carried them to the sink, banging them down hard.

My fork tore through the lace. I stared at the jagged tear and heard his voice: they'll say it's all your fault, no-one will believe you.

My mother stood, completely still. I heard her whisper, 'No, no.'

She crossed the room to stand in front of Alexis. 'What do you mean?'

Alexis was silent. My mother lifted Alexis' chin with her thumb. They were almost the same height. 'What do you mean?' Alexis shook her chin free and turned away.

My mother walked over to where I sat. I put my hand over the tear. She started to kneel beside my chair. She held on to the edge of the table with one hand and placed the other hand on the floor, put one knee down first then the other. I put my hands out to help.

I hung my head and did that thing with my mouth that makes my lips sore.

'Tell me about it.'

'I don't know what Alexis is talking about,' my voice shrill. 'It's not true; it's not fair, you always believe her.' I stopped.

My mother repeated, 'Tell me about it. What did he do?'

I knew what he said was true: she wouldn't believe me. She looked into my eyes. I looked back into pain and fear.

Alexis began to noisily stack the rest of the dishes.

I shook my head. My tongue worked away at my lips. She put her hand up and stopped me.

'Tell me.'

'I didn't do anything, but will I go to Hell like the Catholics?' What I really meant was would she send me away?

'Of course not,' she murmured, adding, 'don't tell your father.'

I put out my hand to help her up, she brushed it away and grasped the edge of the table again.

She put her arms out to me when she was standing but I ran out of the kitchen and up the stairs to our bedroom. I heard her call after me, 'Ruth, don't go. I want to talk to you. I'm not cross. Please Ruth, come back.' She would have a go at Alexis now, but she wouldn't get far.

In the bedroom I crouched on the floor, making myself as small as I could, Teddy wrapped in my arms. He didn't mind not having a name, said he knew he was special. I was a good mother. Teddy loved me. No-one else did.

I heard my mother's footsteps and held Teddy as tight as I could and wiped my nose with my dress then remembered it was my Sunday best.

My mother tried to hug me but I wouldn't let Teddy go. Again she asked me what Alexis meant.

'He hurt me.' Hard paddles and fingers. I would never say those words, ever. 'He said I was his princess.'

I let her hug me. 'You're my princess,' she said. 'Always.'

I shook my head.

'You will never see him again. I promise.' I saw a half smile. 'Cross my heart… You must tell me if anyone hurts you,' she said. 'Promise me.'

She undressed me, put on my pyjamas and tucked the sheet and blankets up under my chin. She sat slowly on the side of the bed.

I turned away, my back to her. I didn't believe her.

The next day she was quiet, just sat with her dead eyes playing those two sad records over and over. I threw myself at her, cried out that it was not my fault. She did not reply; did not speak.

Early the next morning. The clock said 6 a.m. I didn't want to wake.

I heard my mother weeping. I pulled the bedclothes over my head. Alexis was still asleep. I don't know how much later it was that I heard my father's car. I pulled on my dressing gown and ran downstairs. I started to run towards my mother and stopped. She was dressed in white. She was wearing a white dress that came down to her feet, her bare feet. It looked like the dress in the photo that was on top of the piano. I ran up to her, flung my arms around her legs, clung to her. She patted my head then put her hands to her ears. She was singing her songs about fate and death.

My father pulled me away.

I waved and waved but she didn't look back. All I could see was her moving mouth and her hands over her ears.

Towards dawn I fell asleep. My mother crossed the kitchen – a lifetime of crossing, a slow, fearful walk – to kneel in front of me, her bright beautiful face, ugly with fear, her eyes an almost perfect match to my own full of pain and bewilderment. 'Tell me about it,' she said.

The cold woke me. I was sitting on the floor of my mother's room, leaning against the wall.

She didn't hug me when she left and I didn't see her for twenty-seven weeks. I counted them. And the minutes.

School started without me. I felt dizzy, unable to move. Each morning I laid out my uniform then put it back on the hangers and placed my new shoes back in the bottom of the wardrobe, the clean socks back in my drawer. My father said my mother would come back. I didn't believe him. Alexis dressed me, took me by the hand (just as she had done for my first school) and led me to the school bus.

The pain and fear in my mother's eyes never left me.

Everything is given away or packed awaiting collection. I leave the spare keys with the estate agent and tell them to try for a quick sale.

I chuck the dying flowers from my mother's grave and think about families. How many secrets make up a family; brick by brick? How many secrets to pull it down? And the little intimacies, kindnesses that add up to so much more.

I tell her that soon I will leave here for good but I shall take her with me.

PART IV

Chapter 26

1992

Ten years ago I fled the hills for the sea, an inane way to choose a university, almost like sticking a pin on the donkey's tail, blindfold. Almost, for I hold in my head the picture of Clare with the bay reflected in her eyes. A different sea, a colder sea.

I found a bedsit on the coast. It was small and shabby but I had the sea outside my window and treated it like the desert, part of the journey to myself.

I needed a subject that was to do with life. The blurb said social anthropology was all about what it is to be human across different societies and cultures. That appealed.

In December of my first term at university I travelled to the Greenham Common peace camp to protest against American cruise missiles, joined 29,999 other women and held hands with two strangers to form a human chain fourteen miles long. We were called misguided and naïve. I joined CND and the Labour Party in my second year and organised a protest march in support of the miners' strike. The same people were at CND and Labour Party meetings.

I spent three years thinking about culture and society, power and its range of relationships; and reading Weber, and Foucault and Marxist analyses and ending with global trade policies and neo-liberal capitalism. I worked hard, making up for lost time.

I enjoyed my life, wore the same clothes, washed enough to

be decent, wandered the beach and was happy in a low-key way.

I met Cat on the doctoral programme. I decided on a PhD in much the same way that I decided most things: because it was there, obvious. And I liked books and ideas.

Catherine, known as Cat. There was something feline about her: the way she walked and her impenetrable eyes. And in the way she dressed in brightly coloured clothes that clung to her thin body, undulating with her as she moved.

She introduced me to Sue, Lizzie and Tessa. Their quartet became a quintet and I rediscovered my love of music.

The five of us had fun and laughter and played wonderfully eclectic music: Handel, Scott Joplin (a favourite), Mozart, Nielsen, Faure, and works from the musicals and much more. We didn't stay long on any piece. The university gave us a room one afternoon a week and Cat's parents let us use their cottage by the sea. We went there for the weekends and played on the beach. If it was windy we set up our stands, pegged down our music and played in a beach hut. People stopped to listen and called us the 'beach girls'.

Cat and I watched *Spitting Image* together. We hooted and booed the cigar-chomping, cross-dressing Maggie and vampire Edwina. Geoffrey 'talking-to-a-dead-sheep' Howe was another object of our derision, derision untroubled by the facts.

We walked along the warm sand watching the sun set, and spoke of what we might do with our lives.

'I want to explore the brain,' Cat said. Her eyes shone. 'That's where the future is.' She added, 'Oh, and a beautiful man.'

'You've had all the beautiful ones around here,' I laughed.

We found a sand dune and sheltered from the wind.

'Me too, the beautiful man bit,' I said, wriggling my bum further into the sand, shading my eyes from the low sun. I asked myself over and over: why was I still afraid? I could love and be loved. And make love. It would happen. It must. But still I kept alone.

146

'Kids?' I ask.

'Don't know. Perhaps. You?'

I shook my head.

Clare was growing up. I still carried an undercurrent of loss, of longing.

The Berlin Wall came down. I wanted to go to there and climb on the wall, chip away at it, hand out flowers to those crossing from the East, some just coming because they could, then going quietly back home, not quite understanding how their world might change. Cat and I planned a flight to Berlin but it was only talk.

1989 ended. Cat and Lizzie left: Cat for research into neuroscience in London and Lizzie for more music in Edinburgh. The musical thread that connected us tore apart despite our protestations. Reluctant to leave the sea I dallied, teaching and researching.

I travelled by train to London from the south-west, staying weekends with Ben and Alexis, longer in the school holidays. The three of us went to the cinema, took boat trips on the Thames or Ben and I roamed the museums.

For a year or two it was the Natural History Museum, the dinosaurs. Ben said their name meant terrible lizard. His favourite was the stegosaurus – roof lizard, nine metres long with a brain the size of a tangerine. He giggled and put his small hands together to demonstrate. His next favourite was the tyrannosaurus, the tyrant lizard. 'Like Mr Guy,' he said, naming one of his school teachers. But the real thing has sixty teeth, each eight inches long. He got out his ruler to show me then held it against the side of his own small teeth. Sometimes we visited the blue whale or we took the boat to the Royal Observatory in Greenwich.

He went to boarding school and did well there, just as Alexis predicted.

To leaven the science I bought novels for his birthdays and Christmas. I have a long list of books waiting for him. I measure Clare's life by his.

We spent Christmas together, usually in London. Sometimes they came to my cottage by the sea. Not at all Alexis' style but she didn't say anything.

This was to be my last Christmas here. I had accepted a job from a university in the northern city near my old village, a job too good to turn down: light teaching and generous research funding.

Alexis brought some of the food with her and had the rest sent down from her kitchens: ham, Christmas pudding and brandy sauce, my favourite chocolates. And much more. A feast.

'Survival,' she said when I thanked her.

I'm a lousy cook. Always have been.

We sat on the beach after lunch, as long as it wasn't raining and watched Ben. 'Two mother hens,' Alexis said.

The sea was never too cold for Ben. He did his best to get us in with him, running up to beg us, splashing about to show what fun it was. We clapped and laughed and stayed sitting on the sand, a rug over our knees, shoulders touching. They were usually brisk winter days with a weak sun pretending warmth.

Alexis' business was flourishing. She mentioned large corporations. Big budgets; new, bigger kitchens. She made it sound easy. 'I've got more money than I can spend, but...' She trailed off.

'What's missing?'

She looked away.

'A man,' I said, wondering which of us I was talking about.

'Oh, I have plenty of them. Nothing serious,' she said. 'Just fun.'

There was something in her tone that made me doubt.

'And you?' she asked.

'Too busy,' I said, and wondered if she believed me.

'Clare?' she said.

I shook my head.

'She will find you one day, I'm sure of it.'

'Beth,' I say in reply.

'Perhaps, one day.'

I bought a small cottage a hill or two away from Lower Newhouses with what remained of my mother's money. On the strength of my new salary I got a mortgage for a small flat near the university.

The cottage was scabby with neglect when I bought it: a sturdy two-up two-down Yorkshire stone cottage, mid-Victorian, built for function, squatting in a small garden enclosed by a grey stone wall. Two spinster school teacher owned it then it fell into the abyss of inheritance fallout.

A father and son team from the nearby village repointed the cottage walls and turned or replaced the heavy stone roof tiles. Inside I painted all the walls white and thoroughly scrubbed the stained flags that covered the floors of the two downstairs rooms. My mark on the cottage and its surroundings was to be light.

In the kitchen I scraped back layer after layer of brown shiny paper from a fine stone mantel and surround. Two old armchairs flank the fireplace. Workspace, sink and stove, and a few cupboards take up the remainder of the room except for a rectangular dark oak kitchen table where I work when I am not out roaming the hills or sitting with a book in front of the fire. The table seats six but there are only four chairs. Two good-sized windows above the sink look into the garden, another to the wilderness. The garden is also paved with stone flags from the nearby quarry.

The other room downstairs is a rarely used sitting room. Upstairs are two bedrooms, both with a working fireplace. They overlook the hillside with its crags and bare stone. Large chunks, some the size of cars, sprawl over the lower ground.

The flat, in a newly built block, has two bedrooms, a kitchen with dining area and a decent-sized sitting room. The Persian carpet looks too grand and my mother's piano has pride of place. Ben and I play duets together when he comes up.

The flat came fitted with luxuries, by my standards anyway: washing machine, dishwasher, microwave and latest cooker and hob. My furnishings are sparse. I sleep weekly on alternate sides of my double bed and change the sheets fortnightly. What I call the gnome's room is furnished with a bed and small bedside cupboard. Ben calls it his room, says he makes a good gnome at over six feet.

Lucy helped me paint the walls, a neutral cream shade. We went shopping for a small sofa and two comfortable chairs. She presented me with some large floor cushions which add softness to the sitting room. I bought some prints, standard wallpapering stuff: Cezanne, Monet and Jackson Pollock.

I took possession of the flat and Lady Murasaki on the same day. When Murasaki is her most delicate and stand-offish I call her 'Lady'. Sometimes I put her on a lead and take her to the park. The kids there love her. Otherwise she spends her time sleeping or gazing out the window. She has a luxurious plaid cat basket in the sitting room but prefers my bed. In the late afternoon sun she sits on the windowsill, her white feet tucked neatly in, and her delicate face staring out the window waiting, so I delude myself, for my return.

Ben declared me a dinosaur, insisted I buy a television and threatened not to visit if I didn't. Bluff, but I gave in.

Ben is fifteen now.

Chapter 27

Spring 1993

Maria waves to me as I step through the door. Not a profligate overarm movement or a parsimonious coy flick of the wrist, but an elegant hand action. She smiles, bright vermilion smile. Her red hair is tied back and fastened with a black velvet bow. As always she wears a slim knee-length black skirt and a white blouse with frills at the cuff and neck. Her hands sparkle with rings. Today her necklace is shades of green. Venetian glass, I guess.

'Ciao Maria,' I say, with a smile.

'Ciao Ruth.'

We kiss, air kisses, both cheeks. Our little ritual pleases us both.

She takes *The Guardian* from under the counter and hands it to me. When I leave I will put it with the other papers. I have a rule of only reading the news at Maria's otherwise it would take over my whole life. The rule is frequently broken.

I slip into my usual seat in the back corner. When I open the paper I give a silent cheer: a woman, Betty Boothroyd, the first female Speaker of the House of Commons for 700 years. This augurs well for the day.

Even at 8 a.m. a few customers are demolishing the signature sticky meringues with fresh strawberries and piles of whipped cream, some delicately combining a little of each on the spoon, savouring, anticipating, others gobbling, using a motion more akin to shovelling.

We regulars – loners, workaholics, waiting for our lives to begin – nod to each other and sit on our own.

A few months back a Japanese lady entered bowing to everyone, entrancing us with her grace and her smile. I invited her to sit at my table endeavouring to return her bow but it was a poor thing. Everyone smiles when she is here. Now she and I share a table at the weekends. Her husband's a scientist and works every day. She doesn't mind, says that he's a good man. She belongs to a reading group and sometimes asks me what some of the words mean. I come away from those mornings feeling lighter, more decorous.

My double espresso with its layer of cream across the surface is exquisite. The kick and the reassuring opulence are the same every morning. This morning I reject my usual croissant and go for brioche and mascarpone cheese. I had a hard run earlier and have earned the treat.

My route to work takes me across the park. It is not much more than a piece of green, but I think of it as mine. It's a long walk but I enjoy it and don't often take the car. On the other side of the park I pass several blocks of three storey terraces with long narrow gardens and little evidence of plant life, then down a busy road populated by student coffee bars and fast-food outlets.

My office is on the first floor of three, about halfway down from the central staircase and on the left-hand side. The rooms and corridors are a little tatty. The cream brick building houses the sociology staff and two other departments.

The ground floor of the building is given over to lecture rooms and computer services. Attached to the right-hand end of the building, like a carbuncle grown overlarge for its reluctant host, is a lecture hall built to reflect our most recent strategic direction: bums on seats, especially if they are well-heeled, overseas, fee-paying bums. Across from my building are more lecture halls, the library and the large and airy glass refectory. A little further away, the administrators, the dean's office and the senior common room.

I breakfast at Maria's, then most of my waking hours are spent in my office. Its walls are a murky yellow brown and it is replete with bookshelves and a standard issue grey filing cabinet. It's a large room by university standards. Windows run along one wall and open on to a stand of trees and an etiolated back lawn belonging to one of the houses in the street behind. My desk takes up half this wall. At the right-hand end is my computer, printer and a stack of paper. The remainder of the surface, except for a space immediately in front of my chair, is covered with stacks of journals and papers and separate piles of books. They look random but are not.

Teaching has just begun again after the late Easter break.

My e-mails first: several students asking for meetings to discuss modules for next year. Lucy reminds me we are meeting next week. A chapter from a doctoral student – he's extremely bright but his research into social networks in inner city communities has not yet reached the interesting stage.

A new e-mail flashes up: from the dean confirming the substance of our meeting last week, and reminding me of the gathering this evening. I look at my notes from nearly six months back.

The dean, a small man with hamster cheeks and slickly combed back black hair, sat behind his overlarge desk and placed the fingers of his right hand on the exquisite walnut desk top, one finger at a time, a piano scale movement, revealing in the process, an inch or two of fine white cotton cuff under the sleeve of an expensive navy suit. His small eyes are brown behind his black-rimmed glasses. Gossip is, that the cost of the recent refurbishments of his office would pay for two new lecturers.

'An opportunity for you,' he proffered lifting his hands from the desk and placing them in front of his chest, matching finger to finger to arrive at a semi-prayer position, one, two, three, four, and then the thumbs, 'to make your mark. It'll help with promotion.' His hands parted and he pulled down his short arms into his overlong sleeves, adding, 'Now that you have your publications in the pipeline.'

We both knew that the fastest route to promotion was via publication in the top international journals. It would be smart of me to duck this job, recognise the dean's flattery for what it was and put everything into my research. The men here are tougher than us women; we are natural suckers. But I was hungry for a senior lectureship and he knew it.

He interpreted my quizzical look. 'We don't have long to get the MA in place. It starts September next year.'

The deal we struck at my interview fifteen months ago hung over us, cartoon bubbles: one year's light teaching with no administration to get the publications from my doctorate.

A copy of the course outline sat on his desk: MA in Research Methods. It's long-winded, encompassing all eventualities. In weekly sessions over the academic year it would cover all major aspects of research methods.

He stood, not tall.

Chapter 28

The Evening

It's a late spring afternoon but the north is niggardly with its warmth. I dashed back to the flat to exchange my jeans and sweater for a light blue cotton dress and high-heeled sandals. I slung a cardigan over my shoulders, switched handbags and grabbed my car keys. At the last minute I tied my hair back and had another go at my make-up.

A blather of voices, some a little drunk already on the dean's good wine, bounce off the walls of the senior common room, a room unsoftened by carpets or curtains and once a gathering place for monks. The sun filters in through the blues and reds of the stained-glass windows set high into the plain stone walls.

I immediately feel sleepy in the crowded airless room, shift my weight from foot to foot and look around at my mostly dull colleagues. I'd like to slip away to my office and finish a paper. Its conclusions are in my head. An hour's hard work would do it but tonight is the official launch of my MA course.

It is shaping up nicely. I've nursed it through endless committees that thrive on obstruction and pedantry; have written course outlines: formulaic jargon-ridden things, and spent many hours getting the right teaching in place.

The dean is talking to one of his acolytes on the far side of the room. He sees me and nods, expecting me to join him. I don't. I spot Gill and Rosemary and wave. They have both agreed to teach on the programme. Rosemary is a brilliant statistician.

I take a glass of white wine and I pick up the usual snippets: protests of plagiarism, too many scripts, too many courses, too little time for research?

'Good turnout,' says Gill.

'If it doesn't go on too late we could eat at the pub,' Rosemary puts in.

'Not there,' I protest, 'too many students.' I suggest a reasonably priced restaurant not far out of the city. 'I have my car.'

They both look pleased and I resolve to be less of a loner.

Not so long ago Alexis said, 'You're hiding yourself away; you need to get out.'

'Where to?' I asked. 'Anyway I'm happy.' I knew what she was really asking: men. None and a non-existent sex life. I've almost given up. I try not to think about it. And fail.

'I'll send Ben up to distract you,' Alexis said.

'I'm thirty-four,' I said, 'and can look after myself but I'd love to see Ben.'

A stranger strolls through the door and pauses, surveys the room.

He's wearing a navy suit, pale blue shirt and striped blue tie. Expensive. His eyes are wide set and a deep azure or… I run through the possibilities: cerulean, the colour of clear sky and calm sea; no, gentian, the wild flowers on the Swiss mountainsides where I have walked the summers past. He looks a vain man but vanity can be intelligent or dumb. This, I think, is the clever variety. A dangerous, beautiful man.

I surreptitiously straighten my clothes and see Gill pull her lipstick out of her handbag. Rosemary runs a hand through her hair.

He moves from group to group, an actor on stage. I watch defences fall, conversations grow animated. He leaves the dean till last.

The dean puts out his hand then proffers a glass of wine. Too

156

eager, I murmur to myself. The stranger continues to look around the room while the dean leans close, his lips moving, his hand fluttering. The blue man turns in my direction and smiles. I don't have time to look away. His eyes, blue enough to burn, lock into mine. I move a few steps from Rosemary and Gill.

He saunters over. 'So you are one of the new stars.' He puts one hand in his pocket, sips his wine, wrinkles his nose slightly and puts the almost full glass back on the table. His nails are trimmed and painfully clean. I tuck mine away. They are a little grubby.

'The Dean won't like that,' I say. 'He prides himself on his wine.' I cast a quick glance across the room to see if he has noticed. He has.

The blue man thrusts out his hand, 'I'm Daniel Phillips and you're Ruth Bishop.'

His eyelids droop a little giving him a sleepy look and behind that, amusement and a slither of ruthlessness. The tilt to the right of his nose is offset by a large flesh coloured mole. If uniformity in facial features is beauty, his face is at the other end of the scale: interesting, attractive features that do not fit easily together.

'He,' Daniel inclines his head towards the dean, 'has asked me to teach on this programme of yours.'

In my head I go over the list of lecturers. Daniel Phillips is not on it.

He reads my face. 'He didn't tell you I see.'

I shake my head. 'He does that.'

Daniel Phillips laughs.

'What do you teach?' I ask him.

'IT strategy, databases; the sexy stuff that they can't get enough of,' he says. 'Postgrad. Teaching helps my consultancy.'

'Could be useful,' I say and wish I'd left my hair down.

'And you, what's your area?'

'Power.' I keep my expression neutral although I'm longing to laugh, wildly.

What is power? That question fills most of my waking hours.

Real power is not always obvious, not the power of money, that is obvious, but the power of exclusivity, clubbiness. Get a grip, I tell myself and say, 'How organisations interact,' and throw in Max Weber.

'Don't know him,' he says, his eyes wrinkling at the corners.

Round one to you, I think and wonder where his self-confidence comes from. Not public school. I'm enjoying myself. 'And trust, between organisations,' I add. 'Partnerships.'

What's happening to me? Giddy. Not me, surely. Where has this creature, me, come from? Too many years head down, all work. Ambitious, successful years, I judged them, until now. Lucy has given up on me with men, tells me I have something missing. I almost believed her.

I shove casual into my voice and say, 'Perhaps we can help each other. IT strategy and databases could be a useful addition to my course.'

'Perhaps,' Daniel says. His eyes run over me not bothering to hide their journey. He likes what he sees. 'You know everyone here?'

'More or less.'

'Any I should meet?'

'You've already done that,' I say. 'Working the room.'

Daniel's laugh, deep, prolonged, is so loud that some turn to look at him.

Oh to bottle his deep warm voice with laughter in it. I'm in danger of becoming a mewling idiot. I want to carry him away to some secret cave and keep him captive to gaze upon, Calypso to his Ulysses but I want more than seven years, earthly immortality for us perhaps. I have to turn away, shake up my thoughts, hoping they might rearrange themselves into something rational.

I must be mad. I want his hands on me; I want to touch him. Wonder is in my heart and something else. How quickly, quickly.

He looks at his watch. 'I'm catching a train to London soon.

That's where it all happens.' He taps my arm. 'I'm a northerner so I know.' The word 'losers' hangs in the air.

'Then what are you doing here?' I ask, looking straight back. The room suddenly feels cold. I glance around. Rosemary and Gill are smirking. 'You'll be telling me next that Maggie Thatcher is just what the country needs.'

'She is,' he grins. 'But don't take it like that. I love the north but my office is in London and I have a meeting first thing tomorrow with a major client.' He names a large multinational and looks around the room as if waiting for the applause. He leans forward and places his hand on my arm. 'I'll find you. Soon.' He takes his other hand out of his pocket while continuing to hold my arm. His hand is small and neat, a few dark hairs on his knuckles. 'A quick word with him,' he points in the direction of the dean, 'and I'm off.'

The light from the stained-glass windows mottles his face and clothes blue and red as he walks across the room, bouncing off the soles of his shoes.

Just as he's reaching the door I call softly. 'Perhaps I'll be here.'

He turns round and laughs.

'Not for me,' I tell myself and feel like crying.

Not long afterwards I make my excuses to Gill and Rosemary, promising another time, and slip away.

I throw myself into my work and two weeks later leave for a conference in Edinburgh. I have all but erased the blue man, shut down my dreams.

The university is in the old town and accommodation is, as usual, in student rooms. I've seen worse but it's pretty grim: cold worn linoleum on the floor, a small bed and scabby desk, and marks on the walls where posters and other bits have been taken down and a washbasin with bathroom and toilet down the corridor. It will be bearable for four nights. The conference centre is a short walk away.

My first day I spend exploring the castle, wondering at the wealth of Scots history and my ignorance, and walking the Royal Mile to the Palace.

The second day goes well. I present my paper to a large audience: 'Who is in control? Power and trust.' I say that it's never a relationship of equals, always pragmatic. I slip in a reference to my book which just happens to take pride of place on the publisher's table.

At question time a researcher from Manchester says he has just divorced so where does that leave him?

'A demerger,' I say. 'You lost power. Perhaps you used punishment instead of reward.' We all laugh and later at the bar he buys me a drink. It's my sort of conference: serious and fiercely competitive but fun. Perfect.

Two more days of papers and networking. There's interest from researchers at Penn State and I'm invited to collaborate with a researcher here at Edinburgh. He has an excellent reputation. With colleagues I take in Edinburgh's pubs.

On the train home I begin planning a week's walking in Switzerland. I might persuade Cat to join me.

A light tap and my office door opens. It's exactly a month.

He wears jeans and a plain blue sweatshirt with a cream roll-neck top underneath. It's the first week of June.

'Hello Ruth Bishop,' he says.

It sounds like school roll call. I look into his sleepy eyes then down at my clothes. This morning I put on my best black trousers, a pair that fits well and a turquoise top. I looked in the bathroom mirror: good mouth, shapely nose with a slight tilt at the tip, high cheekbones, reasonable to good figure. Eyes: strangers have to look deep to find me. The mirror said 'better than OK'. But for what, I asked myself.

'Hello Daniel Phillips,' I say.

'Good,' he says, looking at my trousers. 'You'll do.'

'For what?' I throw back at him.

'Artemis.'

'Ah, the twin sister of Apollo, daughter of Zeus,' I murmur. 'The goddess of chastity, an eternal virgin, surrounded by virgins,' I put my hand lightly on his arm. 'Men who saw her naked were punished gruesomely, then death.' I am lighting up like a taper put to dry brittle grass. Fires are not safe.

'I shouldn't ride her then,' he chuckles. 'A mate suggested the name. Sounds as if I've been set up.'

I stay seated a few moments, see his leathers and assume Artemis is a motorbike. I pick up my handbag, lock my office and follow him.

We walk to the staff car park.

A gaggle of students cluster round a motorbike that etches itself deep into my imagination: bright red and yellow, low, sleek, potent. There's joy in its understated elegance, the powerful stealth of a rarely spotted jungle cat, crouching, ready.

'A Ducati,' he says.

'Italian,' I say although it's a wild guess.

His grin tells me I'm right.

'It, she's beautiful. You chose well.' I laugh, 'The name I mean.' The only thing I know about motorbikes is that they have two wheels.

The students move away. A few recognise me and smirk.

'Yes.' He strokes Artemis with the tenderness of a lover and hands me a leather jacket, trousers, gloves and a helmet. They are too small for him. I wonder who else has worn them. I wriggle into the jacket and trousers. They feel odd. The gloves come halfway up my arm to my elbows.

'You need to wrap up. Don't be fooled by the sun.'

I tuck up my hair beneath the helmet and adjust the chin strap. It feels like a house on my head. Daniel puts on his leathers and helmet and sits astride. He half turns and pats the seat behind.

161

'Hold on to me,' he says. 'Let me know if your feet get too cold.'

For the first ten minutes I sit upright, stiff and terrified then something in me gives and I lean the side of my helmeted face against his silk-smooth leather jacket, tighten my arms around his waist, and press my knees against his hips.

We sashay through the city, coast past the queues of gridlocked cars and large stone buildings in the centre, markers of a more prosperous age, and further out boarded up shops, graffiti and rubbish. We seize the moment and the gaps and on through the suburbs of semi-detached houses. Daniel swings the bike round the corners, beating the lights and muscling past the slow moving traffic. By the time we reach the sweeping switchback country roads we move as one.

In one or two dales there has been an early harvest. I smell the cut hay strewn in black plastic rolls looking like chunks of liquorice thrown on to straw coloured trays. On a stone wall a little owl inspects the shorn field for rodents. One field is replete with hundreds of lapwing and plover; others fields uncut, lush and green.

Small daggers of cruel wind find unprotected gaps. I press myself more tightly into Daniel's back and shout that Artemis is great but the noise and the gelid wind snatch my words and toss them away. We dance over the hills, joined together in the adrenalin rush of the deep mean bends, leaning forward down the steep hills, then up again.

We stop on the western edge of the Pennines where bikers gather. I start counting and give up at fifty-five as still more draw up. Motorbikes of every colour, black leather-clad men, a smattering of girlfriends (not me, I think, not yet,) and a roadside van. Daniel takes off his helmet and helps me with mine. There is blue excitement in his eyes. He bends and kisses me on the lips as if we are already lovers, have always been lovers. This takes me by surprise. I hold him tight.

My feet are freezing. A small thing, I tell myself and wriggle my toes, flex my ankles until I feel some warmth returning. We drink tea from the roadside van. Daniel knows some of the men, most of them much older. He introduces me but the names don't stick. They admire his bike and speak an Esperanto of bikers. Daniel glows. I stand a little to one side, overwhelmed. Daniel later explains that bikers are to be found wherever there are long, fast roads and sweeping hills.

On the way back we stop at traffic lights near the centre of the city. He turns his head towards me and says. 'We could go somewhere to eat or go to my flat.' He points off to the right. 'It's just over there.'

I nod and don't bother saying I'm not hungry.

Daniel puts two separate locks on his bike, punches in a code for the outside door of a block of smart apartments, then holds my hand lightly and slings the two helmets across his other arm. The hallway is pristine and a gunmetal and wood staircase leads upwards. He points to a lift. It's small with mirrored walls. We stand close and hold hands. The dance of the hills is still in me.

The late afternoon sun invades the bedroom and a shaft stabs a king-size bed. Deep vermilion floor-length curtains are drawn back from French doors that open on to a tiny terrace. The fading sky is tinged with wistful salmon pink feathers.

Two or three feet from the bed stands a large white bath, not the plastic baths of modern houses but a serious heavy creature with bold claw feet: deep, very deep, and long.

I kick off my shoes, sit on the end of the bed and hear the plop of a cork being eased from a bottleneck, the same noise a frog makes as it slips into a pond to hide. Perhaps I will lay myself out, piece by piece and he will take me as floods engulf parched dry and barren earth. Perhaps I will taste him all over the way cats do their kittens and put flesh on the ghosts of my dreams. Or perhaps I will put my shoes back on and flee.

163

Daniel places a wine glass in my hand. I drink deeply. He takes the glass from me, pulls me up, unbuttons my blouse, unzips my trousers and pushes them down to crumple round my ankles. I step lightly out of them, undo my bra and slip out of my knickers.

Thirty-four and afraid.

He undresses swiftly. My hands are on my mouth, too often there like hesitant butterfly wings. He takes them, holding them in his own: delicate, oddly small hands for a man who is not small. He pulls back the bed covers and we lie down, facing each other. Our lips touch, fleetingly at first, his fleshy mouth and perfect white teeth hover over mine, lips brushing then taking flight, teasing. I feel the soft muscle of his tongue forcing open my lips.

He holds me gently, carefully, as if I am his most precious possession. I tremble at his touch yet I exist only to fit my body to his, to fill up his spaces, have him fill mine. His skin takes up the colour of the curtains, the colour of lust.

I draw back, pull away. My heart is thumping. I'm back in the dark outside the church hall. 'Don't be dumb,' I tell myself. 'That was half a lifetime ago.'

He's puzzled. I'm not a teenager.

I whisper, 'Be patient.'

I shut my eyes and trace the first two fingers of my right hand around his face, faltering at the unexpected dimple, right cheek only, my fingertips softly circuiting his deep-set eyes, forcing the eyelids to close, tracing his cheekbones, and the touch of uncertainty, of girlishness above his brows.

We touch each other.

I trust him.

He takes his time; we take our time and much later he enters me, filling me. I unravel.

Dusk falls and a small bedside light with a red shade mingles with the twilight. The room is blood red.

Smiling, he turns me around to face the direction his hand points.

I lean back on his chest, the warm water enfolding us, moving with us: a baptism.

On the wall beside the bath is an enormous mirror. I wave one wet arm at it. Daniel disentangles himself and steps out of the bath pulling me with him. We stand in front of it, glistening and reddened in patches.

What do I see? A man and a woman fitted together like the final piece of a jigsaw. His thick brown hair, a shoreline at the nape of his neck, the unruly whorls of body hair, the strength of his shoulders and his arms and his eyes, the colour of the Swiss meadow flowers. And the naked woman curvaceous, firm full breasts, legs not overlong but not short either; her arms holding the man tightly as if he might turn out to be a mirage and slip from her arms. Perhaps I really am that woman: eyes full of joy and wonder and a flicker of surprise.

A hint of dawn. Daniel eases himself half out of bed, turns back and kisses me gently on the lips then throws off the black and white patterned duvet, roots in a drawer and tosses me a large blue woolly sweater. He puts on a deep blue dressing gown.

'Dawn is good from the terrace. There's a couple of cushions over there you can take out for the chairs.' He points to two very large cream and red cushions on a small armchair in the corner. 'The chairs are a bit cold and hard on your bum otherwise.' He grins, 'I'll make us some coffee.'

I tear myself out of the warmth of the bed and put on his sweater. I snuggle into its smell, pulling it down over my thighs. On the terrace I place the black wrought iron chairs side by side and cover them with the cushions. The early morning air is chilly so I tuck my legs into his jumper.

We each hold a mug of strong black coffee and he puts his arm around me as we gaze at the city beginning, like a nervous young girl, to show itself. Intermittent car grumbles and people murmurs from the street six floors down float up. Minute by minute the cityscape glows and comes alive.

The coffee warms me. The grumble and voices become continuous.

Daniel stands and stretches. 'I'm catching a flight to London in a couple of hours. I'm there for the rest of the week, then New York.'

He kisses me on the forehead and puts his hand down to squeeze my bum. 'I'll find you. It'll be a couple of weeks.'

I believe him.

Chapter 29

Spring into Summer

Children play in the street, excited happy voices and the tatty bedding plants lean out of their soldierly ranks and wave. The delicate evening light hovers until the sun settles a last muslin glow on the city.

I dream of his hands and his eyes the colour of gentians. All my instincts shout danger but translate into excitement. 'Get a life,' I tell myself. 'You'll be an old maid soon.' But another voice says, 'he's not for you.'

Everything changes. I stop and watch the kids in the park. They are bemused. My doctoral students' research seems fresh and exciting. I don't even mind the marking. I have to go back and re-mark some scripts. I've been absurdly generous. I smile at everyone and they smile back. Maria guesses instantly. 'It's a man,' she says.

I decide to take work to the cottage. It will ease the waiting. Cars blast their horns. I'm driving badly but don't care. A fat-backed capital C cloud sits in the dirty sky a little above the quarry edge. I try to turn it into a D and fail.

I hear my first curlew of summer. Its fluty melancholy call echoes across the moors and I neglect my work. I no longer recognise myself. This pleases and disturbs me. I put on my tracksuit and run and run, wildly, joyfully, forcing myself to exhaustion and beyond.

I pick wild flowers and take them to my mother's grave. I give her my news, tell her about my job, then whisper, 'He's called Daniel; he's beautiful.' I don't tell her that we barely know each other. 'He makes me feel good, safe,' I say.

I leave the cottage after two days.

I drift through the park and talk to the kids. I ask their names: Kevin, Jon ('with no h,' he says), Jeanette and Alison. They must be two or three years younger than Clare. They have two more years at school and are solidly indifferent to most things. Politely they ask me what I do. When I tell them they point to Alison and say she's the clever one, will go to university. She smiles and looks down. They have seen me out running and are more impressed by that.

The girls boss the boys; just how it should be.

I chat to the two old women about the weather, their health, and their grandchildren. They are on their bench in the hopeful sunshine. They tell me I look pretty. I'm inclined to agree.

I am all amiability, to pluck a word from my childhood. It must have come from one of my mother's books. I was always searching out odd words.

Lucy leaves a message: 'Where are you? What about lunch?' I don't return her call. Instead I go to town and buy a large mirror for my bedroom, stand naked in front of it and imagine his hands upon me.

The flat looks drab, needs a good clean and Murasaki complains of neglect, alternating between sitting on my knee, dribbling with pleasure, gouging wheals into my thighs and refusing to come near me. The couple from the flat next door have a key. They come in to feed her. They too love her but I like to think Murasaki is a one woman cat. I try bribes of special treats but she is too wise to be so easily won over.

I go on a spending spree: new curtains, bed linen and a deep turquoise bedspread.

I have my hair cut, just a little, and throw myself into work.

The dean e-mails me. Daniel will not be teaching on my programme. 'We can't afford him,' he writes.

I change the route of my morning run to pass his block of flats. It's a massive detour. Stupid tears wreck my rhythm. No more, I tell myself.

The campus is quiet. In search of company I find Jonathan, one of my doctoral students. We have coffee together. Jonathan is looking at the role of bank lending in the housing market following the Tory deregulation of the City. He is enthusiastic but I remember little of what he says.

Late May and the last departmental meeting of the year. Out of 120 academics about forty attend. We don't sit together but spread ourselves around the overlarge lecture theatre.

We suffer the usual exhortation for a push on publications. No-one bothers to point out the obvious, that increasing student numbers with new courses to match does not allow time for groundbreaking research. Morale is low. We have lost our five research rating. I switch off and examine my colleagues and think about trust – not a lot here; power and dependency in spade loads, but complicated. Power: the dean of course, and the department administrator, a tough mature woman and, in day-to-day terms, the one to watch; then eight professors and plenty of others trying to scramble up the ladder.

Course heads, including me, deliver reports. My course will start in September with a full complement. I make the report as brief as possible.

'Delayed in New York. I have a few days free at the end of next week. Do you like the Hebrides? D.' The e-mail leaps out from a dozen others.

It's exactly three weeks since our night together. I force myself not to reply immediately.

Two hours later: 'Never been to Hebrides but love Scotland and the sea. You're on. R.' My best laconic.

Eight days to wait, each one an eternity. I rearrange a couple of meetings, change appointments and buy new clothes from a shop so expensive I'm almost ashamed. I tell Alexis.

'I'm proud of you,' she says. 'There must be a man.'

I fob her off. It's too soon. For the same reason I put off dinner with Lucy. Guilt makes me pour hours of love into Murasaki and find the best and most expensive cattery for her holiday which she will hate.

It's almost the longest day. Artemis carries us across the ancient grey-green hills of the Pennines, rounded and worn. We sweep through the Lakes: jagged, individual hills clad some way up by a soft down of deciduous woods. At their feet run rivers, or cold, still lakes, some long and skinny, others wide. We push on, over the horizon into Scotland, through more hills, different again, but more like the Pennines in their bald breast-like roundness; soft, green and deceptively unchallenging.

Daniel has bought me a full set of leathers including hideous boots. I am snug.

The first night we stay in a small exclusive hotel set among lime green woods above a long thin lake, its surface disturbed only by wild ducks and geese. White and grey clouds reinvent themselves in the lake. The woods are mellifluous with birdsong.

Daniel is welcomed at the hotel as an old friend. The bedroom is large and overlooks the water. He flings himself on to the bed, waiting for me to follow. The next day we cruise up the motorway, circle Glasgow, and speed towards the purple high mountains in the distance then ease west. The sea, like a young girl on a first date, offers itself in small parcels, glistens, beckons and is gone; another hill, another offering. We follow the sun, jousting with the wind until the sea is a throw of a ball away. The wind takes us up, like a baby in its mother's arms, and carries us north.

We stay three nights on Islay, one of the smaller Inner Hebrides islands. The few houses are plain and severe, squatting white and low against the Atlantic gales. On Sunday the swings are locked.

Our small grey stone hotel has sweeping lawns, few flowers and shrubs, and is set back from a largely empty road. Its six bedrooms bravely face on to the windswept western sea, aquamarine in full sun, but today sombre and crepuscular. The Outer Hebrides pluck chunks out of the far horizon. Daniel says we might go there one day and tells me about the 'lazy wind' on the islands, too lazy to go round so goes through.

Hand in hand we stroll down the lawn to the rocks and the seashore. I point out the cormorant drying its wings, the diving gannets, the kittiwakes calling their own names just as the chiffchaffs in the woods back home call theirs and, just once, high in the sky, a sea eagle, a flying white barn door. Daniel knows nothing about birds, a city boy. The promised rain holds off and a few random clouds scatter across the gunmetal sky like brown blots on the faces of the old.

Later I watch him sleep, his hand on my thigh, a slight smile on his lips, lips puckered a little from the pressure of the pillow; ambition closed down.

He teaches me about my body, about love, although we have not yet spoken the words. I explore his body, run my fingers through his body hair, place my white arm against his olive-skinned one with its light covering of dark black hair. I learn what gives him pleasure.

Daniel has food sent up: small, elegantly arranged dishes with a different wine for each course. I discover new foods. He shows me how to examine the wine's colour, find its bouquet, taste it on the sides of the tongue, accompanied by a sucking noise. He explains the tannin/acid balance and how to look for sweetness with the tongue's tip.

We are sitting up in bed, backs against the pillow, holding hands. My face is flushed and Daniel is smiling and soft.

'What food or wine would I be?' I ask.

'Cool, sweet wine, chilled on the outside, a burst of taste and surprise on the tongue,' he responds quickly. 'And me?'

I use my newfound knowledge and say confidently, 'Shiraz; a robust confident Aussie Shiraz.'

A flicker of disappointment passes across his face. Too late I realise he was hoping for one of those stratospherically priced clarets – a Margaux or a Lafite, the aristocrats of the wine world. I know the names, not the wines. He speaks of them with longing in his voice.

Like artichokes we unpeel ourselves leaf by leaf, each layer more succulent until the lush slicing of the teeth through the muscle-firm core, the thing that is.

'An only one,' Daniel says when I ask him about his family.

'Weren't you lonely?' I ask. 'I can't imagine my childhood without my sister, Alexis. I bet you were spoilt.'

'Not really. Mum was great,' he says, a tinge of sadness in his voice. 'She was always fun but no cook.' He adds, brightness filling his voice, 'She bought us both bikes and we cycled together in the holidays. She made me feel special. I'm glad there was only me.' He swirls the wine and buries his nose in the glass then raises his head looking pleased. 'We lived on fish and chips and takeaways, mostly Mum and me. Dad wasn't home much.'

'Mine neither,' I say, 'work and God.' He squeezes my hand.

'They divorced and I was packed off to boarding school.' He's partly talking to himself, his voice sounds faraway.

'What was boarding school was like?' I ask, feeling a little jealous.

'It was OK once I learned to look after myself. It wasn't a very good one; cheap and full of kids like me whose parents were somewhere else.' His mother is dead now, he says and his father lives in New York. He sees him sometimes when he comes to London.

172

'My father pushed me,' I say. 'Always had to be the best. Second or third were never good enough.' I don't say that I was a bit of a show-off. I see myself in the classroom, always first hand up, always calling out the answers before the rest of the class even heard the question.

I speak briefly about my years by the sea – the desert can come later.

'I wanted to be a chef when I saw Keith Floyd on telly. Always a glass of wine in his hand. University was a waste of time,' he says as he swings his legs over the edge of the bed and pours two glasses of wine. 'My father insisted. I taught myself the IT.'

We are both silent a few minutes, each wrapped in our own memories.

'What does she do, your sister?'

'Alexis has her own business catering for big companies, lunches, dinners. Her prices are astronomical but she gets them without much trouble. She's good.' I stroke the hair on his arm backwards. 'She left home as soon as she could.'

I tell him a lot about Ben. I leave out Beth.

'You obviously care a lot about this Ben.'

'I do.' Daniel must see the smile on my face.

We move the pillows and lie down, holding hands. I want to tell him about Clare. 'Too soon,' I caution myself.

It sounds overloud when I say, 'I loved my mother; my father was closer to Alexis and she would give you a completely different version. That's families.' Then I remember that Alexis is unlikely to speak to anyone of our childhood now. 'But I'm a bit of a loner.'

'Me too,' Daniel says quietly. 'Perhaps that's why we're so good together.'

We take pleasure in dressing for dinner, looking beautiful for each other and for ourselves. My new dress is a deep red, silk. I put my hair up. Daniel whistles when I emerge from the bathroom.

At night I curl up tightly against his body, my arm across his

173

chest, fingers curled in the whorls of his chest hair, my skin stuck to his, my curves fitted into his, his bum against my stomach, my breast soft on his bone-hard shoulder blades. Each morning I'm disappointed to find that we have untangled and I'm lying facing away.

The weather changes but we still sit on our rock and wait for the otter, our hands on each other. Our exploration, each of the other, never ends. I could come if he willed me to, looking into his eyes and giving me his naked body to gaze on. We never put it to the test; we can't withhold our touch.

The next day we take a small motor boat on to the flat grey mackerel sea lit by eddies of light from the pewter sky above. On the horizon, islands: two hill, three hill, solitary lumps, the bump of a pregnant woman on her back, and other low flat mounds. Flocks of gannets dive into the sea, machine gunshot from above; storm petrels swoop, cresting the waves and guillemots accompany them with their mournful cries. We return just as the moon hovers on to the horizon early, impatient for the declining sun to depart.

A storm threatens. The roiling waves build and envelop everything they touch, carving their own inexorable path. We go to bed, abandoning the tempest to its play and get up after midnight, leaving our warm bed. It's our last night. The storm has blown itself out and the meniscus of a silver/gold moon flecks the sky and the argent sea. We run down the hill to the boat. We don't feel the cold.

He rows quietly on the loch; splash, drip, whoosh, sing the muffled oars. The slip of a moon, a lucent promise of beauty to come, is overwhelmed by a phalanx of stars. Shadows populate the loch. The oars sparkle with bioluminescence, the wake glistens, every droplet incandescent, as Daniel's body comes out of the night-black water, his limbs shining, flashing. An otter's nose and whiskers break the water at the same time a few feet away and we hear seals slithering down the wet rocks to join us. Slender new moons will always remind me of this night.

174

Later, we creep back to the hotel, shower, crawl into bed and snuggle up for warmth. I lie awake and think about love: it is being fully awake for the first time and yet it is a dream. It is madness and it is being caressed by the unreal, the taste of joy. It's written in the sky, sung at dawn by the birds and it fills the air with the scent of blossoms.

It is being naked for all to see and it makes gods of us. It is feeling safe.

I am mad.

The drive home is long. Pressed tight against Daniel's back the world has lost its angularities, its acerbic voices. Everything is resonant with Daniel.

At Daniel's flat our lovemaking continues: the weaving, moving to the point where we might fall, ever down, then rising and clinging to each other's abandonment. I come to know myself through the tracery of Daniel's hands. I feel his smile when his fingers find the parts he loves best. He tries to put his hands round my waist. I have a small waist and big breasts. His hands are too small, but he doesn't give up trying.

Daniel doesn't immediately leave for London. We say those three words and spend long days in bed with good wines. I begin to pride myself on my discernment, although Daniel laughs at me. In the mornings he brings me strong black coffee and feeds me pieces of fruit cut into bite-size pieces. After dinner we take the finest French chocolate to bed to slip into each other's mouths. I bite through the bitter dark shell, then my tongue pauses before tiptoeing through the fresh cream filling. We sip twenty-year-old Sauternes and tongue it from each other's bodies.

I tell him of my time in the desert but he's a city boy and doesn't understand.

'Almost six years,' I say.

'So long,' he says, questions in his voice.

'It was wonderful,' I say. 'Hot, empty and every day new people trying to cross the desert.' I tease with the truth.

He looks puzzled so I say, 'I came back when my mother died,' and don't mention Clare.

I speak of my mother's depression, her absences. I am calm, use pseudo psychoanalytic words. I don't tell all.

I say that I would like to see a world with less poverty, more equality. I'm carried away with the moment; I tell him I'm a paid-up member of the Labour Party and that I hate Maggie Thatcher.

He laughs. 'Politics are a waste of time.' He calls me 'My armchair socialist,' or 'Red Ruth', says I am like his mother, an impossible dreamer. I take it as a compliment.

'New York,' he says. 'One day I'll have an office there.' He has a long way to go but things are moving quickly.

I'm aiming for a chair, a small cohort of good researchers and papers in the top international journals.

He plays music of pop groups I don't know. He abandons them and offers me jazz and I grow to love the melancholic notes that at any time might be taken over by an exuberant alter ego. I want to learn more.

I collect my CDs from my flat and play Mozart and Wagner. He's bewildered so I offer the lost loves and dying heroines of Verdi and Puccini and take him to the opera. He tries hard to like it.

I have to believe that our love will keep us safe from our differences. They are many.

Daniel infuses every second of my day. I sing him in my head. It's messy, intrusive and I'm not prepared for the takeover.

Two weeks pass and I have to go back to the university and to Murasaki whose displeasure at her abandonment is marked.

Daniel returns to his clients. They're clamouring for his services. He puts his fees up and they clamour more strongly.

I perch on a stool in Daniel's kitchen and telephone Alexis. While I'm waiting for her to pick up I gaze around the kitchen. With its straw-coloured floor tiles, cream worktops and cupboards and brass fittings it's on a different planet from my flat. On the wall behind the worktop are ferocious looking knives. Daniel is proud of his knives, sharpens them obsessively. Next to the knives is a small television set. He watches TV while he cooks, a news junkie: BBC, CNN, Sky all of them. The kitchen is his domain. That suits me.

Her voice reverberates down the phone. 'You've got it made.' She's stirring something on the cooker. 'Lend him to me: a man who doesn't get under your feet, makes you wonderful meals, buys the best wine, takes you out to expensive restaurants, doesn't want you to clean or to iron his shirts. Heaven, if you ask me. When am I going to meet him?'

I dissemble and don't tell her that Daniel spends most of his working week in London.

Later in the year two boys, Jon Venables and Robert Thompson are tried and convicted of the brutal murder of James Bulger. Daniel and I have our first argument.

'A travesty,' I say of the trial in an adult court.

'Think of what they did to that little boy,' he says.

The Sun newspaper campaigns for a longer sentence.

Daniel and I do not let our falling out linger.

Chapter 30

1994

Maria brings my double espresso and a small jug of cream and sits with me and talks about Italy and her family there. She misses her grandchildren and the sun.

Outside it is a raw January day but I am like a hot spring, bubbling warm and excited.

I sip my coffee and watch the door. It's lunchtime so none of the breakfast regulars are here.

A couple arrive so Maria leaves me. The man is tall and skinny, in cycling shorts, lanky, my mother would have said, with legs not much thicker than a girl's arms and soggy looking cream skin. His girlfriend holds his hand. She has a strong, tanned face. An Alice band pulls her blonde wavy hair back off her face and she wears a full flowery skirt with a plain white cotton blouse. They take a table near me. The woman – Jeanette would be a good name for her – coquettishly eats a fat succulent pastry, and drinks a cappuccino, the froth lingering on her top lip. She intermittently plucks a small flowery handkerchief from the depths of her skirt to wipe her mouth. Skinny man sips an espresso.

A young woman, with long slim bare legs, sits with a small dog on her knee, feeding it blobs of whipped cream from the tips of her fingers. Maria approves.

An old lady dressed in pale pink, including a pink beret with 'silly old cow' picked out in darker letters across the front, fumbles in a capacious black leather bag, peering perplexedly for something. The skin on her neck is collapsed and folded, a palimpsest of the life she has led, or of too much reckless sun.

Lucy is late.

Her boys are now four and two. Ryan (named after her grandfather) is dark-haired and solemn. Mattie is a wonderful laughing toddler, fair like his father Dave but other than that is all Lucy. She's not going to try for a girl. Both boys are at nursery until 4 p.m. and Lucy works part-time. Until recently I saw them most weekends.

At last, Lucy.

She swings through the door, glancing kisses to Maria and speeds, a colourful, laughing thing, to my table. Most look up. She has had her hair cut very short. It stands in short spikes all over her head. It suits her.

Her boys have changed her little, except that she always looks tired.

'You have no idea Ruth. Boys never stop,' she says, echoing her mother, 'and there's my job.'

She's right, I don't have much idea.

Lucy's questions trip off her lips in the middle of our hug. 'You have some news, the gorgeous Daniel that you're keeping hidden. When am I going to meet him?'

'Soon, I promise.' I look smug and can't help it.

Maria places Lucy's latte in front of her, and waits until she looks up, 'One of your almond slices please Maria.' Lucy never orders the same cake, which upsets Maria who prides herself on knowing all her customers' tastes.

'So tell me all,' Lucy says, as she eases herself more comfortably on the wrought iron chairs.

'My favourite boys first,' I say.

'Wonderful, what else? Come and see them this weekend. They're insisting and I've let Dave off for the football.'

'I don't know,' I say, stalling.

179

'Daniel,' she says and adds, 'you look great, by the way; that blouse, very smart. You've been lashing out. Has Alexis been up?' Lucy and I usually go shopping together so there's a hint of disappointment in her voice.

'No. I've been adventurous and you weren't around.'

'So it's all for him, a new Ruthy,' she teases. 'Come on, spill.'

Maria stands over us, a brightly coloured mother bird. 'I've been waiting for you to try a new cake Ruth.' She places a small delicate cake in front of me and another in front of Lucy plus her almond slice. 'They're new.' She pats my hand. Without looking at Lucy she glides back to her station behind the glass cabinet of delights.

'We can't offend Maria.' I point to the cakes.

Once the thin dark chocolate coating is sliced through, after carefully removing a white chocolate fan on the top (Maria expects no less care) four different coloured layers are revealed, moist and creamy. I anticipate the soft resistance of the layers, each promising a different consistency and taste. I slip a piece in my mouth and seconds later I give Maria the thumbs up. White teeth flash between vermilion lips and she nods. Lucy demolishes her cake in a few mouthfuls.

'It's about time I met this wonderful Daniel,' Lucy says as she drinks her latte. 'We don't see much of you now.'

Ryan and Mattie stayed with me some Saturday nights at my flat if Lucy and Dave wanted time off. Mattie crawled through my books, toppling them and shouting with delight. We read together and played in the park, snuggling up in my bed for the night. Or I spent weekends with Lucy and Dave and the boys, playing silly games or watching the telly, all of us lying on the carpet. I miss their touch, their unsullied eyes and their small hands. Lucy made space for me.

'Can't drag yourselves out of bed.' Lucy giggles and puts up her hands. 'I can just about remember those days. My boys put a stop to that.' Her face belies her protest.

I wonder if she realises how much she sounds like her mother when she says, 'my boys'.

I lean back from the table and cross my legs. 'He's great. I don't care if it's just weekends as long as we are together.'

How to tell her what it is that quickens my heart: his laugh and the way he throws his head back and opens his mouth wide, careless of who might be around, his habit of walking into a crowded room and standing still; his hands with their short, careful fingers, his mole and the cleft in his right cheek, his deep blue eyes and the narrow river of short curly black hair that runs down his flat hard belly. The litany is long: his fingers curling through mine as we walk or his habit of running his forefinger down the side of my face and the feel of his hair under my hands and the joy of lying beside him, watching him sleep, seeing his lashes curl on his cheeks.

I reach across and squeeze her arm. 'I've moved in with Daniel.'

'This is sudden,' says Lucy, her mouth still full of cake and her lips chocolate coloured. 'Moving in, I mean.' Crumbs spray.

'You'll be the first to meet him, I promise. And you should see the flat. Daniel had a design firm do it,' I say.

I stand up, gulping down my coffee. 'Come on, let's go there now.'

'What's the hurry?' says Lucy. She reluctantly finishes her coffee, wraps the almost untouched almond slice in her paper napkin and shoves it in her handbag.

I grab her arm, pay the bill, bid Maria a quick goodbye and we half run the fifty yards to Lucy's car.

By the time I reach the top floor landing Lucy is a couple of flights behind.

'Why didn't we take the lift?' she pants, catching her breath.

'Good for you, the exercise.' We grin at each other. This is old ground. I let her catch her breath then take out my keys and open the oak door.

181

I lean past her, switch on the light and follow her gaze past the kitchen and down the short hall to the sitting room where the sun is pouring in through the large French windows. She moves a few yards to the kitchen and fingers the edge of one of the knives. 'Aren't you tempted to put just one in the wrong place?'

'OK,' I say and lift off a delicate 4" boning knife and place it beside a whopping 10" giant killer.

Still looking over her shoulder at the knives Lucy walks into the sitting room. It's large and doubles as dining and sitting room with a six-seat mahogany dining table. She runs her hand over the table's silk-smooth surface. 'I like this,' she says. 'And these.' She points to embossed leather floor tiles then spots them repeated in the glass-topped table.

'The same as in the kitchen,' I say, like a letting agent.

The sun hits the TV right in the centre of its 42" screen. 'The boys would love that,' she points.

Lucy picks up the photograph of Daniel: his MBA graduation. His mortar board is under his arm and beneath the black gown he's wearing a navy suit with white shirt and a pale blue tie. His smile is wide. 'No wonder you've kept him quiet.'

She's being ironic but I'm still pleased. 'The other photograph is his mother and father.'

'They don't look poor,' Lucy says and moves to the other side of the room.

'Now, this IS good.' She has stopped in front of an enormous abstract oil painting: yellows, reds and browns. Expensive, I bet.'

It has always reminded me of Australia.

The wall opposite the painting is glass from floor to ceiling, the heavy cream curtains fully drawn back and in front of it a large rug. Lucy wanders over to gaze at the city. We stand side by side.

'I want to see this bath you've talked about,' she says.

I grab her hand and lead her into our bedroom.

'Wow,' she says, lying back on the bed. 'A bit different from your flat.' She laughs, 'And my house.'

Her house is always chaos – the boys, she says – and my flat isn't much better. Bookshelves on all the walls: novels (I've left the 19th century and am digging deep into modern novels), poetry, biography, current affairs. I make my bed each day and keep the kitchen and bathroom clean and that's about it.

Lucy and I are thinking the same: no Ryan and Mattie here.

Back in the sitting room she points to a door. 'And there?'

'Daniel's black hole.' I walk over and push open the door.

Some ten feet away, is a black rectangular table taking up the back wall except for a three-drawer filing cabinet to the left. A padded, high-backed executive chair sits in front of the computer. The room is windowless and a small bookcase on the side wall holds a dozen or so books. His computer stands aloof. Each year it's traded in for a faster, sexier model.

'A couple of Vietnamese women come in to clean on Fridays,' I say.

Lucy takes one of Daniel's books from the bookcase, his latest, and carries it through to the sitting room. She throws herself into one of the armchairs and reads out loud: 'Daniel Phillips: Winning Leadership: My Rules.' She opens the book and looks at the back flap. 'Mr Gorgeous himself,' she says, and flips through it while I get the coffee.

Lucy and I sit opposite each other in the armchairs and I force myself to look relaxed. Where has the excitement of Maria's gone? I sip my coffee. Lucy sits upright, her arms crossed, her drink neglected on the glass table near her elbow, the book on the seat beside her.

'What are you going to do with your flat?' Don't be rash is written across her face.

'Let it, probably, but I'll need to get it decorated,' I say, 'and spring cleaned.'

'Don't sell it.'

She doesn't have to spell it out. I look around. For a second or two I see the place through Lucy's eyes.

'When I bring my things it'll look different,' I say, but can't think of anything much except my clothes and most of them are already here. A large chunk of my books line a wall of the spare room.

'I've never felt like this before. It will work, does work.' I don't say that no-one, nothing else matters. 'He and I are different, that's all.'

Lucy flashes me a look and says, 'I've gathered that.'

'Work is tough at the minute. The dean's a bastard. Daniel supports me. He doesn't have to be here to do that,' I say. Then I lean over and lightly touch her hand. 'I won't change how I think about things, what I care about.' I lighten my voice, 'You and Dave are an old married couple.'

Lucy picks up her coffee looking troubled. 'Dave and I believe in the same things, want the same sort of world. He doesn't seem your type.' She takes a sip of coffee and looks straight at me.

'You haven't met him. You'll like him.' I want to believe that. 'We argue sometimes,' I say slowly, 'but we're not going to change each other.' I believed, once, that I might. I smile as I say, 'In some things he's to the right of Genghis Khan but we can work it out. Other things matter more.' In some ways, important ways, Daniel and I are as different as two people can be. I can't see betrayal in his eyes.

Lucy looks at me with love and dismay.

'I'm working on him,' I say. She is making me cross and I refuse to say more. But, after a few minutes, long minutes when we avoid looking at each other, I get up and sit next to her, our bodies touching. 'I love him,' I say. The words are too small to carry their weight. 'I feel safe.' She can't possibly know how important those last three words are. 'And he loves me.'

'That's OK then,' she says.

We hear the raised voices of a couple float in through the open French window. They are arguing about which film they will see. We both listen to the heated discussion. The girl will win.

'No Murasaki,' she says looking around. 'I take it he doesn't like cats.'

'Adores them,' I say. 'Hates them. Can't bear to touch them.'

'Murasaki?' he'd said. 'What sort of name is that?'

Murasaki was sitting on my knee, looking her best. I got up and held her out to him. He shrank back. I placed her on my chair and walked to the bookshelves. '*Tale of Genji*: *Lady Murasaki Shikibu*,' I said, holding out the book.

He looked briefly at the book and shook his head. 'Just me. I can't stand cats.'

That was a tough one.

There might have been another tough one: Clare. I waited and was not sure why.

'Will you look after Murasaki?'

'You're giving up Murasaki?' Lucy's astonishment reverberates. 'Ruth, you and she are a couple.' Lucy looks around. 'I have to admit that this doesn't look like a Murasaki flat.'

'She's just a cat,' I say, of that loyal, loving thing that waits for me in the evenings and sees me off in the mornings, listens uncomplainingly to me and is neglected on the weekends.

'OK. Murasaki and I are fans and you'll have visiting rights. The boys love her. I'm her second mother anyway.' She laughs, 'Third if you count the original.'

There is silence from the couple below. I am faintly curious to know who won.

Getting up to look out the French windows I place my hand on her shoulder. She smiles up at me and the backward action stretches and elongates her face creating a different Lucy. The couple have moved on.

'The piano?' I say sitting back down. She has a large Victorian house with a couple of large spare rooms. My piano will fit nicely in one of them.

Lucy takes a large dollop of cream, hovers over the sugar, sighs and puts her teaspoon down without taking any. 'I'll take that too. Pity I can't play.' Her face lights up. 'Perhaps I'll get lessons for the boys.'

'I won't offer to teach them but we might play together.'

'If you can find the time,' Lucy says a little sharply. 'I'll kill him if he hurts you.'

'We'll all get together,' I say. 'Soon.'

'About time,' she answers and settles back on the settee.

After Lucy leaves I unpack the glass girl and place her on the small table near the photos. They are big, oversize and my glass girl is a delicate five inches tip to toe, reflecting the light from the window, taking it to herself, greedy for it. Sometimes she shines with a curious reddish glow, the light and colour of the Australian desert.

On Friday Daniel picks up the glass girl, a questioning look on his face.

'I brought her back from Australia. An old man in the desert made her for me.'

He carefully places it back on the table saying, 'It looks fragile.'

Six weeks later, Lucy and Dave and the boys meet us for lunch at Pizza Express, Mattie's choice. It goes well. Daniel is great with the boys, especially Ryan. Daniel turns out to be good with crayons. Dave and Daniel talk about the City and football, although Daniel isn't really into football. Lucy and I take over entertaining the boys.

Lucy e-mails that Daniel and I are good together.

Chapter 31

Not long after moving in I take him to my cottage.

Cirrus clouds mottle the sky. I point to the high green hills with their rocky crowns and to the woods beside the road still carpeted with bluebells with their unruly heads and dark secretive ways. I motion to Daniel to stop. We walk through the woods and breathe in the silence. It bewilders him.

Artemis manages the rough track magnificently. My cottage remains unnamed although I'm sure it has a name on a map somewhere. The locals call it the quarry cottage.

I slip from Artemis while Daniel is still pulling off his helmet. He stares around at the dull grey day, a wrinkled sky day.

The cottage looks a little neglected. The few shrubs cower from the wind and rhubarb grows untended in one corner under the shelter of the stone wall. Other years I've made crumble from it in May when the stalks are tender and not too acidic. It will soon be ready for picking. One day I'll put real money into the cottage, show Daniel it can be comfortable; teach him country ways.

I suggest a walk. The ground is dry as we stroll towards the quarry face. I point out the old platforms, the cut and abandoned stones, the remains of the engine shed, the robust retaining walls, the layered stone, majestic in size and age. I love its scale and grandeur. Here and there stunted trees and grass soften its effect.

He looks around, bewilderment in his face. He hugs me, 'I need people, buildings.'

'What about the rides on Artemis, the countryside then?' I say although I know the answer.

'That's the roads; the twist and turn, the speed,' he says.

'And the Hebrides.'

'Great but I couldn't live there. This is all so lonely, so depressing.' He sounds defensive.

I want to speak of the wind soughing in the trees and the sky, most of all the sky. Sky is a mean close-fisted thing in cities where the weather is moderated by the press of citizens and buildings. I say none of this. Lucy doesn't much like the cottage either. 'No creature comforts,' she pronounces. 'Not me.'

We don't stay long. He turns to me as we get on to Artemis. 'I'm sorry Ruth. I know you love it. I just can't.'

'I forgive you,' I say, masking my disappointment.

I'm promoted to senior lecturer and I have a paper accepted in one of the top three international journals. My book, *Power Bases of Corporations* is favourably reviewed. I have said most of what I want to say about power. I'm more interested in trust now. Trust is complex and not without risks. Trust is about partners creating value for each other. Does one person ever completely trust another?

I've been doing the reading for a year now, firming up my research questions. Now it's about getting access to data. Daniel offers to help and sets up access to six of his largest clients. Data pours in.

Friday nights. I listen for his footsteps, the soft plop of his bag on the floor and the sound of the lock dropping. He stands on the landing, his bespoke suit a little crumpled, his briefcase at his feet, his eyes telling me he has come home to me. I run to him, fling my arms round him, murmur into his neck, whisper that I have missed him.

'Hold out your hands.'

I hold them out and shut my eyes. A small present: chocolates, a wine I like, sometimes a scarf, or just occasionally a kiss on the forehead that tells of a too busy week. If he has to go abroad and cannot get back he sends flowers, beautiful extravagant armfuls, but I hate them.

Daniel showers while I make coffee: stovetop espresso pot. A mix of fruity Ethiopian and high mountain coffee beans arrives in a box from London every month. I grind it, tamp it down and pour the water into the bottom section, taking care to leave half an inch before screwing the top section on. I shall buy him an expensive coffee machine for his next birthday; the one he likes with its severe lines, and expensive branding.

While I am still engrossed in the coffee ritual Daniel, still a little damp from his shower, steps in the small space behind me, nuzzles my neck from behind, his chin fitting between my shoulder and collarbone. He reaches round me and pours two glasses of wine, dry white for me, red for himself. Coffee first, wine for later.

Daniel cooks. Food is transformed: cold-pressed organic olive oil poured in patterns across the ridges of the grill pan and chicken breasts marinating in the same oil with a sprinkling of garlic, oregano, thyme, (herbs picked from the pots on the terrace), and lemon zest and pepper. Steamed whole beans and small new potatoes, the potatoes lightly tossed in unsalted butter, followed by a small but unusual cheeseboard, mostly local cheeses. My only regret is the absence of something sweet. I'm a sucker for cream and chocolate.

He sips his wine as he cooks and watches the news. He doesn't offer to teach me. I accept his exquisitely flavoured food as love offerings.

We stay in bed until the sun labours round the cityscape to embrace our terrace. Tentatively, gently, it eases through the windows, enfolds us. Later we sit on the terrace, the two chairs padded and joined by cushions, our hands wrapped round cups of coffee, tearing apart croissants. We hold each other and garner strength for the gym or a run or yoga. If the sun fails us we put off the day.

Daniel joins my yoga class. I promise him he will love it.

'I can't do it,' he says. 'The body is not meant to do that stuff.' He means the headstands and stretching that he's seen me practise.

We run across the park on a Saturday morning, holding hands, trying to ignore the banging of our mats strapped to our backs. He's the only man and Barbara, the teacher, makes a fuss of him. I place our mats together so the other women know he is mine. He looks good in shorts and tee shirt. He likes the stretching and is surprisingly good at it, gets into positions that I can never hope to reach. He considers the meditation rubbish, religious hoo-ha. We join the girls for coffee afterward or jog into town to Starbucks. He doesn't like Maria's, thinks it's a place of oddballs, loners. I tell him he's right and that's what makes it great. He's not into cakes. Or Maria.

I try to teach him to dance but we abandon it. Unexpectedly he's shy and awkward. We take it in turns to choose films at the cinema. Warm evenings sometimes lure us out for a run through the park, along the quiet streets and through the deserted main university campus. For fun we go to my office and make love on the floor.

One Saturday morning, when the sun is finding its way in, too early, announcing a bright summer's day, Daniel jumps out of bed, and returns a little later with a coffee.

'Come on,' he says, bending down to kiss me. I put my arms out. 'The races.' He pulls a suit from the wardrobe, selects a deep blue tie and a white shirt. I am buried in clothes.

'The Members' Bar,' he says when I look askance. We both like to slob out on weekends.

190

The night before he studies the form of the horses he wants to back: number of races this season and wins, trainer and loads more. He says it's a science. I'm the opposite. I have a lucky number: five, Clare's birthday. I'm a bit ashamed but it's fun and works often enough.

We meet his friends there. They rarely bring their girlfriends. They call him 'Dan' which doesn't suit him. They all have short names: Pete, computer techie, self-employed, hauling in the cash; Dave, manager in M&S; Mick, a litigation lawyer (the sort I suspect who advertises on the back of the toilet doors in motorway service stations); Dick a small business consultant; Pete 2, (he came later to the group) an estate agent in the City and the source of Daniel's speculative property purchases; Joe, PR consultant to a major bank and Jon, a marketing manager for a start-up IT business. Plus one other, a closed circle of eight. The G8 I call them. They like that.

We troop to the pre parade ring to see the horses. The men offer expert judgments. Daniel places serious bets. His horses win more often than they lose.

In the Members' Bar we drink lakes of champagne. I love to watch the horses with their strong legs, their restless eyes, their spirit. For a very short time they are gods. I shut my eyes and drown in the deep thunder, their need to be first across the line. I always wear the same earrings for luck, not that I bet much. It's the horses I go for.

The weekends are never long enough. I store their memories as a camel stores food and draw on them in need. When Daniel comes home the clean sharp lines of the flat soften and pulsate. We eat and drink, laugh and make love and start over again.

He tells me about his clients, about the chief executive, overconfident, bullish, that he pairs with the timid but clever senior manager and waits to see what happens.

'Usually a humbling,' he says.

191

'Which one?'
The chief exec. of course. Then I build him up again.'
'Wiser?'
'Hopefully.'

Weekdays I revert to my pre-Daniel life (except for his nightly telephone calls, usually when I'm in bed so I can imagine him there with me). I stay late at my office except on Wednesdays. Those evenings Lucy cooks and I play with the boys. Mattie is really good on the piano. I take my clarinet and play duets with him; we relax with silly games and Lucy and I talk far into the night. She asks about Daniel. I give her edited versions and she dissembles. We're still best mates.

Daniel's music is in me and I chastise myself for behaving like a teenager. Songs I didn't think I knew, songs about love, run through my head on permanent repeat. Sometimes, greedy for him I open his wardrobe and bury my face in his sea of blue shirts, play his jazz, keep busy. That's how children deal with time, wish it away.

The clock strikes. It's my present to Daniel, a Harley Davidson clock. Every hour it plays a different motorbike sound. It has a light sensor so is silent after dark and will not strike again tonight.

At night, in bed, it's his hands I feel: sure, gentle, undoing my bra and slipping my knickers down my legs. I look at myself in the mirror and smile, seeing Daniel's love. Sometimes I run my hands over my body, finding it soft and pliable, rounded and lovely and marvel that it has taken me so long. It's Daniel's touch.

For a time on weekdays we exchange e-mails about the things we hate most. The rules are no more than two at a time.

His first are: crap food and fingerless gloves. I bounce back: men who wear their hats in the car, pogonophobia.

Daniel: girls' football (they are rubbish), cloth caps. Me: men with hairy backs, Mr Bean. Mr Bean is a wind-up. It's Daniel's favourite TV programme.

Daniel: screaming kids, Freemasons (girls in aprons); me: men who insist on exposing wobbly fat bellies, the big woman who stands in front of me in yoga.

I break the rules and send a long one: the supermarket: wrong time of day, packed with elderly husbands frogmarched there by bossy wives; old men blocking the shelves. I want to run my trolley over them, or trip them up and leave them floundering helplessly on the floor, like the little babies they have become.

After a while it gets boring and we give up.

A cold November day. We stand side by side in the kitchen, hip-to-hip, with Daniel's new brochure spread out on the worktop and a glass of wine in our hands. Underneath the brochure is his latest book: *Corporate Leadership: The Winning Game Plan.* A long list of courses and venues, all five-star hotels: Edinburgh, Manchester, Birmingham, but most of the course dates are in London. He takes his clients' companies and repackages them into digestible bites, a week's worth, promising better profits, rational management and leadership and competitive advantage.

The kitchen smells of the duck cooking in the oven.

'It's practical,' he says. 'They can take it away and apply it tomorrow.'

The photograph of his London office reveals a glass-fronted building with large sparsely furnished rooms. Daniel's photograph shows a man with gravitas, a man who has something to tell you, a man you can trust, a good-looking man, young but not embarrassingly so, the right age for new ideas, innovation, thrust. He's sitting at a regency desk and looks reassuringly expensive. He's wearing glasses.

'You don't wear glasses,' I say wonderingly.

Daniel looks a little coy. 'They make me look more serious.'

I can't stop laughing. 'What do the clients think when they see you without them?'

'I wear them sometimes,' he says, refusing to smile, 'clear glass.' His clients, he says, are some of the most powerful men in business and he has to look the part.

He recovers himself a little, grins and puts one arm around my shoulder. (How I love that grin; the way it starts slowly then attacks his eyes, bringing small wrinkles to the corners, deepening his dimple.) I give him a hug and take him to bed.

Chapter 32

March 1996

Sixteen small children killed at Dunblane. The killer had four handguns and 743 cartridges. The numbers stick in my mind: 16. 4. 743.

It's an unusually warm and sunny Saturday evening in late March and there's a clamour in the background from the pub down the street. It's been a bad winter in the north so the weather is causing some excitement. A long spring stretches invitingly ahead.

'I'd like to see Ben. Let's have him here for a weekend,' I say to Daniel. 'It's ages since I've seen him. I miss him.' I turn around and lean my back on the terrace railing. Daniel's nostrils flare like the lithe Arab horse we saw win at the races earlier that day and I almost hear the stamp of hooves.

'There's the spare room. It's small but he won't mind,' I say.

'I need my weekends, just you and me, not strangers. I work too hard during the week.'

I poke him gently in the ribs and say, 'So do I and he's not a stranger to me; he's my nephew and I want you to meet him.'

One of Daniel's long silences follows. They are usually his route to capitulation.

'I want to show you off.' I lean forward and kiss him on the mouth. It's hard, unresponsive. 'He's smart and fun, into astronomy. What about the weekend after next if he can make it?'

Daniel gets up and walks into the kitchen. His heels strike the floor, then there's the noise of the dishwasher being stacked.

The full moon sails across the sky leaving a golden path over the city, marking its trail. Daniel sticks his head inside the bedroom door. 'OK, just grumpy me. I'm going for a ride; want to come?'

I nod.

The station is prosperous and sombre, wealth from a bygone age that has come full circle. It's crowded. The concourse is chilly and my cotton dress blows round my legs. I wrap my cardigan around me and wait.

Ben is moving unhurriedly through a thick soup of babble and bodies. He spots me and lopes over. Compared to Daniel he looks half-finished although he's less gangly, has put on muscle. He wears contact lenses now but something about his eyes still gives the impression of wearing glasses. His face has the same classic proportions as my sister, except that his mouth is generous and full. He wears baggy knee-length khaki shorts, an old striped tee shirt, and brown sandals on his long thin feet. His eyes are pure Alexis.

The day is beginning to wear itself out. The overconfident sun forces its way through the churlish city air and jousts with Ben's hair, parting it, burrowing under the curls to create a spectrum of reds from deepest auburn to teasing ginger, lighting up his pale skin like a street lamp glowing in a shadowy street. He is a singular looking boy/man.

He bends to kiss me on the cheek and holds me in a huge hug.

'You look posh, Auntie Ruth,' he grins as he releases me.

'You noticed,' I riposte, copying his grin and fingering my necklace. I'm wearing matching earrings. 'Daniel and I had lunch at a brasserie near here.'

He looks at his watch. 'A long one. Pissed, so the clothes aren't for me.'

I punch him lightly on the ribs. 'We can go straight to the flat

196

or have coffee in town, although I've bought some of those buns you like.'

'No contest,' he grins, 'besides I want to see what you exchanged for Murasaki.'

I dig him in the ribs again and realise how much I want to touch him.

'It's only ten minutes away. Daniel is at the gym and won't be back until later.'

Ben hauls his rucksack on to his back and we weave through the crowds to the station exit.

'Mum sends her love.'

We stop outside the door to the flats. Ben gazes around while I punch in the code.

'This is Artemis,' he says, pointing to a shape under a black plastic cover. It is easy to make out the handlebars.

I smile at his excitement, 'Yes.'

'Daniel will take you for a ride later.'

Ben drags himself away as the door clicks open.

'Great,' he bounds up the stairs. We race.

'The top floor,' I shout after his disappearing legs.

He waves over his shoulder, already at the first floor. At the top he stands back and waits.

'You've got longer legs,' I puff, unlocking the door, then lead the way in. He dumps his rucksack just outside the kitchen and stares around.

'Who watches the telly?'

'Daniel, while he cooks. Wait until you try his food. Go on then.' I give him a shove.

He pauses briefly in front of the TV in the sitting room then sticks his head through the door of our bedroom. 'I like the bath.' His voice teases as he adds, 'And another telly.' He steps out on to the terrace then turns to me. 'Three tellies. Does Daniel have any games?'

'Yes,' I say, 'and he's bought a new one recently but I've no idea what it's called.'

'Where, where?'

'Have a look,' I say, as I open the door to Daniel's study. 'There,' I point.

Ben almost runs across the room.

Sometimes Daniel stays up far into the night playing his latest game. He doesn't need much sleep while I need the regulation eight hours. I hate waking up and feeling the bed empty beside me, a precursor of my weeknights.

I go to the kitchen and get the coffee and buns.

Ben throws himself on the sofa. 'Well, I can see why you abandoned Murasaki.'

'Enough cheek. Buns and coffee?'

'Just buns.'

I bring in a plate with four large iced fruit buns. He picks one up and takes a huge bite. He looks around. 'No piano. Shame, mind you I probably can't still play.' He holds out a book. 'I found this in there.' He grins, turning the book over in his hands, running his fingers over the title. 'Do they work?'

'Does what work?' I ask although I know exactly what he means.

'His rules.'

'The same clients keep coming back and recommending others. All his courses are booked up for two years and he's taking on another consultant.' I sound like a promotion leaflet and Ben detects it.

He points to the *Daily Telegraph*. 'I take it he's a Tory.'

'Yes.'

'You got to me early. I hope you haven't gone soft,' he says, with a grin so wide it threatens to split his face. He stands and walks to the window to look down on the street below. 'I expect he's making loads.'

'I expect he is. Put your bag in the spare room. I've cleared out

198

some of my stuff.' I point to the door. 'You can read my books,' I grin.

Ben strides off, bag over his shoulder; a young unladen walk.

'I'll take the buns out to the balcony. Through my bedroom,' I shout.

'What does your mother think? About school, being sent down,' I ask. 'You must have done something really dumb to get sent down,' I say. 'Not like you.'

Ben's legs are stuck out in front of him. Coffee and one remaining bun sit on a small table between us.

'I haven't told her. She thinks I've got extra time off for the exams.'

'Don't change the subject. What did you do?'

'I put a virus in the school computer network.' He can't stop himself grinning. 'It was chaos.'

'And you couldn't resist boasting about it.'

He nods, the grin fading just a little.

'What made you do something so stupid?' My anger takes him by surprise and wipes the smug look from his face. 'In your last year,' I say. 'What was all the work for if you are going to do something childish like that?' I sound shrill. This is not a good start so I try again. 'Your exams are only two months away then it's university in October.'

He looks away, 'I was bored.' He pulls his legs in and sits up straight. 'I'll work at home. I've already covered most of the syllabus. No big deal. Cosmology, that's the exciting thing now. There are brilliant guys at Cambridge and London and I'll be working with them.' He pauses only to take a breath, 'The stars and the cosmos, no beginning and no end and billions of stars to find and explore; black holes, dark matter, dark energy. Doesn't it sound exciting? We don't know enough. I'll change all that.' I run out of breath before he does. His hands wave about erratically, finally wrapping around his coffee cup, the flush on his face fading at the same time. 'You don't see the stars in London. And I might join Greenpeace and help stop the whaling.'

Helpless under the onslaught of his ridiculous naiveté I smile.

He laughs, 'They'll take me back.'

I don't want my surrender to be too obvious. 'You'll have to tell Alexis some time. I expect they have already written to her.' I add, 'As soon as you get home.'

'We'll eat first then I'll show you something you'll like,' Daniel says to Ben. 'It'll be daylight for hours yet.'

'Artemis?' Ben says, his smile spreading.

'Yes, and something else.' Before Daniel turns back to his cooking he gives Ben a giant bowl of crisps to put on the coffee table.

It's going well.

Ben lays the table then takes a handful of crisps.

Daniel pours more wine and tells Ben to sit at the end of the table. Daniel and I, as usual, sit opposite each other.

'Great soup,' says Ben. Then, his eyes bright, both hands curled round his wine glass, he asks, 'What would you do if you ruled the country? Absolute power.'

Before we have time to answer he almost shouts, 'I'll start. I'd abolish private schools.'

'Including your own?' Daniel sips his wine and winks at me.

'Of course,' Ben says.

'The poor get bugger all,' Daniel says. 'It's always been that way. You just have to make sure it's not you.'

'As simple as that,' I say, and tell myself that he's winding us up.

'More or less.'

'That's stupid Daniel.' He hates being called stupid. 'It's not a matter of choice. The poor don't have the choices.'

'Privilege,' Ben says. 'The kids at my school get ahead because their parents have money.' Ben is clearly enjoying himself.

Daniel looks carefully at him. 'I'd send my children, hypothetical kids of course, to the school that gives them the best chance.'

'So you are buying privilege.' I come in to support Ben.

'Man always does, school is just an obvious case.'

'And that's an adequate reason for perpetuating inequality.' I say then remind myself that it's a game. 'What would you do?'

He rubs his nose. 'I'd take away as many regulations as I can and not just economic ones.'

'Dog eat dog, you mean,' says Ben.

'Survival of the fittest,' Daniel carries the bowls into the kitchen and returns with grilled skate wings with ginger and lime and a green salad that looks so beautiful in its high-sided glass bowl that it's a shame to mix it. 'We should take from life what we want, no-one will offer it on a plate,' he says, as he mixes the salad and passes it to me. 'What would you do?' he asks once we've all helped ourselves.

'I'd lock up all Tories,' I laugh, 'or put them on an island somewhere.'

'That's not serious,' Ben says and adds, 'with man-eating tigers.'

Ben pushes back his chair and looks around. 'That was great. I'm stuffed. You should meet my mother.' He looks at Daniel. 'She's a great cook too; it's what she does. Kensington Gourmet Food her business is called.' He gives Daniel a quick glance and then turns to me, adding, 'She charges a lot.' Pride flushes over his face as he sprawls as much out of the chair as in.

After dinner Ben suddenly asks, 'How many eggs did the *Titanic* take on board?'

He loves these silly games and has a remarkable memory for the odd.

I guess, wildly, 'Ten thousand.'

'40,000. And how many bottles of beer?'

'20,000,' Ben says, 'and 7,000 cigars.'

'Come on. I'll show you my new game,' Daniel says. He kisses the top of my head and they go to his study. The rest of the evening is filled with whoops of joy and groans.

I read and go to bed around midnight. Shortly after I hear the susurration of Daniel's clothes and the soft thump as they hit the carpet.

'Have fun?' I ask.

'He's good,' Daniel says, 'too good.'

'Poor you,' I say. 'You'll survive.' I turn towards him. 'Do you like him?'

'He's OK.'

I grin, 'Leaving aside that he thrashed you.'

The next morning, surprisingly early, I find Ben sitting on the sofa reading one of Daniel's books. His camera is on the chair beside him.

'He gave it to me.' His voice rises slightly as he holds up the book.

'So this is the surprise.' Ben's disappointment bounces off the walls of the building. 'What will happen to Artemis?' His voice cracks and wavers like a current struggling over rocks. He's clutching his camera.

There's laughter in Daniel's voice. 'Artemis, oh I'll sell her.'

Ben is silent. I feel a rush of love for Ben.

'Don't be daft; I'll keep her for fun. We can go for a ride now if you like. I thought you'd prefer the new machine. She's Artemis on four wheels.' He points to a low sleek sports car. 'It cost a bit,' Daniel murmurs.

'It's great.' Ben's doubt changes to awe. 'Yeah, I'd love a ride, as long as you are keeping her. He points defiantly to yellow and red Artemis who somehow looks a different inferior creature now.

'I haven't named her yet,' he motions at the car. 'Perhaps I won't, or you can think of one.'

I murmur, 'Attila.'

He ignores me, 'I was lucky to get it. A mate fixed it otherwise I would have had to wait twelve months at least. She impresses the clients. They like to drive her so I let them.'

I wonder why cars are usually female for men, then look at Attila and have my answer.

'Mum would love it. You must show it to her when you are down.'

Ben gets out his camera and takes considered shots of the car and Artemis. He hands me the camera to take a photograph of him on Artemis.

'Come on Ben,' Daniel puts his hand on Ben's shoulder. 'Let's go and you can think of a name.'

'So what's the name?' I ask a couple of hours later.

'We couldn't agree. Ben suggested all these crazy star names. We're still debating.' Daniel grins.

Chapter 33

April 1996

The park opposite the flat runs across several streets. There are formal circular gardens of bedding plants in summer, green or bare in winter and a good-sized pond. Tucked away in one corner is a fenced off children's play area with swings and a slide, a couple of small rocking horses.

Daniel prepares a late breakfast. It's Monday. Two days to May and the hope of summer. Unusually we are both home. Outside it's cold and miserable. Hesitant rain falls as if holding back some secret. We're both in tracksuits but have given yoga a miss. My eyes stroke the curve of his bum, pausing on the change in contour, the rise between his cheeks. His bare neck looks vulnerable.

We're sitting at the table, slowly bringing ourselves into the day when Daniel jumps up and turns up the television sound, turning it up so loud that it drowns out the rain. The decibels and the urgency in the commentator's voice surges.

'It's Australia,' Daniel says, and pats the seat beside him. Bodies, too many, are being carried away covered but not hidden. Some are small, children. I remain standing as if that will help me get to the scene, be there.

The reporter states that a man, carrying a blue sports bag and a video camera walked into a café at Port Arthur, the old convict settlement at the bottom of Tasmania. The man ate a meal, talked about European wasps. He opened a bag and the slaughter began.

In fifteen seconds twelve were killed and ten wounded. A car park, a tour bus and cars: indiscriminate carnage, no time for 'Why me?' The man is described as quiet and a loner. We see a young, unexceptional looking man with shoulder-length fair hair. During negotiations all he asks for is a ride in an army helicopter. Thirty-five dead. No names released.

Daniel is also standing now, a coffee in his hand. 'God,' he says. 'That's bad.'

I imagine the killer pointing his gun at Clare. She does not flinch but speaks softly to him, holds out her hand. He fires.

My head tells me she's not there. Everything else screams that she could be.

My sobs drown out the commentator. Daniel turns quickly, and takes me in his arms. I can't stop crying.

The TV commentators are now greedily feeding off experts' opinion as to why the boy with the long blonde hair might have done things so casually incomprehensible. Bystanders are adding their accounts, real and imagined.

He reaches round me and uses the remote to switch off the TV sound.

I have to believe that Clare is safe; anything else would mean insanity. She turned twenty in January. The dangers I have imagined for her are mundane: sibling rivalry, unhappy love, although I hope not yet. I may never know if she died on this day, on holiday with friends. That stupid murdering bastard.

I touch the side of Daniel's face with two fingers, take a deep breath and walk across the room. He starts to follow. I turn. 'I'll be back.' In our bedroom I drag my sweaters out of a drawer and find what I'm looking for. I sit and wait for my crying to subside, tell myself this is the time to be strong. I can do it.

We sit side by side on the sofa. He murmurs something about me being a softy and hugs me close.

'There's something I need to tell you.' At the same time I'm asking myself why I haven't told him sooner. We have never talked

205

about the past, his past girlfriends, my non-existent lovers. He doesn't want children, says there's too much else to do in life. I've gone along with that, made work and him my life. We both live and work in childless worlds.

I've moved on, I tell myself. Not far enough.

I move out of his arms to perch on the edge of the sofa. He waits, his arm on my left shoulder, one finger and thumb gently massaging my neck then takes out his handkerchief, wipes my eyes which no longer need wiping, and looks directly into them. I pull a framed photograph of Clare from between the seat and the arm of the sofa and hand it to him.

He holds the photograph close. His surprise flickers and is extinguished.

'She was just under six weeks.'

'Tell me,' he says, at last, and pulls me back to rest on his chest. I take back the photograph.

What do I say? That I fled to Australia and gave my daughter away. I sit up, hold his gaze and tell him, but not all. He listens carefully.

I describe Clare: her curled gripping fingers and her chubby legs and feet ready for growth and her smile.

He looks a little puzzled but I carry on. I try to ease the pain from my voice when I say how much I miss her.

'Why Australia?' Daniel's voice brings me back.

'Lucy had an aunt there.' I half laugh, 'I was desperate.'

Before he can ask I say, forcing my voice into matter-of-factness, 'The father, I didn't tell him. I was young, sixteen.' I want to get it over with and forget. 'Only Lucy. No-one else knew.'

I feel calmer.

'Your mother?'

'I couldn't tell her.'

He looks puzzled. 'I've told you,' I say, a little irritated, 'about her depressions. And you don't know what my church was like. Twenty-one years ago,' I say. 'A different world.'

'Your sister then. She would have helped you?'

I almost laugh. 'She disappeared in London, didn't answer my calls.' I want to get this over with and move on.

'It must have been tough out there, on your own. I can't imagine it.' He holds me tightly to him.

I start to say that I've wanted to tell him. 'Hush,' he says. 'You've told me now.'

I pull myself up and look into his face. His eyes smile.

'Would she be there?' He points to the blank television.

'I don't know,' I say, and accept my madness.

The silence between us is overloud without the television sound.

'It's alright, she won't ring the bell any minute.' I sort of laugh, a stupid empty sound, and add, 'She's in Melbourne. That's where she was, anyway.'

He pulls me back and I rest, limp against his chest.

'We could find her,' he says, 'if that's what you want. It would cost, but a private detective could do it.' He turns and kisses me lightly on the forehead.

How I love him for that offer, even if he is hoping I won't accept. I take his head between my hands and look into his eyes. 'I love you Daniel,' I say, and don't speak of the times I've almost looked for her. 'Believe me,' I say softly. 'I long to find her but I must not.' I try to sound casual. 'If she wants to she'll find me.'

Daniel stands up. 'Thank you for telling me,' he says. 'Not such a softy after all.' He moves towards the bedroom.

I put the photograph of Clare on the table with that of his parents.

Chapter 34

London Autumn

'It will be interesting to see the two of you together, especially as I don't know anything about this sibling thing,' Daniel says, as we sit on the sofa, feet up on the glass table. He twines his fingers in my hair. He loves to get his hand behind my neck and run his fingers through my hair down my back. I am pigging out on the chocolates he's brought. It's a late autumn evening.

Alexis has invited us for a weekend. This is not the first invitation but the only time I've been inclined to accept.

I warn him, 'She's bossy.'

'Well, she won't boss me.'

'No, my shrinking violet but she'll try.' He doesn't like being teased but he's learning. It is a standing joke between us that his mother, anxious he might be shy as an only one, worked too hard on the confidence bit. 'Overkill,' I told him.

'Very nice,' says Daniel, peering into a bright yellow Porsche soft-top, with a recent registration outside Alexis' house. I take his arm and pull him up the path to the front door.

The early evening sun, low on the horizon, is slinking over the houses and setting fire to the large windows of the houses opposite.

Daniel carries a small overnight bag and I'm clutching two bottles of the best vintage Taittinger.

I stand at the door with Daniel feeling as if it's trick or treat night. I've barely raised my hand before the door opens.

Alexis' fair straight hair is cut short, chin line. Her make-up, a discreet layer, might have left her looking pale were it not for her deep crimson lipstick. She wears a low-cut silky red top and a long black skirt that clings over her hips. And black patent high-heeled shoes. She looks great.

We hug and she shakes hands with Daniel. 'Ruth has kept you hidden away,' she says.

I put the bottles in her hands. She examines them then smiles her thanks, and walks ahead of us into the house.

At the foot of the stairs she says, 'Ruthy, you're sleeping upstairs. I've converted the attic so keep going on up. We'll have a drink when you come down.'

We climb the stairs past the door to Alexis' room. Another floor up and we stick our heads into Ben's room. The toys and wallpaper have been replaced with complicated looking maps of stars on the wall and a stack of games, almost as big as Daniel's, beside his computer. One wall is now covered in books. Daniel walks in and runs his fingers down the games. 'He's got a better selection than I have,' he grins.

The attic room is bright and airy with a large double bed, a small wardrobe and a door leading to the en suite. We dump the bag and I use the bathroom, renew my make-up and change for dinner into my perfectly fitting designer jeans, a cream silk blouse and a delicate gold necklace, inlaid with small green stones. I'm tempted to put my hair up, but leave it down. I pull Daniel to me and kiss him hard before we wander back down to the kitchen.

Alexis runs her eyes slowly over me. 'Nice,' she says. That, from Alexis, is a serious compliment.

'Daniel,' I say, and finger the necklace.

Alexis gestures to chairs at a very large scrubbed wooden table. 'Dinner is nearly ready.'

'I could do with a kitchen this size,' Daniel says as we sit down.

A door at the back leads into a small garden that has room for a wooden table and chairs and over a dozen pots of herbs. A rose scrambles up a trellis on the side brick wall.

The smells from the oven are heady.

'Smells good,' I say. I'm bubbling with excitement.

'Ben was full of praise for your food,' Alexis says to Daniel.

'And he for yours,' he smiles back at her.

With a last look in the oven she leads the way down the hall.

The drawing room is now painted cream: walls, cornices and woodwork. One wall is replete with serried columns of paintings, each lit with discrete lights. Covering much of the floor is a red/blue Persian carpet about twice the size of my mother's. A sculpture of a graceful young man stands in one corner, catching and holding the eye. Above the marble fireplace is an immense gilt mirror. The curtains have been replaced with full-length cream shutters, fastened fully back. Ben's photos are still there with a couple of recent additions.

Alexis pours three glasses of white wine, from a bottle sitting in an ice bucket. 'We can have the champagne later,' she says. 'It's a bit warm still.'

'Keep it for some other time,' Daniel replies and waves his hand. He sits down in a large winged Regency chair. It's covered in a velvet material and an exotic red/gold/blue/yellow tapestry is draped over the back. He's too far away. I want him close to me, touching distance, but I sit on a large cream sofa and Alexis perches a couple of feet away on the ottoman, her legs crossed and then wound round each other below the knees.

'This is perfect,' says Daniel, waving his glass at Alexis. He leans forward to look at the label.

'I'll put you in touch with my wine merchant,' Alexis says.

I've told Alexis about Daniel's wine collection, boasted.

'Where's Ben?' I ask.

'He's gone with a friend to an observatory somewhere.'

Alexis turns to Daniel, 'He couldn't stop talking about that motorbike of yours. He called it something.'

'Artemis,' I say softly. 'Daniel has sold it. I suppose that's yours outside.' I wave a hand towards the yellow creature at the kerb.

'Of course.'

'The Porsche.' Daniel struggles to sound casual. 'It looks great.'

'It is.' She unwinds her legs and gets up briskly. 'Stay here. Help yourselves.' She points to the bottle. 'Dinner in five minutes.'

The dining room is shuttered and painted deep green. The table is laid with silver cutlery on a cream damask cloth, extravagant amounts of crockery, candles and a couple of bottles of wine, one already open with the cork lying beside it.

Alexis seats Daniel at the head of the table, herself on his right and me opposite. She places a square plate with exquisitely arranged scallop mousseline in front of each of us and sits down. She shakes out her napkin and places it on her lap. The candlelight flutters across her white breast.

He tastes a small forkful, 'Wonderful.'

The table could seat ten. The flickering candlelight transfixes, beguiling with the ghosts of others who might be seated here. My father would be eighty-six now, an old man; my mother seventy-six. And Beth: unaged.

Alexis tops up our glasses and raises her own. 'Lovely to have my little sister here again.'

We smile at each other. She looks happy.

'And you, Daniel.'

'The food and the company.' I watch his lips hold the glass's edge as he drinks. My sister looks away.

They talk about their clients. Daniel mentions a couple of multinationals.

I want to tell him that he doesn't have to try so hard. Instead, I say, 'He's good, has them eating out of his hands.'

'They like my style,' he says.

211

Alexis responds with her company turnover, a figure so large I wonder if she is lying. I look closely at her and decide not.

'Wow,' says Daniel. 'Ruth didn't tell me that.'

'Ruth didn't know,' I say and we all laugh.

'One of my clients introduced me to the Carlton Club,' Daniel says with his mouth not quite empty. 'Useful.'

'That's news,' I say. 'When?'

'Oh,' he shrugs, 'some time ago. You have your Labour pals.' His voice softens the words.

'It's useful, the contacts.' He turns to Alexis, 'You could join as a Lady Associate Member. Good for business.'

I know a little about the Carlton Club, thanks to Maggie's well publicised membership. A gentleman's club: old, elite, right wing. 'A Lady Associate Member sounds second class to me,' I say.

'I've got all the business I can manage thank you,' Alexis says, her tone moderating the words.

Daniel lets it drop. 'My father says he knows you. You did a luncheon for his company.'

She chuckles, 'He's a good-looking man.'

'He said the same about you,' he laughs. 'Well you know what I mean. And you'd love the food in New York and the restaurants are great,' Daniel says. 'Perhaps there's a niche for you if you ever get sick of London. I travel there a bit.'

'Perhaps, one day,' she says.

'We're going there soon,' I say, excitement making my voice loud. 'I've submitted a paper to a conference near there. I'm pretty sure it will get accepted and we'll add on a few days in New York.'

Alexis collects up the dishes and motions to us to stay seated. She returns with a rich venison casserole, potatoes, spiced red cabbage and a green salad. We help ourselves and Daniel pours red wine into fresh glasses.

Daniel leans forward, resting his forearms on the table and surprises us both when he says, 'I can't imagine having brothers or sisters. Ruth says I've missed out.' He drains his glass.

'What he's trying to say is that he was spoilt,' I cut across, 'by his mother anyway.'

'Ruth and I were close as kids,' Alexis says.

I wonder if Daniel notices the missing years.

I reach out my foot – I've long since kicked off my shoes – to touch his. He returns the pressure.

Alexis and Daniel compare recipes for the casserole. I half listen.

Five minutes pass and I'm beginning to think we should have done this sooner when Alexis says, 'My mother wasn't Harriet, Ruth's mother. My real mother gave me away.'

I stare at her and Daniel looks at me, puzzled. I tell myself that this is just Alexis and her games.

The silence sits and waits.

'Well, that was dramatic,' I say at last. 'Perhaps you'd better tell Daniel the rest.'

She stands, colour in her cheeks. 'You can tell him,' she says as she walks towards the door. 'Later,' she throws back.

Daniel raises his eyebrows but she's quickly back, carrying home-made ginger and spice ice cream and a bowl of cherries.

We help ourselves to the ice cream. Alexis picks at the cherries softly punctuating the silence with food talk. Then she starts on about living life as if every moment is the last. I wonder if she has found some fashionable guru.

Daniel agrees with her but they don't get round to specifics.

'The West is too greedy. The 'I want' syndrome,' I say, but lightly. It's old ground for Daniel and me.

'I'm not ashamed of wanting,' says Alexis. 'Why should I be?'

I raise my hands in mock surrender. Now is not the time.

'A great dinner,' he says.

A clap of thunder rolls around outside and Alexis gets up to close the shutters. 'Would you like to see my portrait?' she says to us and walks towards the door before we can answer.

We don't move.

She looks back, 'Come on.'

Daniel stands. I move quickly around the table and take his hand.

Alexis is standing at the foot of her king-size bed. The top half of the bed is a drift of gold and red cushions. There's a deep-pile cream carpet to wade through. The walls are painted soft cream and on one wall stands a very large light oak wardrobe. A door leads off one corner to her en suite bathroom. A dark gold armchair in the opposite corner has a pair of tights slung over the back. The only light in the room comes from lamps with mulberry coloured shades either side of the bed. Mulberry floor-length curtains are pulled back from the windows. Shafts of sunlight are ambushed by the lush reds and gold of the furnishings.

Alexis takes Daniel's arm and with her other hand points.

On the wall behind the bed is a life-size portrait. Alexis. Her portrait-blue eyes lock into mine, her painted lips stretch lightly into a provocative smile as she looks over her shoulder. She's sitting back on her heels half turned away from the viewer, on a piece of gold material in front of a deep red backdrop. Her long blonde hair hangs down her back. She tantalises, revealing her left breast, her bum and a body that challenges the viewer to love what is revealed and regret what is not.

I get out, 'Who painted it?'

'Oh, someone in London famous for portraits, his signature is there.' She points to the bottom right-hand corner of the painting. 'I found the best. I wasn't paying.' Alexis gives me her most sisterly smile and sits on the bed. 'He did,' and she motions to one of the silver-framed photographs.

I turn to look.

Quickly I look away and say to Daniel, 'An old man.'

The rain smacks the window, uncertain of its strength at first, then individual rivulets roll down the glass like fat slugs.

The real Alexis stands there smiling. I stare at her and want to strangle her.

Finally, Daniel says, 'It's good.'

Later, when we are in bed wrapped round each other, Daniel's right thigh across my left, his right arm cupping my breast, he says, 'That was something.'

I know what he means but ask, 'What?'

'The portrait.'

'Yes, it's good,' I say and mean it but wish he hadn't seen it.

'And who was the guy in the photo?'

'An old man,' I say again. 'Her lovers are old men.'

His body is hot, although the room is cool.

'What do you think of her?'

'She's something,' he says. I hate to hear the admiration in his voice. 'But not my type.' He yawns. 'The food was great.'

'You got the full works tonight.'

Daniel kisses me, 'She's too hard, tough. I like softies like you,' he murmurs.

We make love. When Daniel falls asleep I gaze at his body in the light that slithers through and around the dormer blinds, creating a harlequin of his nakedness. I would like to sculpt him.

The wind dies and I get up and close the shutters to keep out the street light.

Much later I put my hand on Daniel's thigh. He wakes and turns towards me with sleepy, vulnerable eyes.

'It's true,' I say. 'My father was unfaithful.'

'I thought she was making it up,' he murmurs, reluctant to wake.

'My mother left a letter. He brought baby Alexis home to her.'

Daniel doesn't speak and after a minute I say, 'She was called Beth. My father said she couldn't look after Alexis and there was a lot of stuff about God and forgiveness.' I pause. 'The woman wasn't a believer. He didn't want his daughter brought up by a heathen.'

'God,' he says, then laughs. 'And your mother bought it?' He's awake now.

'She wanted a baby. I don't know. They'd been married nearly five years. I was born two years later.'

He runs his hand up my belly. 'So something was right.'

'I hated him when I found out,' I say. 'Perhaps he really wanted to be with the other woman, Beth. Alexis would have told you more had you asked her,' I say. 'That's what she wanted.'

'It was embarrassing.'

Has Alexis told anyone else? I think not. She seemed to be testing out the words as she spoke them.

He asks what Beth was like, how old was she?

'I don't know. Alexis doesn't know.'

Before Daniel goes back to sleep he murmurs, 'Families, eh.'

The next morning Daniel leaves before Alexis is up. Ribbons of sunlight find their way into my sleep, coloured and playful.

'I like him,' Alexis says.

There's a faint thrum of traffic noise. I pour myself a large mug of coffee.

'He's good for you. It's about time you had someone like him.'

Chapter 35

1997

A Labour government. I'm crying with excitement. A landslide, the end of eighteen years of Tory rule. I'm thankful Daniel is in New York. Our local Labour group met at the pub for election night. We expected victory but not a Tory rout. Lucy and Dave got in a babysitter and joined us.

Maria and I kiss, air kisses, both cheeks, then we hug and air kiss again. She's smiling broadly and so is everyone else. I slip to my usual seat. I lean over to nearby tables and offer comments, approval. The air pulsates with excitement and loud conversation, although there's a tiredness underlying the buzz. I expect most of us stayed up through the night, savouring the moment. This is not the usual tranquil self-contained Maria's. Only the man in the suit sitting in the back corner opposite me is looking glum. The 'no mobiles' rule has been temporarily cancelled.

They ring jauntily, triumphantly; their ring tones – Beethoven, Mozart, pop tunes – marking out the owners. With every ring, Maria jerks round to shake her head gently but firmly at the user, remembers, and smiles broadly instead. Ben telephones. We crow together in triumph for a few minutes. He's on his way to Downing Street. I'd love to be with him. Today is exceptional in every way.

Lamont, Rifkin, Portillo all lose their seats. Tony Blair at forty-three is the youngest prime minister this century. We have a majority of nearly 200. Tory cash for questions dominated the campaign. Life for many will be different from today. I'm sure of this but hear Daniel whisper in my ear: dreamer.

Daniel stays away a day longer than expected: 'Give you time with your pals, to celebrate,' he says, without rancour over the phone.

When he returns Daniel is more interested in Labour's win than I expect. He doesn't quite come out and say it but he admires Tony Blair and thinks the Tories were dumb to get caught with that sleaze.

Five months later I go to Lucy's to watch Princess Diana's funeral on the telly. Daniel is away.

"The people's princess" Blair calls her. He has a way with words. Ryan and Mattie are in another room with their games.

Maria closes her café for the day.

The death of a princess has brought tens of thousands to the streets and the pavement outside the Palace blossoms. I break my 'no newspaper during the week' rule and scour the papers avidly. Temporarily I become a TV junkie.

There's change in the air as well as grief: Dolly, the sheep is cloned, a buggy lands on Mars, the IRA call a ceasefire and it's likely that the Scots will say yes to devolution. It's a good time, an exciting time.

Maria gives me her brightest red smile. 'Ciao Bella,' she says. The café is quiet, only half a dozen in. I've just returned from Mexico.

It's one of Lucy's yellow days. Everything, including her shoes, is bright canary yellow. Someone less confident might have looked ridiculous, an oversize fat bird. Her clothes flow as loosely as her skin sits tightly over the flesh. Strangers smile to see her. She suits the café.

'You should get a tan more often, you look good,' Lucy says as she starts on a mountainous meringue liberally doused with whipped cream and raspberries. She leans forward, first sucking the cream off her fingers, and lightly touches my scarf. 'I like this, not your usual thing.'

'I bought it in Mexico, well Daniel did.'

'Ah.'

Just over a month back Daniel stood at the door to the flat, holding out an envelope.

We'd had perhaps our most serious row the week before. He was spending more weekends away. 'Too much work,' he said. 'It won't go on forever; my business is still too small. I need to grow; concentrate on pulling in new clients which means travel, then we can relax a bit and I can take more time off.'

He sent flowers. I refused to accept them, sent them back to the florist.

'It's being fobbed off Daniel; fucking fobbed off,' I told him, when he got back. 'I don't want flowers, I want more of you.'

'I show you that I love you don't I?'

'These flowers are just things.'

He placed his hand on my thigh, his face crinkled in a smile. 'You have me; there's no more to give. It's the way I am.'

That conversation was a cul-de-sac.

He stood there, holding out the envelope. Our fight was still in my head but I wanted to hold him, smell him, touch him. I opened the envelope.

'We need some sun,' he said in that voice I wanted to bottle and keep.

Two tickets for Mexico and confirmation for a hotel; two weeks, two whole weeks. One week had been our longest holiday so far. A little snake in my soul noted that he could get time off when he wanted to.

I gently slap Lucy's arm. The comfortable flesh talks back. 'I don't usually let him buy my clothes.'

'Thank goodness,' Lucy sighs. 'He'd have you dressed like something out of the pages of *Hello*.'

Lucy and Daniel might as well occupy different planets. Daniel doesn't care what Lucy thinks of him but then he doesn't care much what anyone thinks of him.

'How are the little gods?' I ask.

'Exactly what I deserve for all my virtuous living,' she says. 'They're at school.' She smiles that private mother's smile. 'So tell all, what did wonder boy do that made it so good?' Lucy giggles, 'You must learn the art of dissembling, you have your sexy face on.'

Thirty-nine and I still flush like a young girl. 'Well, there was Albert.'

Lucy raises her eyebrows and slips more red and white goo into her small pert mouth.

'He's a rabbit, a big grey thing with long fluffy fur.'

'This is your hotel we are talking about, not a second-rate Disney. It sounds most un-Daniel like. I thought he liked the Hiltons, the smart, the place-to-be-seen hotels.'

'Envy,' I say. 'He knew I'd love the place.' I sip my coffee and let my mind wander back. Primary colours everywhere – deep reds, blues, large cool floor tiles, white painted walls, with Mexican motifs in strips on the walls, the bedrooms around a central courtyard, and coarse grass kept trim by a fat rabbit with a silky grey Persian fur, Albert. Another rabbit, Ted, as thin and long and elegant as Albert was short and fat, perched on the edge of the brick wall of a well, his white wooden legs hanging far down and his long ears shooting up.

'At night Albert was shut in a cage. The vultures might get him if he's out,' I tell Lucy. 'They cruise down from the burnt cacti-covered desert hills. And there are hundreds of dolphins in the sea,' I say. With their sleek flying lines, their blunt noses and

220

sly eyes, they raced the hard white plastic bow of our catamaran, showing us what movement through water might be, sometimes a dozen, sometimes hundreds. We stopped the boat and jumped into the sea, heedless of its cold stretching three miles down, but the dolphins didn't need us for company; we were too ugly and ungainly with our claggy white skins and clumsy movements.

We found whales and hurtled towards them in the dinghy. Their ears must have screamed at the obscenity of our outboard motor. They can pick up the song of other whales over a thousand miles away.

We looked into their eyes, wondered at the curious markings on their sides, smiled at the small fish attached to them and held our breath as their huge house-high tails rose and thrashed the sea as they dived. One evening we lingered into dusk, the sea silk-smooth, the burnt-brown cactus-dotted hills of the shore ten miles off. The sun procrastinated. A hundred yards away two or three whales circled, blowing. Long slow blows spouted dozens of feet into the cherry-pink sky and the whoosh of the exhalation broke up the stillness.

I start to tell Lucy. She looks confused. 'I'll e-mail some pics. I've sent a few to Ben. He'll like fat Albert.'

This holiday was Daniel's gift, our secret place.

The university, largely empty through the summer months, fills up with noisy, excited students at the start of the academic year. The first day of the semester I spend seeing my new personal tutees, offering a mix of advice: establish good work habits from the start, work smart but not all the time and embrace all the good things university life has to offer. I don't mention the negatives. They'll find those for themselves. I advise two girls from China to attend English language classes. They nod vigorously. I ask are any of their friends from this country; they shake their heads sadly.

Someone else has taken over my master's course. I'm now head of the doctoral programme. I enjoy difficult questions and know that finding the right question is harder than finding the answer.

Daniel is interested in answers not questions. 'Don't do it for them,' is all he says.

I take on two new doctoral supervisions. I love their enthusiasm and try not to temper it.

Josh is collecting his data online, examining the impact of information technology on corporate relationships. He'll find it hard to keep up with the burgeoning technologies. I tell him to come back with meaningful propositions, a research question even.

The other is Australian: Jeanette. Before we first met I'd hoped, ridiculously, I know, that it would be Clare, coming back to me. Jeanette doesn't look the least bit like me and eventually I work out that she's a couple of years older than Clare.

Jeanette's applying game theory to corporate relationships: self-interest and the need to betray the other party rather than trust them. Self-interest determines strategy and is the best solution. If you don't trust your partner, believe they will cheat in the right circumstances then you will get the rewards. It's necessary to deconstruct your opponent, examine their ambitions, their beliefs and attitudes and their most secret dreams. Acts of kindness can be weapons of power and control. Jeanette is using mathematical models and applying them to corporate buyers and sellers locked into different relationships.

Daniel loves game theory and we discuss a multitude of scenarios. It's about choices available to players in the game and it puts individual goals up against the common good. We scrutinise television thrillers, Daniel's clients, politics and politicians. We rarely agree but we enjoy the jousting.

Outside snow falls, each individual flake flattening itself on the windowpane. A single lonely flake sticks, tenacious, then slides slowly down the glass as the heat from inside sabotages its attempts to stay separate. I step on to the terrace, leaving the doors into our bedroom wide open behind me. The curtains sigh softly, swish a little then silence. The snow flutters butterfly kisses on my bare arms, flakes loiter in my hair before settling and melting, running in individual rivulets down my cheeks. The city cleanses itself of its dirt and greyness; the white blanket flushes with pink and reds of the setting sun denying ebony-night its watch.

I love snow. As a child I would get up in the night to check it hadn't gone. This snow dances and pirouettes, bewitching everything it touches with its delicate gentle caresses. Adults and children cavort together in the park and snowballs fly with laughter and screams. The city gridlocks. Warring neighbours become ephemeral good friends and Christmas festivities slip in with the snow and carry on while it lasts. Everything softens.

Daniel and I build a snowman. A chill wind ices its surface. Daniel ties one of his scarves round its neck and I fashion it a vegetable face. It's admired by the kids so I stay to help them with theirs after Daniel goes inside. It's a short generous day.

I send Ben three books for Christmas, all favourites: *Le Grand Meaulnes* – a story of teenage love and romanticism; *Voss* by Patrick White – Voss' mystical nature is one Ben will empathise with, a bit old for him but he'll manage, and a Ford Madox Ford novel.

We've made some changes to the spare room. It now has a chunky dark blue desk squeezed between the bed and the opposite wall is lined with bookshelves. The single bed is only used when Ben comes. Usually it's a repository for my papers.

Earlier in the year Daniel bought a large basement room in our building and converted it from one dusty sprawling room that ran the length and width of the building into two. The larger space he made into an air-conditioned gym complete with the most up-to-date equipment and computerised programmes. His personal trainer comes to him but I still go to our old gym. I like the buzz and the friendship.

The other room Daniel shelved with wine racks and a special temperature-controlled fridge to take his wine although the room is kept at a steady fifty-five degrees Fahrenheit. Wooden cases line one of the walls and open wine racks another. They're all carefully labelled. There's a separate small wine rack of bottles that I use when he is away. We joke about 'my wine rack'.

On Christmas Eve Daniel walks through the door carrying a long thin parcel, an etiolated silver Christmas tree made of paper-clad wire. He erects it in the corner of the sitting room where it stands six feet tall with a meagre eight or ten wispy branches. He bought it complete with eight blue glass balls for decoration.

'There, it looks good,' he says, stepping back and looking pleased.

I prefer the old-fashioned real green tree.

In the middle of the night I creep out of bed and place Daniel's presents under the scrawny silver thing ('tree' is to endow it with too much reality). They're wrapped in plain gold paper: a new watch with touches of blue in it, a couple of razor-sharp carbon steel knives for the kitchen and the latest computer game and CDs. I sit a while in the darkness. It gets cold. I don't go back to bed but bring my knees up to my chest, wrap my arms around them and think of Clare. Time is eleven hours ahead in Australia so she has probably already opened her presents. I tick off a list I might have made for my twenty-year-old daughter: books, lots of them, clothes – pretty, stylish, extravagant and perhaps a bracelet made of old gold from a watch chain, like the one I wear. I wish her unimaginable happiness and most of all that we might meet, that some need for me might be in her.

Chilled, I go back to bed.

Another pile is under the tree in the morning, professionally wrapped in silver and blue paper. Chocolates, three novels, a book by a left-wing writer on the state of the world, perfume and a handbag I admired when we were strolling late one evening past closed shops in town.

Christmas Day we sit cross-legged on the floor, our breakfast on a tray on the carpet. I have put on his bulky blue sweater and he wears his tracksuit. He hasn't shaved and the dark shadow on his cheeks and chin turns the blue of his eyes to peacock. We open our presents, interspersed with coffee and croissants. Afterwards we make love on the rug.

Chapter 36

1999

Daniel helps put together my case for a chair. It's successful. Our lives still mesh only at weekends when the hours are sweet.

Outside the wind jousts with the black afternoon. I hate these days even though spring is not too far off. The sun is barely in the sky before it starts slipping away again like a whore telling the client he's had all he paid for. There's no-one else in the building.

Someone knocks and pushes open my office door.

'Hello Ben. This is a lovely surprise.'

Anxiety flits across his face and he flushes. 'You got my e-mail?'

'Only just but it doesn't matter.'

I give him a hug. He has to bend some way so our faces can meet. He hates jokes about his height.

He looks around my office. 'Cool. This is much swankier than the old one, Prof.'

'It goes with the job.' I smile. 'People here take more stock of that than the papers I write.'

Ben grunts.

'I'm joking, don't look so serious.'

'What do you do?' he asks.

'Research, the doctoral programme, that's me. If you don't count the endless boring committees where most grovel to the dean.'

'Not you.'

I love his loyalty. 'No, not me. I fight,' I say. 'But I thought you were still away. Your mother's away isn't she?'

'She's back,' he says.

'How's uni?' I close down my computer, and move to the round table, motioning to another chair. He's twenty-two and just started on his doctorate.

He shrugs, 'Busy, lots of lab work but it's good.'

University hasn't given him any greater sartorial style: a pair of jeans, torn I suspect from overuse rather than a fashion statement, old sneakers and a burgundy sweatshirt.

'Relax.' I lean over to lightly touch his arm. He's an inveterate sprawler but today he sits upright, his long limbs looking improbably tidy. Sprawling suits him. He looks tired. He's always been a hard worker: too enthusiastic.

'Let's go to the pub for a drink?' I say.

He starts to say something and stops. 'Can we go to the cottage? Just for the night. It's great there,' he says abruptly.

'You can go back to the flat and take my car.' I wave at the papers piled on my desk. 'What's wrong?'

He looks down at his feet. 'Can we both go?'

Ben's timing is bad but I start packing papers into my briefcase. 'Sure, just wait while I gather some work together. Daniel will be home tomorrow night. We'll pick up takeaways and other food on the way. It'll be cold.' I hadn't expected to be going to the cottage until well into the new year.

'It's OK. I've left a couple of jackets there and some boots. Perhaps it'll snow.' He sits up looking pleased for the first time. 'This is cool, Prof,' he repeats, looking more cheerful.

'Let's go.' I jump up. The work can wait.

He nods.

We walk through the campus. The few students around stare curiously at the two of us, some going out of their way to get close enough to say 'hello', as if in passing. I smile at them all. Ben carries my briefcase.

We leave the grounds and walk three blocks up the dull busy road and across the park.

Ben looks pale.

'We can take Daniel's car if you like. It's faster than this thing.' I pat my car lovingly. Daniel is always on at me to change it. I take Ben's arm and wonder if everyone who knows him wants to touch him?

'Yours,' he says.

I pack some wine, salad and fruit and a few clothes and try Daniel on his mobile. He's not picking up so I leave him a message. We buy food and beer on the way out of the city. Ben doesn't care much what he eats although Alexis has taken him to restaurants from an early age, telling any who would listen that's how French children learn to behave in restaurants and develop their palates.

I concentrate on getting out of the city.

When we leave the suburbs Ben turns on the radio, fiddles with the dial to get a pop station and stretches his legs. We turn off the A road and begin the last thirty miles through small back roads. Ben points to the sign to Lower Newhouses. We drive on and cross the small humpback bridge, pass a gaggle of houses and one small church then climb the narrow steep hill, the car protesting at the effort, and begin the half mile along the farm track to the cottage. I'm relieved we've not come in Daniel's car. It would struggle with the uneven ground and the bumps and deep ruts on either side of the grassy middle strip. The ground drops steeply down on the driver's side to a ragged cluster of trees that bend and strain against the prevailing westerlies. On the passenger side crumbling high stone walls keep in shaggy and windswept sheep. Below, the valley is in a mist no lights can puncture. The cottage stands solid and alone.

Alexis has never been to the cottage. 'Took me years to get away from there, why would I want to go back?'

228

We pull up on the only flat piece of ground and Ben unwinds himself from the front seat.

'Be careful.' I point to the flagstones, covered by a plaque of moss.

The sky is pewter coloured and a storm threatens.

'You get the coal in and light the fire,' I say. 'We're going to have to huddle round it.'

Ben grunts assent and takes the bucket and shovel for the coal and puts on one of the jackets that hang behind the front door. 'I'll light a fire in your bedroom as well,' he tells me. 'I don't need one.'

Living with Daniel has made me soft.

The wine and beer keep out some of the cold until the fire gets going. It's always been a difficult one to light but soon the flames are leaping, greedy for the coal and small logs. I can still smell the firelighters.

Most of the ready meal I put on Ben's plate, including a mountain of rice. We eat off our knees, pulling the battered armchairs close to the fire. Ben never wastes words, is often silent before answering, thinking over the exact response. Sparsely he describes university life: good times with friends, a wonderful library. No mention of a girlfriend. He looks at me earnestly as he talks of astrophysics. Usually I make the effort to understand him, ask sensible questions but the fire is making me sleepy.

He spent the summer in India: loved the teaching and the children and hated the poverty. He launches into a speech about the evils of the free market and exploitation by the West. I want to hug him.

The fire collapses a little and sighs as the coal spreads and another log catches. What is Daniel doing right now? I've left him a message but there's no signal here. The thought of seeing him in twenty-four hours warms me.

The storm builds. There are few trees so the cottage takes the full force. It would be difficult to stand up outside. The kitchen windows rattle and groan. Small sharp draughts of cold air lurch their way in. I love to hear the wind, to feel the strength of the small solid building as it shrugs it off.

I drink half the bottle of red and Ben drinks all the beers. The fire will stay in until morning. Its shadows leap and dance over the walls, red and sometimes malign.

Ben sinks into one of the chairs besides the fire, wraps himself in a duvet and disappears except for his face that his beanie frames, accentuating its strong symmetrical features. I put on a gilet. He catches my gaze and pulls the duvet up higher. Now I can only see his eyes.

'What's wrong?' I ask.

He doesn't reply but swings his legs round from where they are draped over the arm of his chair and sits up. There's a fug in the room now and he has shed beanie and duvet. I'm looking forward to the warm fire in my bedroom. I love watching a fire splutter and blaze from the warmth of a bed.

He digs into a pocket and hands me two small pieces of paper. I take them from his slender fingers. They feel glossy: photographs. We have long since turned off the hard white ceiling light and have been talking by the flickering firelight.

I peer at the first one and just make out Albert, rabbit Albert.

'I sent it to you last year,' I say.

Ben's tension is palpable. 'Look at the date on it.' His voice is harsh.

The firelight is not bright enough so I start to get up to turn on the light.

'Don't,' Ben shouts. 'I'll tell you the date, it was last year, 10th September and it's not your photo, it's Mum's.' He leans back in his chair, the flush of the beer gone from his face. 'That's what I came to tell you. Mum and Daniel. He's a shit.'

I don't want to look at the other photo but I do: Daniel and my sister on the beach, arms around each other. Stupidly, I wonder who took it.

The wind ceases. Ben looks around surprised, trying to work out what is different.

I sit and run the date through my head. Daniel was away last September for over a week.

I take one of the photos between the forefinger and thumb of each hand. The muscles tighten. I look at Ben. His eyes widen; he nods. I tear it into pieces and tear the pieces again and again and throw them on the fire, watch dully while the fire feeds itself on the pieces. I pick up the second one, hesitate and slip it in my pocket.

I offer Ben a fixed rictus smile. You stupid fucking idiot, I tell myself. The guru on trust and commitment. I swallow laughter, wild, hysterical laughter.

The scrape of his chair as he pushes it back is like a fatal wound, a scream of permanent ending. His body unscrambles. He leans on the mantelpiece. The fire is too close but I can't speak.

'He's a shit.' He points a long angry finger at the last flicker of burning photograph. 'He's a fascist, Ruth.' He flushes and sits down.

He's never called me Ruth before.

'Does your mother know you are here?'

He shakes his head.

'Thank you Ben, that was hard for you.' I tell myself it's not fair to ask the next question but I do. 'Do you know when it started?' Does it matter, I ask myself.

The Grand March from Aida runs through my head, majestic, solemn. I try to shut it out. A living death for Aida, the cave's mouth closed with a stone. But Aida had her lover. I will not. Perhaps I am truly my mother's daughter: mad.

'All I know is that she was away for over a week and came back with a suntan,' he says. 'She showed me pictures of this hotel and Albert. She said the hotel was quaint but she didn't like it much. He doesn't come to our house when I'm there.' He bows his head. 'She'll kill me for this.'

'Go to bed,' I murmur gently. 'I love you Ben. Adults do terrible things to each other.' My head is filling up again. I prefer the vacuum. 'I'll stay down here a while.'

Ben replies softly, an attempt at a smile, 'I've lit a fire in your bedroom.'

I nod. His tread on the stairs is that of a fat old lady.

Would it be better never to have a sister?

I slide off the chair on to the floor, knees up to my chest, arms wrapped round them, trying to shut out the truth.

The melancholy wind sobs at the windows, does the crying for me; tells me what a fool I've been. Oh, Daniel, how could you? And my sister. She could have any man. Not Daniel, my Daniel.

I go through all the possibilities, all the explanations. I choose a scale with even numbers, eliminating the weasel central territory, the neither agree nor disagree, the five point scale so beloved of researchers. A mistake, another Adolf: one out of ten on the unlikely side of the scale; a temporary liaison, seven out of ten. Where does that leave me? Back to one of the key questions: will I have him back? Out of ten, seven or eight, or one. Mischief-making by Ben: impossible, off the scale. Alexis went to our hotel in Mexico but not with Daniel. For a short time I give that eight or even nine, then it slips. The date fits. That's all I can make fit.

And there's the photograph.

The odds don't matter. I can't imagine life without Daniel. I'm not yet ready to tell myself that I have to.

I store all the happenings in my life to talk over with him: the jokes, the little stories, my work successes (and failures); the latest outrageous demand of the dean, the walk through the park. He listens, comforts, laughs, chides, and tells me some of his clients are just like the dean, can't bear to be stripped of their status, their power and that's exactly what he does. They can't bear to fail.

We have rows, of course we do. Not about the state of the world, politics, poverty. We blank those out. It's mostly the same subject: not enough time together, more holidays, no weekends apart.

Have I been naïve, stupid, not to question his absences? I might call some other woman a fool.

Game theory, power, trust, relationships. A joke.

It is sometime in the deepest shadow of night when I go to bed. The fire has lost heart and dulled. The storm takes out the electricity and tears at the fabric of the house. Thunder joins in and lightning throws itself through the cracks in the curtains, slashing the dark of the bedroom like fairground lights. The fire jousts with the walls, peopling them with demons. I put more blankets on the bed and wonder if Ben is warm enough before falling into fitful sleep.

I still don't believe it.

I wake utterly lonely.

Ben looks haggard and chilled. The cottage is cold, the fire black; the wind rages and now it frightens me. Or is it anger.

I scrabble in a cupboard for a gas jet and heat a saucepan of water to make a large pot of tea.

'Are you OK?' I sit opposite him, grown old overnight: a young man and an old woman in front of a blackened fire.

He looks down, wrapping his hands round a cup of tea, 'Will you have a go at Mum?'

'Yes.'

I walk over to him, place my hands on his shoulders. We move to hug then hold back. 'It's a brave thing that you have done.'

His voice trembles, 'What will you do?'

Already he sees me alone. 'I don't know. I haven't taken it in properly yet. Couples come through this sort of thing. Sometimes.'

I move briskly. 'Come on, let's go. It's too cold here.'

This time we do hug.

We drive back to the city through an inky sky. The thunder is personal. I flinch at every clap and fear its soulmate.

It's midday.

Ben drags himself up out of the car. I feel my own exhaustion in his laboured efforts. I ask again, 'Will you be OK?'

'Yes,' he says, not looking at me.

I touch his cheek. There's no strength left for kissing. 'Look after yourself. I'll e-mail you, but not for a day or two.'

He walks away, a small wave over his shoulder.

Chapter 37

Confrontation

I am still lying on the bed, our bed, seven or eight hours later. I don't phone him.

There is no contingency I haven't covered.

My sister. I had grown to love her again. Trust her. Almost. Has he taken her to our special places, spent days in bed with her in the same expensive hotels? Have they laughed at my naiveté? Has Alexis told him her life story the way I unpeeled myself, layer by layer? She will have kept secrets as have I.

Time to think the worst, find excuses, revisit my arguments, work through every nuance.

The light fades, the darkness scrambles in. The marshalling of the arguments in favour of innocence in the daylight is less compelling in the black night. Have I been the instrument of my own downfall? Too busy, too intent on my own career. A weekend partner. Or just stupid. I recall Lucy's words: 'Dave and I believe in the same things, want the same sort of world.' Daniel and I didn't.

I turn on the light and follow its flight on to the balcony. Couples are sauntering along the street below.

Back in the bedroom I scrabble in a bottom drawer and find my diary for last year. I drag a cushion on to the cold metal seat on the balcony and start to read. Work stuff, worries about promotion, joy of Daniel. I flick through. I haven't imagined it:

good sex, passion, tenderness, love. Have I been naïve, stupid, not to question his absences? Daniel and I discussed shrill, nagging partners and agreed we would not be like that. We promised to be honest. Past girlfriends; plenty I guess. He always said that none of them moved in with him and I believed him. We never talked about marriage and he's always been clear about children: none. I put down the diaries.

Rigid with cold I go back into the bedroom and dress, catching a glimpse of myself in the mirror, a passing blow: my swollen face, empty bloodshot eyes; my brown hair lank.

Daniel stands at the door.

'Forgotten what I look like.' His eyes crinkle. A couple of days earlier I might have traced the lines with my fingertips.

'How was the course?'

'Good. Nothing unusual, except not a very lively group, in fact, boring old farts.' That's one of his favourite expressions. Strange, I hadn't noticed it before but now it irritates me.

'Where did you stay?'

He looks surprised. 'My flat. Why do you ask?'

'We need to talk.'

'Can't it wait?' His eyes scan my face. 'I see it can't.'

He strides into the study and dumps his briefcase. The set of his shoulders indicates impatience. He comes back to the sitting room and sits on the sofa. He waits for me to sit beside him, patting the empty space. I refuse the sofa and sit in the big brown chair, at right angles to him. The lightning taunts our building. It's close, very close. There will be a deluge of rain soon. The storm has followed me.

Daniel sits, waiting for me to begin. He thinks it's something to do with Ben.

I force myself to meet his eyes; I uncurl my fists and place my open hands on my lap. He reaches over to take one of my hands but I refuse to surrender it.

236

He shifts his bum on the sofa. 'I'm all yours, but I need to change.' He waves towards the bedroom.

I pass him Ben's photo.

'A rabbit. What's this all about?'

'Albert,' I say.

'Albert? What the hell does that mean?'

'A grey furry thing in a garden in the middle of the desert. Remember. The vultures.'

His face gives nothing away.

'Do you love me Daniel?'

He looks surprised. 'Of course, you know I do.'

'I tell you that all the time, too much I expect, no scarcity value,' I say.

Daniel sits, his shoulders hunched.

'He's popular is Albert. My sister likes him also.'

There's a long leaden silence. He doesn't bother trying to lie his way out.

'How did you find out?' He recrosses his legs and folds his arms across his chest.

I want to leap at him, scratch his face, hit him. I want him to tell me it's all a mistake, that Ben is lying, a dreamer, away with his stars. I will my hands to stay where they were, one on each knee. My anger is drowning me.

His feet shuffle, he turns his head to look at the storm and gets up. There are beads of sweat on his face.

'I'm getting a drink,' he says.

I lean across and grasp the glass girl.

Daniel returns with two glasses of wine and a small bowl of my favourite nuts. I push the nuts away.

'Who told you?' He looks puzzled then his face clears, 'Ah, princeling Ben.' His nostrils distend and he gets up and puts on a disc, I hate background music. The clarinet whispers to me, of being alone, lost, of pain that is exquisite but still pain.

'Turn that thing off.'

'I thought you liked this piece.' He turns it off and sits down again.

'If you're going to shack up with his mother you had better get to like him more. The 'blue man' he calls you.'

Daniel puts his hand to his pale blue shirt, looks down for a fraction of a second and stalks to the French windows. 'It just happened.' He speaks to the rain outside.

'Fuck you Daniel.' I enunciate the words deliberately, loudly. 'Nothing just happens. There's action and reaction, cause and effect. So you have two women, her weekdays, me on weekends?'

'You haven't given me a chance,' he snarls and takes a slug of wine. That's not like him. I slug, he sips.

'Fine.' I sit back and cross my arms. 'Is she the first?'

'Yes.'

'Why should I believe you Daniel, believe anything you say?'

He half moves towards me but stops when I shrink back in the chair.

'When did it begin, your philandering?'

'I don't remember,' he says irritably. 'And don't call it that.'

'What would you call it?' I say. 'When?'

'Last year,' he says grudgingly. The rain threatens to implode the glass windows.

I realise that I have never looked at him with anything but love. Little irritations, yes, minor fights but none overwhelmed the love. This has changed. So soon.

'I thought we were good together,' I say quietly.

'We are good together,' he says. 'I'm sorry.' He sits down on the sofa, holds out his hand.

I leave it there, in the space between us.

'For what? Sorry I found out? Sorry for fucking my sister? How the two of you must laugh,' I say. 'Who made the first move?' Stupid the way that matters. It won't change anything. Did she want him because he was mine?

He doesn't answer.

'My sister, I expect. She has a history. Is she a better fuck than me?' I wish I hadn't asked that. I can't stop, don't want to stop. 'Do you like to shag us both?'

'Work,' he says. 'She had some clients she thought might be useful.'

'Ha, I see. Useful, that's Alexis.'

'It just happened,' he repeats.

'Nothing just happens. She's my sister, she's taboo. Don't turn away from me.' I shout, and take pleasure in the noise I make.

I take a large mouthful of wine. It tastes sour. I put the glass back down.

'Do you tell her you don't do it with me any more? That's what most cheats say, isn't it.' I look straight into his eyes. 'Or did you think you could just carry on? Have both of us: weekday and weekend lovers?' I search his eyes and wish I hadn't. 'You did, didn't you? Oh Daniel.'

'We don't talk about you,' he says.

'How honourable. And that makes it alright except I don't believe you.'

He says nothing.

'Remember you are in a long line of old men and won't be the last.' I grab his arm, my face red, ugly with rage. 'Do you love her?'

He pulls away and stands. 'I love you.'

'Then you'll have to choose.' I stand, inches away. 'That's if I'll still have you.'

'I'll make dinner.' He turns away.

'This isn't over Daniel, not until you tell me why, and I don't want any of your fucking dinner.'

The Harley Davidson clock revs up for seven o'clock, and resonates forlornly.

I follow him to the kitchen. 'We've never shared the same dreams but I thought we could work around that. Have you ever loved me, Daniel, really loved? Anyone?'

I look around. There are few signs of me in the flat. It's as if I've been passing through.

'Look at your flat, so anal, sterile, so nothing. That picture there.' I move back to the sitting room and point, although he can't see me, 'I've never liked it but you say it's worth ten grand. You tell me what everything is worth, or you wear the labels so everyone knows.' He strides back into the room, a tea towel in his hands. I move towards the picture and see him tense. 'Don't worry. You should know me better than that.'

The rain has stopped and the sun filters through the pewter sky, a watery pale swathe of pink-orange that lights up the trees and grass in the park and the solid grey stone buildings, like abandoned old men, flaunt their rain-sodden stains down their fronts.

I grab the glass girl and walk quickly into our bedroom. He follows.

'We can sort it.' He stands in the doorway, already a leaden pared down version of that quick gorgeous man who, six years ago, walked through my office door clutching two crash helmets.

I shove an arbitrary selection of clothes into an old rucksack that I've pulled from the bottom of the wardrobe. 'I'm going to the cottage.' I need time to get my head round this.

'Don't go,' he says, not meeting my eyes.

I close my rucksack and dump it on the bed. 'I'll be back next Friday. You can tell me then what you have decided. Meanwhile I'll think about whether you are worth keeping.' I straighten my shoulders. I too, am pared down. 'Stay away from her unless that is where your future fucks are.' I laugh one of those unreal laughs again. 'You know where I am.'

'I've a new company starting, a new course. I have to be there.' He sounds worried but is there a tinge of relief in his voice?

'OK. Run. I suppose it's in London, this new course,' I say. 'You usually get away with tweaking the old ones. You are so good at it, the author of three leading-edge books, your inspirational tracts, the same old stuff repackaged with sexy titles. I'm amazed the punters don't see through it all. They will eventually.'

He flushes.

I start to close the wardrobe but pause, running my fingers over his clothes 'You and your blue wardrobe. Don't you see how pathetic it is? Live dangerously.' I wrench clothes off the hangers and throw all the shirts I can grab on to our bed, a medley of blue. 'Try cream, yellow, pink. Your trousers are cut to disguise your short legs. Your legs are too short. My sister has long legs, but you know that.' I add trousers to the pile.

He leaves the room. The coffee machine, my present to him last Christmas, noisily works its way through its cycle. Daniel returns with two cups of coffee, places them on the bedside table then sits on the bed.

I ignore the coffee and remain standing.

'You'll need that if you are driving to the cottage.'

I pick up one of the coffees. My hands shake.

'You're like her aren't you?' I say slowly. 'Take what you want; money buys anything. For you I have become another person and I don't like some of the makeover.'

I drink the coffee standing.

'Do you touch her in the same way as you touch me?' I start to cry. 'She won't love you as much as I do or is it did. I don't know.'

He shifts his small feet, moves towards me. I put out my hand. He stops.

'Cat got your tongue?' I say. 'You don't even have the good grace to look guilty.'

'I am guilty.'

That startles me so I look deep into his eyes. They show nothing but I catch the tiniest of shrugs that he tries to cover by moving to pick up his coffee.

'I've never promised you anything.' His hands push the heavy air away then rest on his thighs.

'Of course you have. Our life together was that promise,

241

although I see now what a fool I've been to settle for what you offered.' I place the half drunk cup of coffee on the bedside table and lift the rucksack. 'So what are you going to do about it? You let me think we were in it for the long haul.' I pick up the glass girl on the bed. I pick her up, wrap her carefully in some knickers and put her in the bag.

I considered getting pregnant without his knowledge but despised that trick. That didn't stop me fantasising about having children, a child, another Clare. I can only think of babies as girls.

It's dark outside. Coruscating lightning courses up and down the distant buildings. There was other lightning, far north, when Daniel and I ran naked and unafraid into the sea.

'I don't think you can love anyone Daniel, other than yourself. Be careful, very careful, remember Narcissus.' Narcissus, Narcissus.

The tears are there, dammed up. I will cry later, crying that is best done alone. Only once before have I cried like that. That time also I was alone.

An unknown solitary whale in the Pacific sings songs that other whales do not know. It has a life no-one can understand; no other whales answer its call.

I sit in the car and call Alexis. My message is short: I never want to see you again.

Chapter 38

I don't recall getting out of the city. The fields are drear and ugly and I get stuck behind a tractor, along with a dozen other cars. Miles later, when I tear past, I give the farmer the two fingers.

The rain, which has been jogging along behind like the exhausted last man in a marathon, catches me and sprints ahead. I slow down. The lightning is close and deadly; the earth waits, sighing, resigned to the next barrage.

Three sweaters and I'm still cold in the cottage so taking a bottle of wine and a plastic tumbler to the bedroom I fall into a freezing bed and drink. The feeling sick stage passes, numbness takes over.

At dawn, nauseous and exhausted I punish myself and the hangover by going out into the cold to clean and restock the bird feeder. I don't light the fire but walk the hills, over the unyielding brittle spikes of silvered white grass to the small reservoir perched high on the hillside. It's frozen over. Sheep totter to its white rim and wander off again. My wet clothes cling, water streams off my head, snot mingles with the heavy-bosomed matronly rain. The dun coloured sky does not lighten, but presses down and down.

The electricity fails so I light the fire and it plays tricks with the room's shadows and corners. Two days pass, shapeless days like a fat lady in a shift. I walk the hills and revisit the past five years. The wind jousts with me.

As a child I was afraid of wind. It got mixed up with God and sin and guilt. My father tried to explain the physics, told me that it is just the flow of gasses that make up the atmosphere, that air flows from areas of high pressure to low and the rotation of the planet is key. I listened and pretended I understood. My mother took me in her arms and described a gentle fairy patrolling the skies, and when the wind was especially strong it was her anger that chased away the wicked ones. I asked what the wind fairy looked like and she smiled and said I must imagine her for myself. I thought the wind fairy must be just like her.

I weep through the night and send my cries out to the starless dark and dream of Clare, her tiny fingers clasped around my large one. She is smiling and kicking her chubby legs. I put out my free arm to Daniel, to show him.

Nothing changes with the daylight.

A tree is struck. I mourn us both. Rock-hard frost lingers in the crannies of the stone walls, distempers the flags outside, paints, in intricate detail, the squares on the wire fences, and outlines every branch, twig and leaf of the wounded tree: a white-clad beauty. The windows are traced over with frost flowers.

Later in the day the sun creeps out, ashamed of its cowardice but makes little impression except to loosen the frozen ice droplets covering the bare trees so they fall, brightly glistening, to the ground and lie pearly there.

Another long dark night.

What might I have done differently? Everything, nothing. I put too much of myself aside. It's still here, left luggage to be reclaimed. The part of himself that Daniel chose to give me was small, small enough to be slipped to another.

Was it because he was the first man I trusted?

I lived with him in my head, in the books I read, the lectures I gave and in the endless boring meetings. Our love was a creature that curled into a knot in my stomach and round my heart and took the air from my lungs; was light. I opened myself to Daniel. Too far. Like the early wildflowers piercing the snow in the Swiss mountains, I rushed to soar out of the lonely snow into the sun. That's what I believed love was.

The thaw wanders slackly into a dirty dawn.

I scream at Alexis, as if my voice might fly out of the hills and slip into her house, drop poison in her ear while she sleeps.

Will she tell him all the stuff that sisters share, the never-to-be-told outside the bond, the total, brutal honesty of siblings? Even if she does her stories will be different.

Alexis and Daniel, Daniel and Alexis. The words stick in my throat. I stretch, pull back my shoulders, throw my breasts forward, thrusting them away from the hills of my hunched shoulders.

Outside the sun is low on the horizon, spreadeagled over the hills, layered apricot and grey.

Two days later Daniel arrives with the thaw and the electricity. He must have left the car at the road. He glares at the mud on his shoes.

He offers me a mean-mouthed kiss but I turn away from it and we stand like dummies until I step back and let him pass, motioning to the chair opposite mine in front of the fire. None of my pain is mirrored in him. He's all walled up. Duty, not love, has brought him to me. I am an inconvenient puddle.

He ignores his trail of mud across the floor. We sit either side of the fire. It stains the right side of his face.

He doesn't ask how I am although I must look terrible.

He gets up. 'Where do you keep the coffee?'

'Stay there.' I stand up. 'I'll get it, this is my cottage.' It's only instant so it doesn't take long. He grimaces when he drinks, which pleases me.

'It's too late,' I say. 'There's no going back, for me.' The words surprise me but they are the right ones.

He gets up and leans on the mantelpiece as if it's his house and he's about to offer me a cocktail. 'I'm going to live in London,' he says. 'I'm selling my flat.' He notices dust on the elbow of his sweater, brushes it off and sits down without looking at me.

'Ah,' I say. 'With my sister. The end of the northern adventure.'

Two words: London and I. The 'I', a tiny insignificant thing but an exclusive pronoun, no room for manoeuvre, no looseness of understanding, unlike 'us' and 'we'. He's not come to take me back, ask my forgiveness. Once my spider-lady sister catches her prey they are hers until she chooses to let go.

The inconsequential part of my brain wonders if she's tired of old men.

Daniel leans forward and gazes into the fire.

'My sister doesn't do live-in lovers,' I say. 'Who does the cooking or do you take it in turns?' Fury has this nonsense dribbling out.

He takes the question seriously, 'I do. She says she does enough with her business and she likes my cooking.'

I laugh, loudly, derisively. 'You always did take yourself too seriously, Daniel.'

I push back my chair. It scrapes across the stone flags and startles Daniel. I stretch out my legs. 'We weren't together much were we? Friday evenings, unless you were delayed, with a wonderful meal. Our Saturdays were magic, I give you that: our run or yoga – how you lapped up the attention – then more sex.' I draw in my legs and sit up straight. 'Sunday, two separate papers and we don't discuss them because we won't agree. A pact: no politics. Sunday evening you were usually preparing for the next week.'

I'm on a roll. 'So a quick tot.' I use my fingers, 'Two days, but good quality, I grant you. Oh, and snatched holidays, more of the same only somewhere hot.' I look straight at him. 'I've never been first in your life even before my sister.'

This is not his sort of conversation.

'Have I changed you Daniel?' My tone sounds like a happy seaside exploration of life's possibilities. I marvel at it.

'No don't answer. I'll tell you. Of course not and I doubt she will.'

I hear the plangent grouse call: go back, go back. 'You're a shit Daniel.'

Daniel turns toward the window. 'What's that?'

'A grouse.'

'It sounds lonely, sad.'

'Go back, go back,' comes again from outside. The wind lessens, muting its melancholy moan.

He gets up and peers out of the window into the dusk. 'I don't know how you can stand it here. It's so... so empty, so threatening.'

He leaves the window and sits at the table, hands around his coffee. I'm not going to make it easy for him so I get up and sit at the table, opposite him.

'Where in London?'

He shrugs, 'Does it matter?'

'Of course it bloody matters.'

'I've bought a small house.'

'Ah, of course, a good investment or won't she have you in Fulham? Are you going to live together?'

'Yes.'

I didn't anticipate this. I want him gone before I break.

'My sister is a tart but you know that. Money doesn't change hands but luxuries, entertainment, the high life does. Although she has plenty of her own now, money, I mean.'

I slow down, stop waving my hands, 'She's rich, but it hasn't always been like that. My uncle got her started: with the sex. She was ten.' (I don't mention my own initiation.) 'And she stayed faithful to him until he died.' I half laugh. 'Perhaps there's hope for you. She can be faithful.'

Daniel doesn't look shocked, just vacant, a pair of bookends jammed together, no books in between. He probably thinks I'm making it all up.

'She's fucked up, Daniel.' I get up and my chair crashes backwards on to the stone floor.

'I expect you want me out, out of your flat. It never was mine. I was a fool not to see that.' I take the glass girl from the mantelpiece; hold her a minute or two before placing her on the table. I pick up the chair.

'No hurry.'

'There's something more. I can hear it in your voice.'

He stands and half turns to the window again, his back to me. 'Alexis and I are going to New York.' He flushes, 'We may eventually move there. We're going to look at business prospects. And see my father.' He turns back.

I did not expect a rout.

My coffee cup feels heavy in my hands. Surprised, I watch it move through the air, its trajectory unreal, suspended in time. The seconds slow, almost stop. I start to put my hands over my ears as the cup hits his chest, a soft thud. His eyes widen as it bounces off him and slowly falls, breaking into four pieces on the stone flags while a trickle of coffee weaves its way down his sweater. The broken pieces sigh and settle. I let them lie. He takes a handkerchief from his pocket and wipes himself slowly, looking down. When he looks up his mouth is tight.

The grouse calls, again and again.

'I would have given my life for you, you know, last seat in the lifeboat stuff. But it would never cross your mind to do the same for me, probably for anyone.' I gather myself. 'When did we stop talking? We did stop. TV, games, they did the talking. Perhaps we never really did.'

He reaches out for his coffee. The glass girl falls to the floor.

I stare at the two pieces. I push the hair out of my eyes. I kneel on the stone flag. The break at her waist is clean. I pick up the two pieces and hold them in my clenched hands. Outside the feral wind prowls. I bow my head and let the tears fall.

'I'm sorry.' His voice is paler than his face. He takes a step forward.

'For what?' My voice is brittle. I don't look up. 'This,' I hold up the pieces in my open hands, 'or my sister? I know it's your flat but I expect you gone when I get back. It won't take me long to move out.'

I stand, well away from him and look into his face. It tells me nothing.

I don't see him leave.

A delicate long-legged black spider lowers itself on a silken thread from the slate mantelpiece.

The next day I barely move. Over and over I hear his footsteps, his key in the door, his voice saying 'hold out your hands'. Slumped in the chair I watch the fire splutter and die. It takes a long time. The spider keeps me company. Its web grows more intricate and a half-dead fly stumbles into it. The spider puts it in store for another time, another feast.

I leave the cottage. I have a great idea. I almost feel cheerful.

His clothes are still in the wardrobe, waiting for Friday night, another weekend. I walk through the rooms, avoiding the mirrors. I cannot bear to hear the Harley Davidson clock sing out its memories so I stop it.

A chaffinch crashes into the balcony window and lies on the terrace floor, its neck at an impossible angle. For a second or two I envy it.

Nothing is out of place. Except me.

I trail down seven flights of stairs to the cellar below the building where Daniel stores his wine. It is a dark room, temperature-controlled at 55%.

There's one small rack, mostly New World wines, my rack. Of the remaining wine, over 500 plus bottles, some are more than thirty years old. The cellar is carefully laid out, separated into Burgundy and Bordeaux. He's too much of a snob to drink New World wines. He's been a good teacher so I know which are the most valuable. I quickly locate the first growth clarets: several cases of Chateaux Lafite and Chateau Margaux and a case of Chateau Haut-Brion. Daniel would praise my discernment. Now for the burgundies and the grand crus. I select four cases: Musigny, Corton, Montrachet and Chambertin. Ignoring the open cases I go for the untouched, pristine wooden cases. Daniel says they are liquid gold. I find a screwdriver and wrench them open.

The first bottle tastes metallic. I try three more, opening a new case each time. Finally I select as many as I can carry in my arms, dropping one on the stairs and leaving it there, bloody and broken. For the next seven days I open bottles, try a few mouthfuls and throw the remainder down the sink. A little of the pain and regret washes away with it.

Back at work I stare, stutter and fall silent. I manage not to cry. For some days everything, everyone, seems mute. I panic that I am going deaf. I go to the doctor's for a sick note. I have money in the bank and can go anywhere. Lucy is away.

I telephone Alexis again. This time a recoded message refers me to another number. I call that. A young voice trills, 'Kensington Gourmet Food'. Alexis is away for a month. No, the girl has no number to give me. Alexis' mobile is dead.

I live on coffee, little else.

There's not much to pack. I take his overlarge tee shirt with me, the one I wore on that first night.

My heart is full of fantasy, but is that not what love is: fantasy.

The university is understanding, generous even. I leave the city and wander along the sea on the northern coast, staying one or two nights in small hotels. The beaches are deserted except for the swoop and glide of an osprey. Perhaps it recognises another lonely creature. I ache for its solitary beauty.

I buy a pile of novels, hastily pulled off the shelves. They are vacuous, idle gossip.

I can't go back to my cottage so I rent one at the end of a long dark loch. I leave my car half a mile away. The owner, a kind man, worries that I have so little luggage, offers to bring food for me in his Land Rover. Deep, soldierly pines surround the cottage. There are ducks on the loch. They fly off, squawking indignantly as we arrive.

Lucy visits bringing cakes from Maria's that I can't eat. She says, 'You only had the weekends together, a part-time life. You didn't have a chance to practise on the small everyday things, learn how to work things out together.'

I tell her that I believed I would never be loved, could love, not in the way I dreamt of, until Daniel.

'You're too trusting,' she says.

'That's the price of loving.'

'Four nights away, often more; every week,' she says.

'It worked,' I say, 'until her.' I believed Daniel when he said there had been no others.

Lucy says, 'Your sister is a bitch, always has been.'

'At least I don't have to watch Jeremy Paxman anymore,' I say. We both manage a small laugh.

The ducks outside are still, quiet.

Odd, macabre facts come into my head, to do with death. Edison, that brilliant inventor but who also invented the electric chair. The first victim took eight minutes to die. Ruth Ellis, the last woman hanged in Britain, despite a petition signed by 50,000. A victim of class and her lover, condemned, some say, by her brassy blonde appearance in court. She refused to appeal. Her father hanged himself and her son later committed suicide after defacing his mother's headstone.

I tell myself that my sorrow is little.

The last week I am at the cottage in the forest coincides with Easter holidays. Lucy brings Ryan and Mattie, now young lads with long legs and boundless energy. We do some Munro bagging. Lucy stays in the cottage and cooks food for large appetites.

A day or two after Lucy leaves the squawk and alarmed clatter of the ducks taking off wakes me in the deep dark of midnight. I peer out but can see no-one. I'm afraid. By dawn I think I will survive but I leave that day.

Lucy persuades me that I need professional help. I find a small man who is very old. He has white sweetie powder around his mouth and asks me about my dreams. I tell him about lonely people, of places with no escape, dark bewildering places. I suppose they qualify as dreams but I am awake for most of them. He asks why I gave my daughter away, how I had failed my mother, and what is there in the shadows that frighten me so?

'She knelt down,' I say. 'Her eyes were the same height as mine, the same colour.' I say nothing for a long time. He waits. 'He said no-one would believe me,' I whisper, 'And then she had to go away for a long time, months. He said she would.'

She went away. In a white dress.

I tell him of a recurring dream, of being ground between two giant discs of concrete, the chaff between the grinding stones, and of being stuffed into a hessian bag and carried off.

My cottage is damp so I open all the windows. A pair of wild pheasants have taken over the garden, and are unmoved by my temporary return. They did not expect me back.

The pink hawthorn has lingered late. Most of its life it's a prickly unremarkable thing, a confused bush/tree, but not this year. This summer it is gloriously pink and tree-like. I enclose it in my heart to carry away. The hills are hot and dry and the water, fed by a spring, is running slowly, cautiously stockpiling itself high up on the hill where it collects deep underground.

I wander along the base of the high sandstone walls of the long since defunct quarry with its striated sheer walls unhurriedly becoming carpeted with clumps of grass and small stunted bushes. In another month the moors above the quarry will be a blaze of pink heather.

There's little to pack.

The next morning the raucous 'kork, kork' of the pheasant in the garden wakens me. Without moving from bed I can see the brilliantly coloured male with its red ear tufts, shouting out in triumph at having escaped the rearing pen and the guns, now wild, strutting; free. The early morning sun embraces me through the open window and I mentally tick off the bird calls, not many. Later I sit quietly on the stone wall and watch a fledgling robin the size of its parents but fluffy, dependent, its breast not Christmas-card red but speckled, and consider how Clare must love the kookaburra's laughter.

Chapter 39

2003

The statue of Saddam Hussein has been toppled.

It's Saturday and I'm procrastinating about the gym and the cleaning. If I don't get a move on the others will have done their workouts, had coffee and left.

The flat is a mess, a pigsty my father would have said. He often slips into my head these days.

I've been busy, getting my life back and then work. I haven't been to London since Daniel left me. There, I've said it, albeit in my head, instead of the usual weasel words.

The phone rings. Ben's voice. He hasn't been in touch for an age.

'I know what you are going to say,' he says.

'Excuses then,' I smile down the phone. He sends occasional e-mails, citing too much work, too little time, and Christmas and birthday cards redolent with brief messages of guilt.

'Later,' he says.

'Where? When?'

'My graduation. You can call me 'doctor' then.' He chuckles.

I want to hug him down the line. 'When is it?'

'Promise you'll come and I'll send you an official invite.'

'A deal.' Then I ask, 'Who else is coming?'

'Just Mum. She wants you to come. No-one else.'

We chat a little longer but it's clear he wants off the phone. I pick up Athy, sit down and put her on my knee. She licks my hand with a tongue as rough as sandpaper, surprising given its delicate pinkness. She manipulates my fingers towards her neck. Murasaki stayed with Lucy and I got a new cat when I moved back to my flat. I called her Athena. Overdoing it for a cat but I'm a bit prone to that with names. Athy is not much of a warrior. I have promised her that I will never give her away.

I wonder if I will be able to avoid Alexis.

There are only a few empty seats at the back when I arrive. About three hundred or more BSc students occupy all but the front two of the first fifteen or twenty rows in the hall, a massed tier of black gowns and yellow trimmed hoods draped over shoulders and down the back. Some are wearing their mortar boards while others hold them on their knees. Most of the graduates in the front two rows are MSc graduates. The trim on the black hoods of the MSc graduates is slightly wider. Five other students stand out with scarlet hoods and blue edging: the PhDs.

An excited hum fills the hall. I place my handbag on my lap and open the programme. It's what I expect: pictures of happy students, pages of students' names, an anodyne piece from the vice chancellor and the university crest resplendent on the cover. A cosmologist is to receive an honorary degree. That will please Ben.

The cosmologist tells some good jokes and speaks of the need for more scientists and, at the same time, manages to imply that universities are not being sufficiently selective, that we must bring back the joy of learning, pride in knowledge. I can't argue with that. I don't listen to the chancellor, except to hear mention of a difficult year. That's the same for all of us and unlikely to change.

I spot Ben when he swivels round to scan the audience and I give him a small wave. He returns an exuberant wide Ben smile. I find his name in the programme and the title of his PhD. The words 'black holes' are all I fully understand.

A tall young man climbs the short run of stairs leading up to the stage. The sun, in a single slim shaft, lights up his auburn hair. He waits for his name to be called. Benedict John Bishop receives a beribboned roll of parchment. He stays to chat a minute or two with the chancellor. Then he turns fully around to face us and opens wide his gown to show his tee shirt: Share the earth's resources. Most of the students stand and clap. The parents and families sit, silent. I stand, my cheers part strangled by tears. The people either side of me drag themselves to their feet. Briefly, I wonder if Alexis is standing.

The graduates file down the cavernous hall and up the stairs on to the stage one at a time. Some wave to their friends, making the most of their moment on stage and others hope simply for safe passage, put their heads down and scurry. I clap them all, impatient to see Ben. My hands are sore from clapping and I'm bored. I want to see Ben, give him a big hug for all the time we have lost.

The quadrangle easily accommodates the students and their family and friends. The sandstone buildings have lofty windows punctuating the ground floor at perfectly symmetrical intervals. Above each window small individual balconies of wrought iron run the length of the first floor and above them is another tier of smaller openings tucked under the eaves. In the dead centre of each side is a large portico with finely carved sandstone columns. The quad is hot in the full summer sun and filled with excited conversations, preening families, strutting relieved students.

My eyes linger on groups of proud, happy, smartly dressed families and friends. There's an older couple, small, anxious looking. The father clasps and unclasps his hands gazing up at the young man who has outgrown him by six or eight inches. The mother clearly wants to take her boy into her arms but those days are long since gone and her face mixes joy and awe. The boy stands, fiddling with his gown, looking around. Near them is a woman in her twenties with scraggly blonde hair, long thin legs and a very young baby. Her baby talk drowns out conversation around her. Her husband is stout, and looks to be in his late forties. He breathes heavily, and keeps his hand on his son's shoulder. Two girls in their early twenties stand a little apart; sisters, their touch and looks say.

I thought long over my wardrobe and eventually chose black flared trousers with sharply pointed black boots and a silk shirt with black and cream narrow horizontal stripes and over it a jacket of broad cream and black vertical stripes. I wear my hair shorter now and it suits me but I still sometimes find my hand running through absence.

Alexis is walking through one of the porticos. She stands framed by the columns, waiting, dressed simply in a mid-calf cream linen skirt, a turquoise blouse and skimpy bone sandals. She is wearing large sunglasses.

I walk to the corner furthest away from her.

'Hello Ruthy. I thought you hadn't made it.'

I swing round. Anger flares.

She pushes her sunglasses on to the top of her head and leans towards my cheek. I step back.

I want to say 'You think it's that easy; kiss and make up'. Instead I ask, 'Where's Ben?'

'You look good,' she says and puts her long elegant fingers on my arm. I have to stop myself from flinching.

I feel good. 'And you're a bitch,' I say in an even tone. I've prepared for this for years but now I'm not sure I even care that much.

'You're right sis, I am. That's me, can't help it. But Ben will be here soon.' She touches my arm again. 'There are two doctors in the family now.'

'What family?' I say.

'Wait,' she says. 'This is Ben's day and we can't quarrel now, not here. Come to me for dinner.' There's entreaty in her voice. 'Ben has a party to go to this evening.'

I hold her gaze. She doesn't look away.

'Why?' I ask.

'I'm only here a few days and Ben would be pleased.'

I agree on dinner but tell myself I'm a fool. 'I'm proud of Ben,' I say.

'Proud, of course you are.' The voice, relaxed, confident, comes from behind us. He wraps his arms around both our shoulders. 'My two favourite women.' His eyes are the same loving clever eyes. I want to hold him. He hugs me. 'Hi Aunt Prof. You look great.'

'Yes, she does,' Alexis says.

'Your dress sense hasn't changed,' I say, pointing to his trainers. 'And I like that.' I put my hand on his chest.

He opens his gown to show the message. 'Mum doesn't approve but she's given up.'

Alexis just smiles fondly.

He grins. 'I've missed you.'

'Me too.'

'Come on, I want a photo of the three of us. And of you and me, Ruth.' He starts to move off but stops and turns to me.

'When are you going back?'

'Midday tomorrow, or just after.' I hold his arm.

'That's too soon. I've a party to go to tonight and things to do now. Shall we have breakfast tomorrow? I'll meet you at ten o'clock. Are you staying at Mum's hotel?'

'No, I've got a friend here in the sociology department. He's booked me a room in a hotel near here.'

Ben raises an eyebrow and I shake my head, 'A friend,' I say.

We agree on a nearby café.

Chapter 40

At 7 p.m. I take a taxi to one of Belgravia's back streets and a small block of apartments.

'Fourth floor,' she says. 'Take the lift.'

I hear a buzzer and the outside door opens.

She is standing at her apartment door when I get out of the lift. There are only four apartments on each floor. She's changed for dinner and around her neck hangs a gold necklace densely populated with large emeralds.

I didn't bring a change of clothes. Annoying.

I follow her inside.

'Sling your jacket on my bed.' She motions to a half-open door.

The bedroom has a standard double bed, a small wardrobe, a two bedside cabinets and a dressing table. It's newly painted. Bare walls.

I leave my jacket and find her in the sitting room. At one end there is a dining table and four chairs. The table is covered with a peach coloured cloth.

'It's small,' she says. 'I only use it when I come to London.'

I wonder at 'I'.

'Would you like one of these?' She waves a chunky tumbler containing clear liquid, ice cubes and a slice of lemon.

I'm gagging for a drink but not gin and tonic, 'Wine would be good.'

'White?' she asks. 'It's fish. I've kept it simple.'

I hear her open the fridge and she returns with a tall glass half-full.

I haven't drunk much since Daniel. Those awful days of longing for Daniel, waiting for his touch, knowing my body through his hands, a head full of memories that refused to be dislodged; and anger, with him and with myself, and disbelief that he was with my sister, are gone. His shadow slipped away and I didn't notice its going.

We sit opposite each other in small armchairs.

I break the silence. 'Like the necklace,' I say. I really do.

She hesitates. 'A present from Dan.'

The necklace is not Daniel's taste. 'Is his father is still in New York?' I ask.

'Yes, his apartment is close to ours.' Her eyes challenge.

I only half listen while she describes her apartment overlooking Central Park and fabulous kitchens outside the city. Already I want the evening over, wonder why I came.

'Dan's mother is in a home, has been for over ten years,' she says. 'I went to see her. She must have been beautiful once but she's lost it.' Alexis twirls her almost empty wine glass by its stem, making her rings flash.

So the woman in the photograph isn't dead, except to Daniel and his father, the mother who was great, was fun. Alexis must have burrowed deep. Soon we will be done with Daniel.

'How did you find out?'

'I found some papers.' She looks pleased with herself.

'Why didn't Daniel come to the graduation?' I ask. It feels good to say his name out loud.

She doesn't answer. Then she jumps up. 'We'll eat in a few minutes.'

I get up and wander round the room. The walls here are bare except for one painting at the other end of the room. I stroll down. It's a portrait of a woman, a handsome woman with a strong face.

She looks a little familiar. I move back to the armchair.

A few minutes later Alexis brings in two plates and carries them to the table. 'Bring the wine, will you,' she says, and walks quickly back to the kitchen, returning with a bowl of salad.

We sit opposite each other. My plate has a lightly cooked piece of Dover sole, a few beans and some creamy looking potatoes. I taste the sauce. It is superb.

'Help yourself,' she says, pointing to the wine in the cooler.

I pick up my almost empty glass, reach over and pour myself more. The wine is good. Alexis holds out her glass. I look hard at her and detect little change.

'It's good to see you,' she says.

She's behaving as if nothing has happened. Déjà vu, I think.

I put my cutlery down. 'You set Ben up to tell me that you were screwing Daniel,' I say. 'Was Daniel dragging his feet, reluctant to tell me or did you want him all to yourself?' I rest my forearms on the table.

'It was nothing to do with Dan 'dragging his feet' as you call it. I thought you should know.' She drinks a large mouthful of wine. 'I thought it better for all of us.'

'To force him to choose between us.'

Alexis shakes her head.

Of course, why did I not see this at the time? 'It was Ben, wasn't it? He insisted, so you took the coward's way out and sent him.' I pause. 'Oh Alexis, you should have seen how unhappy he was that night he came to tell me. So cruel.' I push my plate away. 'Anyway,' I say, 'Ben couldn't stand him.'

'He got used to him.'

'Why not just one of your affairs? All those weekdays in London. I may never have found out.'

She's silent. The pause hangs, heavy. 'Dan was different to the others. The others,' she says, 'were just lovers, no commitment, except…' She looks away. 'It just happened. I didn't plan it.'

'Like hell you didn't,' I say. 'You could have stopped it. Did you try? Did you care?' The blankness in her face answers me. 'Obviously not.'

She looks away, looks back at me then says, 'It was partly New York. We were both excited by the idea. Dan was like a kid about it.'

'So you started an affair with Daniel, and then wow, New York was the icing on the cake.' I'm sounding shrill, loud.

She pushes her chair back from the table. 'When this conversation is over you can go back north and never see me again.' Alexis looks down and says softly, 'If that's what you want. I'm going back to New York next week.' She adds, 'He cared about you. Perhaps more than about me.'

'We'll never know,' I say and can't stop asking myself if that is true. Even now I'd like to think so. 'You couldn't bear to see me happy, could you; you had to take what I had.'

She looks away. 'I wanted it to work,' she almost whispers. 'I really did. I wanted a life like yours.'

Neither of us speaks for a couple of minutes. I'm thinking about what she has just said. She said 'wanted'.

'Dan's back here,' she says, 'for good.'

'And you're going back to New York,' I say slowly.

She nods.

'So he dumped you.' I don't bother to hide my pleasure.

Alexis flashes me a look of fury and contempt. 'His business failed. Mine didn't. Then he went to Harvard for six months and I stayed in New York.'

It takes me a few moments to understand. 'So you took Daniel for a fling, oh, and New York,' I say slowly. 'If it had been twenty, ten years even, I might have forgiven you, but not this.'

Alexis doesn't reply.

'A live-in lover, that's not for you. You don't really fall in love, you don't know how.'

'I did once,' she says, so quietly I almost miss it. 'I fell in love once.' She adds in a voice so sad I look carefully at her, 'And it ruined my life.'

262

'That wasn't love; it's called 'grooming',' I say, and add, 'Ben has his hair.'

Alexis looks startled. 'You've never said anything.' She looks sharply at me. 'Ben doesn't know and never will. I have to trust you in this Ruth.'

I nod. For Ben's sake.

'John loved me, told me I was great. No-one else did.' Her bottom lip is stuck out. I haven't seen that expression since we were kids.

'I loved you once.' I pause before I say, 'Far Hill Moor and… A fresh ten-year-old girl,' I say. 'There was no love in what he did, to either of us.'

She pours herself a large glass of wine. 'We were kids. And you could be a pain,' she says.

'A pain,' I say mockingly. 'You were his princess and you made sure it stayed that way by telling Mum.' I don't bother to keep my voice down. 'I didn't understand anything then, except that it was my fault and that was why she left us. Six months is a long time when you're ten. That was worse than what he did to me.'

My mother's eyes come back to me. They haven't haunted me for a long time. She and I made our peace.

'I don't remember any of that stuff.'

'I bet you don't.'

'I wanted John's child,' she says. 'I planned it. He would have been so proud of Ben today.'

'Peter,' I ask. 'The man Ben calls 'dad',' I say.

Alexis glares at me.

'Did you ever love Peter?'

'Yes.' Her eyes fill with tears. 'I don't know.'

I look away. I came to tell her what a shit she is. I didn't expect to feel the way I do: sad, a little lost. For me, for Alexis.

'What's happened to the painting?'

She looks blank.

'The nude.'

'I destroyed it.'

'It was good,' I say, a little grudgingly.

She says softly, her eyes filling, 'He died, just before I left for America. That's one of the reasons I left. His tractor rolled. You remember those steep hills. It was terrible, it crushed him.'

She gets up and takes the plates. 'I've some ice cream, coffee. I haven't had much time to make things.'

'Coffee will be fine,' I say.

'Let's move.' She motions to the armchairs.

She brings in a tray with two cups of coffee, sugar and a small jug of milk.

'She thought she was so clever,' Alexis says, placing the tray on a small table in front of us and sitting down opposite me.

We both opt for black coffee.

'Who?' I ask.

'Harriet.'

'She was clever.'

'Then why was she stuck in that stupid village?'

'Dad,' I say.

'She didn't keep him long.'

Before I can say anything she says, 'I did a search on the Internet.'

What is she talking about?

'Beth. She was easy to find, quite a well-known painter.' There's pride in Alexis' voice. 'She lives in Norfolk in a falling down Victorian house. She's had a couple of exhibitions.'

'You went to see her?' I immediately follow on with another question. I have dozens in my head. 'Had she ever tried to find you, given up hope?'

'Her portrait is over there.' She points to the painting. 'She painted it.'

I get up and stand in front of it. The woman in the full-length dress, with the long hair, rings on every finger. The stranger in the

264

church. I noticed very little that day, except her. I stand and think: my father's change of heart, the air ticket and all the rest. He was afraid. And my mother and the wedding dress.

I pull myself back to Alexis and Beth. 'When, did you go?'

'Soon after he died.' I hear the pain in her voice. 'She came to Lower Newhouses once. She told me. I was in London by then. She saw you.'

I sit back down, tucking my legs beneath me.

'She said that her life was empty after I went. She wanted to keep me. That's what she said.'

I might have used those same words.

'So why didn't she?' I ask. There are two conversations running in my head.

'No idea but I'm glad I didn't grow up there.' She sips her coffee. 'I don't think she ever had much money. You just had to look at the house. She said she wasn't a believer, not into God like Robert.' Alexis laughs. 'You would have thought she was talking about a terrorist the way she said 'believer'. He told her I had to be brought up in a Christian house, in the church.'

'She was better off without him,' I say. 'He might have driven her mad the way he did our mother.' I put stress on the 'our'.

'Harriet was already mad,' Alexis says.

'No she wasn't,' I protest. I can't stop myself asking, 'What's she like?' I'm willing her to go on.

'Seventy-five, smartly dressed; make-up, the works,' Alexis says. There is a touch of pride in her face. 'She was twenty-nine when I was born.'

I do the sums in my head. Five years younger than my mother. 'You told her who you are,' I say.

'Of course. I said I was Robert's daughter,' Alexis says. 'I only saw the sitting room. It made our old one in Lower Newhouses look extravagant and modern. She's lived in the same house all her life, rarely left it. She's lonely; she'd have talked all day.'

I want to cry out, 'She's been waiting for you all her life.'

'She must almost live in one room, the sitting room,' Alexis says. 'There was a divan against one wall, the fire was lit and there was a small table with tea things on it.' She pauses. 'The walls were covered with her paintings, landscapes, all local. She looked after her mother and father until they died. I think they all lived like hermits, shut away in that awful house. No money.'

I stay silent. I don't know what to say.

'She said she loved him. That was why she gave me up,' she says. 'And her painting. I think she loved that more.' There's a tinge of bitterness in her voice. 'Robert loved her, she said.'

'Yes,' I say slowly. 'I think he probably did. What were they like, the paintings?'

'Good.'

She should know.

'There were two paintings over the fireplace: a portrait of a middle-aged man, Robert, and a painting of a baby. She gave them to me.' She waves at the far wall. 'And that one. The others are in New York. You'll have to visit if you want to see them.'

I shake my head.

'Have you seen her again?'

I told her I wasn't coming back.

I feel sick. 'What did she say?'

'She cried.'

Alexis is silent. We both concentrate on our coffee.

'I don't know if I will have time before I go back. Perhaps,' she says, and adds, 'I liked her.'

I want to cry out 'make time'.

I look at my watch. It's nearly eleven.

'That night,' she says slowly, 'Clare, I mean.'

'Rape,' I say, 'is the word you're looking for.' Five minutes, ten minutes, an eternity. People say the same thing about accidents: it was just a minute or two, a second and then… But this was no accident.

'I went outside with Damien because all you kids were

practically licking his boots. I told him to get lost. I knew John would be waiting in his car.' She drains her coffee cup. 'He'd seen you come in. "Quite a young lady now," were his words.' She takes a long hard drag on her cigarette. 'I told him he could see for himself,' she says, 'but of course I didn't mean…' She stops. She punishes the cigarette again. 'I really didn't mean him to hurt you. I wouldn't. I never thought for a minute…'

After a couple of moments she says, 'We had been fighting. I think he wanted to get at me.'

I get up. 'So he raped me to get at you. Have you ever thought of anyone but yourself?'

My heart punches my chest, tries to get out. 'Rape, Alexis? I don't suppose you've known fear like that. People who have a knife at their throat feel the same. Terror, but worse, utter humiliation.' There's more but I'm out of breath.

'Where did you go that night? You weren't home when I got there, when I needed you, thought I needed you.' I see her look away and I know. 'He waited for you, didn't he? Wasn't one sister enough for him? No wonder you left for London before anyone was up. Our Uncle John.' I spit out the word 'uncle'.

Alexis stubs out her cigarette and plays with the cigarette packet.

She holds out her hand to me, palm uppermost, her face puckered, tears in her eyes. 'I loved him,' she says.

'You're not capable of love, you're sick.' My voice is hard, the words are rolling off my tongue, liberated at last. 'He fucked you up Alexis, took away your childhood. He didn't love you. If he had he would have let you go. I'm glad he's dead.'

'No,' she whispers. 'No. He loved me, I know he loved me.'

'And Daniel? Was he revenge? For your lost childhood, for the mother I had and you didn't. Perhaps or perhaps it was just carelessness but you did me a favour.'

She puts her hand out to me. I leave it there and remain standing.

Minutes pass.

'Perhaps we can meet again before I leave,' she says.

I shake my head. 'I'm going home tomorrow and I have a job in Australia, a chair at a good university. I always wanted to go back.'

'You'll look for Clare?' she asks.

'No. But you never know, she might find me,' I say.

'I hope she does. I'm sure she's lovely.'

Alexis pushes her chair back and stands close.

'Perhaps I'll come and see you in Australia.' She stops in the doorway and turns to face me. She's crying.

I have to turn away.

I don't look back.

I walk in the general direction of the Underground. The air is muggy, the night not yet completely dark, a mongrel light. It has been an odd, sad, happy day. It will take me time to sort it out.

My sister: as a kid I called her 'my beautiful sister'. She's still beautiful but with a touch of loss, fragility.

I'm exhausted although it isn't late. Breakfast with Ben tomorrow. Perhaps he will visit me in Australia. I'll take him to the desert, we'll sleep in swags and Ben will name the stars for me even though it's the southern hemisphere.

I finger the glass girl in my handbag. I'll take her to Australia. Glass needs the sun to mend. I'll find a glassblower there; perhaps the son of the old man.

Chapter 41

I'm running late but Ben is even later. The coffee bar is full of students slumped in chairs or draped across the tables. A tired, quiet murmur hangs in the air. I find two capacious armchairs in a corner, sling my bag on one and collapse in the other.

He stands at the door looking around. A couple of students see him and wave. He waves back then strides across the room. He's wearing the same clothes as yesterday. As am I.

Our hug is big although he towers over me now. He's too thin. It's like being in the grip of an excitable skeleton.

I give him a £10 note and he buys croissant and latte for himself and another espresso for me.

'Still feeling cock of the walk? Have you been to bed?' I ask.

'Definitely, and no, I haven't been to bed. There's a concert tonight in the park, a great group.' He waves to a couple coming in the door. 'There are too many things I want to do.'

We grin comfortably at each other.

'I know what you're going to say. I should have been in touch more.' He adds, 'Did you and Mum sort things last night?'

'Yes, to the first and sort of to the second,' I say.

He looks disappointed.

'I've missed you,' I say.

He attacks his croissant, tearing it in two and stuffing one half in his mouth. 'You know they live in New York now?'

Alexis can tell him.

'So talk to me.' I lean across and squeeze his shoulder. 'What have you been doing?'

'What we all do.' He waves around the room at the other students.

I raise an eyebrow.

'Protests? Politics?' I ask. 'And girls?'

'Mostly no.' That grin again. 'Well, the odd dabble with all three but nothing serious.'

He starts to tell me of his research into the space time of black holes. I follow him through general relativity theory and the idea that light cannot escape because gravity is so strong. No paths ever lead out of black holes. They sound like some ghastly incubus from science fiction. I'm beginning to feel claustrophobic just listening. When he starts writing equations on a scrap of paper and explaining the symbols I give up and watch his slender hands waving in the air, his bent head of auburn curls and glimpses of fierce concentration in his face.

He looks up.

I raise both hands in surrender. 'As soon as you started on the equations that was it. I hated maths at school.'

He puts down his pencil and goes off for more to eat. When he returns he says, pointing to his mobile, 'Mum says you are going to Australia. She never could keep a secret.'

'You can come and visit,' I say very quickly. 'I leave after Christmas.'

He sits up and brings his face close to mine. His smile, close up, spreads around the globe and back. 'I'm going to Australia. That's the job I mentioned. I always said we would go together.'

I leap out of my chair to give him a hug. He looks around, embarrassed but I don't care.

My phone rings. I recognise the number Alexis gave me and press the reject button. Daniel.

I will always love him a little but not enough to want to see him again. I smile as I recall the blood-red wine on the stairs and the red river coursing down the drain.

Chapter 42

2003 Autumn

It's a cold autumn day and I dump my handbag on the dining room table, sling my briefcase on to the sofa, take a quick shower and change into tracksuit bottoms and a cotton sweater, not bothering with a bra.

Athy hops on my knee. I am a serial cat-betrayer. I haven't told her yet. Brenda next door has said she'd love to have her. She looks after her when I'm away and calls herself Athy's second mum.

The Australian decision is right. The job is perfect: plenty of research time, exciting courses and a young team.

Here, we are at war: Iraq. God knows where it will end. Saddam Hussein's sons have been killed along with hundreds of Iraqis. Our government has lied to us. I'm beginning to think that's what governments do. My love affair with Tony Blair is over.

I won't miss England, except for my hills. I will run beside the sea. Ben will be in the north and I in the south but we can meet in the desert. I shall go back to the desert soon, to find the old man or his son. He will mend the glass girl.

The coffee machine shudders, grunts and grinds while I open a new packet of my favourite biscuits; nutty ones, anything with nuts. I take the coffee and the post and sit at the table pushing the dining chair back so I can cross my legs. I extract the junk mail.

An envelope with an Australian address. The day is silent and still, a day on hold. I get up and walk to the small white table and clasp the fingers of my right hand around the glass girl.

I open the letter carefully. My daughter would like to meet, Mary Robertson from the Adoption Society writes. Rebecca. She is called Rebecca. I will have to practise. I tell myself to be patient. I can send a letter care of Mary.

There is something else in the envelope: a photograph. The date is on the back: 6th August 2003.

I get up and walk over to my photograph of Ben at his graduation. I place my daughter's photograph beside it: auburn hair both. They look like brother and sister.

I find a pen and paper and start on a draft. It will be word perfect before I send it.

Clare will have her own secrets. I have one, her father. Alexis lies to Ben about his father. I shall do the same for Clare/Rebecca. I don't want her to know the smallest of shadows. She and Ben will be friends. He will call her 'cousin' although he might call her 'sister'.

I hope to tell my daughter that my love for her has never faltered even though I walked away. Not in this letter. I am hovering over the piece of paper. The letter will be short. I will tell her how much I have longed for this, what joy this news has brought me.

I must not overwhelm her. I will find a way of telling her that she has been with me every day of the past twenty-seven years; that I have never missed her birthday. I try not to envy the ones who brought her up. My part in her life is small. Yet birth is not a small thing.

I was her mother once.

There'll be time for us to explore one another's lives, our separate lives. Will she falter under the weight of my love? I want her to be proud of me.

I will give her the glass girl.

I put aside the piece of paper. I will return to it tomorrow, although I must not dally.

I sit for a long time. Just as the room begins to darken I pick up the phone and dial Alexis in New York.

Contacts

If you have any feedback about *The Glass Girl* I'd love to hear from you:
sandyhogarth1@btinternet.com

OR
Tweet me @sandyhogarth1

If you love it, spread the word.

Thank you.

Acknowledgements

I am greatly indebted to Margaret Graham who read an early draft of my novel and helped me generously thereafter including introducing me to her agent, Vivien Green, Sheil Land Associates. When we failed to find a publisher it was Vivien who said, 'self publish.'

And to Debz Hobbs-Wyatt for her advice and belief in *The Glass Girl*.

I owe a debt to three writers, Simon Miller, Nada Holland and Edward Easton, who have critiqued several iterations of *The Glass Girl*. Three of us met on *The Guardian* Masterclass: *Finish a First Draft of your Novel* with Gillian Slovo. A tough but rewarding time. Thank you Gillian.

My family and friends have waited a long time. Well here it is. And my lovely granddaughters, Natalie and Siobhan: thank you just for being there.

The lines from W.B. Yeats on page 36 are taken from the poem: "He Wishes for the Cloths of Heaven'.

The lines from Emily Dickinson on page 78 are taken from the poem: 'It was not Death, for I stood up'.

The aboriginal dreamtime stories are drawn from: Gadi Mirrabooka, retold by Pauline E. McLeod, Francis Firebrace Jones and June E. Baker, Libraries Unlimited.

Lightning Source UK Ltd.
Milton Keynes UK
UKOW04f1840060115

244099UK00004B/242/P